THE SHATTERED BAUBLE

Rachel McLean writes thrillers that make your pulse race and your brain tick. A proud indie author who manages her own publishing company, she has sold millions of copies digitally and hundreds of thousands in print, regularly topping the bestseller lists. She is the author of the Dorset Crime novels and five spin-off crime series, with beloved characters appearing in multiple series. In 2021, she won the Kindle Storyteller Award with *The Corfe Castle Murders*. She divides her time between Birmingham and Dorset and lives with her wife, three children and two cats Cagney and Lacey.

Millie Ravensworth is the pen name of two authors who have been writing entertaining novels together for more than ten years. The Millie Ravensworth books focus on their shared love of crime stories and charming characters who readers love spending time with.

ALSO BY RACHEL MCLEAN AND
MILLIE RAVENSWORTH

The Jurassic Coast Mystery series
The Swimming Club
The Empty Easel
The Shattered Bauble

The London Cosy Mystery series
Death at Westminster
Death in the West End
Death at Tower Bridge
Death on the Thames
Death at St Paul's Cathedral
Death at Abbey Road

RACHEL McLEAN

MiLLiE RAVENSWORTH

THE SHATTERED BAUBLE

A JURASSIC COAST MYSTERY

ACKROYD PUBLISHING

Ackroyd Publishing

ackroydpublishing.com

Printed and bound in the UK by CPI Group (Uk) Ltd, Croydon CR0 4YY

CHAPTER ONE

ANNIE ABBOTT DANCED from side to side on the pebbles near the breakwater as she addressed the group of swimmers. She might not have been their leader, but she liked things organised and was always happy to take charge.

"Brilliant!" she cried over a wind that threatened to whip away her voice. "You were all amazing!"

The group huddled in their dry robes, none of them paying any attention. Figgy muttered to herself, and Helen and Rosamund were exchanging grumbles.

Yes, it had been cold. Yes, swimming in Lyme Regis bay on the last day of November was possibly only for the foolhardy. But Annie was proud of herself, and of her friends.

Even if all she'd done was run in, flap her arms around a bit, then run out again. It was the cold-water exposure that counted.

"That will certainly be my last swim of the year," Helen said as she shrugged on her coat. A deep shiver ran through her body, and she pushed out a shaking breath. "Freezing!"

"We'll all be back here for the Lyme Lunge though?" Annie said, feeling suddenly sad. "We can't miss that."

The Lyme Lunge was an annual charity swim in Lyme Regis bay, on New Year's Day. Even dipping a toe in counted as taking part.

"I'm up for it," Figgy said.

Helen smiled. "Don't worry, Annie. We wouldn't miss that."

"Good. Well then, if anyone does want to brave it between now and then, you know where I am." She turned to Sally, one of two elderly twins who liked to join them. "It's a shame Peg missed it."

Sally shook her head. "She's got a stinking cold."

"Poor Peg."

Sally rolled her eyes. "Oh, don't. I'm sure she'll be fine."

"I'll give her a call later."

Another eye roll. "Really. No need." Sally looked around the group. "Anyone joining me for a warming drink in the Pilot Boat?"

Helen muttered her assent; the Pilot Boat was only a few doors away from the gallery she owned. The two women bid their farewells and made their way along the prom.

"I need to get home," Figgy said. "Work to finish."

Figgy did some kind of computer work that Annie didn't understand. Most of her clients were American, so she worked odd hours.

"Let me know if you want to come out here again in December," Annie said.

"Of course." Figgy threw her a smile and turned towards Monmouth Beach and the caravan site beyond it where she lived.

Annie and Rosamund walked along the promenade

together. The Christmas lights were up, and the pleasure gardens glowed with colour – reds, greens and oranges – uplighting the trees and lending them an otherworldly feel.

They reached Cobb Gate, where Rosamund still parked her car, despite the fact that when she'd parked it there earlier that year, a dead man had found his way inside. If that had happened to Annie, she'd be leaving her car somewhere else. But Annie's home was close enough to walk. Even if a brisk wind was getting up, a wind she was glad had waited until they'd finished their swim.

Annie looked at Rosamund. Her friend had been quiet during the swim.

"Is your ex in town yet?" she asked.

Rosamund sighed. "David messaged me yesterday to say he'd arrived at the cottage he's renting. He's got his new girl-friend with him. Shari. I haven't seen them."

David had abandoned Rosamund and their teenage son Cameron the previous year for his much younger personal assistant. Rosamund had kept it from her friends for months but seemed better since opening up.

"How are you feeling about it?" Annie asked, watching her friend carefully.

Rosamund straightened, her face inexpressive. "My concern is just for Cameron."

I bet. "Of course," Annie said.

"It's been difficult for him."

"Well, you can at least give David a piece of your mind, now he's here."

Rosamund shook her head. "That won't help Cameron."

"He doesn't need to know."

Annie wondered what she'd have done if her Ted had done something like that when he was alive. She was pretty sure Tina and Naomi would have given him pieces of their own minds.

Rosamund pulled out her car keys and gave a theatrical shiver. "Anyway..."

Annie gave her arm a pat. "You take care, Rosamund love. I'm here if you need me."

"Thanks." Rosamund hurried away to her car. Annie watched her drive off up Broad Street, a small waving figure inside the huge BMW SUV.

The Millside Pottery was just past Helen's gallery, near Lyme Regis's old mill. Annie headed towards it, admiring the Christmas lights swinging in the gathering wind. She walked up Coombe Street, little more than an alleyway, and took a left turn into Mill Lane.

As she turned the corner, she was blinded by approaching headlights. She stepped back and threw a hand up in front of her face.

"Turn them down, idiot!" she muttered.

The driver hadn't seen her. She tucked herself in against the side wall of one of the houses as the car sped past, the driver oblivious.

"Slow down!" she cried, knowing her voice would be inaudible above the sudden onslaught of rain.

The car stopped at the junction. Briefly, the driver turned towards her. As he saw her, his eyes widened.

Annie grunted. "Idiot!" she shouted.

She'd seen the driver before but couldn't place him. He was grey-haired, driving a silver BMW.

Annie didn't know anyone who drove a silver BMW. But she didn't know everyone who lived in Lyme Regis, at least, not by sight. This was probably someone who worked in one of the businesses surrounding the mill.

The car picked up speed as it turned the tight corner, showering her with mud.

"Thanks," she spat. "Thanks a lot."

She continued towards the pottery, blinking against the after-image the headlights had left behind her eyelids. "Idiot," she repeated.

Once in the courtyard outside the old stone mill buildings, she forced herself to slow down. Peg didn't need her turning up all grumpy like this.

"It's just a bit of mud, Annie Abbott. Nothing you can't cope with."

The courtyard, a lovely place to sit in the summer, was desolate now. The windows of the brewery, café and sewing school were all dark.

Annie turned towards the pottery and its attached shop. There were green and red fairy lights around the display window, but no other lights visible inside. She tugged at the door. It rattled but didn't open.

She knocked on the glass. Nothing. She pulled out her phone and dialled Peg's mobile.

She looked up at the dark windows above the shop. "Peg!" she called over the wind as she waited for her friend to pick up. "I'm outside!"

Rain trickled down the back of her neck, making her regret not pulling up the hood of her dry robe. It was too late now; the inside of the hood would be a puddle. She wriggled to dislodge some drops.

Don't be a wimp, woman. Just half an hour ago you were neck-deep in water.

The phone was still ringing out. Maybe Peg was asleep. Or maybe...

Annie hammered louder, not caring if she cracked the

glass with her fist. She moved to the window, lifted her hand and peered inside.

The shop was lined with wooden shelving displaying crockery, houseware and artwork. In the dim light, Annie could make out a central table, currently occupied by display pieces but sometimes used for demonstrations and classes. She'd been meaning to bring her grandkids down here.

The room was still. No movement.

Annie heard a bang from behind her.

A door slamming? Maybe a wheelie bin tipping over in the wind. Or had that car come back?

No. She hadn't heard an engine.

She looked round. There were footpaths leading away from here in multiple directions, a rabbit warren of pathways. Charming in daylight, but ominous now.

She listened. Silence, apart from the wind and rain.

You're imagining things, you daft old bat.

But she had to check on Peg. Her friend wasn't responding to her phone calls or door-hammering, and that worried her.

Annie circled the building and stopped. The side door to the pottery was ajar.

The source of that bang?

She approached, swallowing.

"Peg! It's Annie! I'm coming in!"

She eased the door further open and slid inside. In the dim light from outside, she could see stacked boxes and rough shelves. In the corner, lights winked on dark equipment. The way ahead was pitch black.

Annie felt around by the door and found a light switch. She pressed it, her heart thumping in her chest.

An overhead strip light flickered on, illuminating racks of

bowls, plates and ornaments in various stages of production, and the kiln in the far corner.

Annie took a step forward. Her foot brushed against something. She clasped a hand over her mouth to keep from yelping.

She looked down. Someone was lying at her feet, slumped around one of the racks.

"Peg?" she whispered.

She dropped to the floor and grabbed her friend's hand. It was cold.

No.

Annie pulled back. Something caught her eye, lying on the floor next to her friend.

A terracotta jug, smashed in two.

No.

"Peg," Annie repeated, but it was little more than a squeak.

She shifted her fingers to Peg's wrist, feeling for a pulse.

Nothing.

Was Peg dead?

CHAPTER TWO

PC Douglas Anderson hunched his shoulders as he ran from the police station in Hill Road to his car.

Earlier on, when he'd been out in Charmouth following up a report of a disturbance, the weather had been clear. Chilly, but calm.

Now, it was blowing a gale. When had that happened?

He yanked open the car door, cursed the coastal weather and threw himself into the car. His wife Naomi had messaged him five minutes earlier, asking where he was. He'd worked late, finishing up some paperwork, but it had taken longer than he'd anticipated.

Naomi was getting used to this. But he didn't think she was getting any happier about it.

"Sorry, Nai," he muttered as he started the car and backed out of his space.

A second later he slammed on the brakes. "Jesus! What was that?"

Something had flown past in his mirror. He turned off the engine and breathed for a moment, then got out.

A branch lay on the ground behind the car. Just a branch.

You're too easily spooked, he thought, just as the door to the police station opened, and Sergeant Jim Connors emerged. He waved as he spotted Dougie.

"You still here, lad?"

"Almost got attacked by a wayward branch," Dougie called back. He picked up the branch, which would undoubtedly have caused a puncture if he'd driven over it, and heaved it into the bushes beyond his car.

Bloody weather.

"You get home," Jim called. "You can come in late in the morning, make up for it."

Dougie would have loved a lie-in, but he hated getting behind. "It's alright, Sarge. I'll see you in the morning."

The sarge shrugged and headed to his car on the other side of the car park. Dougie got into his own car for the second time.

"Sorry, Nai," he muttered once again.

He waited for the sarge to leave first, then turned out of the car park and up Hill Road. As ever, the junction at the top was challenging: one of the steepest hills in town, coupled with a sharp bend and limited visibility. But he was a uniformed police officer, trained in defensive driving. He should be used to this by now.

Dougie, Naomi and their daughter lived on the south-western edge of town, in one of Lyme Regis's few modern houses. To get there, he could either take the right-hand turn uphill, cutting through to Pound Street along Pound Road, which was little more than an access road, or take the slightly more circuitous route via what passed for the main roads in Lyme Regis.

At this time of night, Pound Road's residents would be

home, and the street, such as it was, would be partially blocked with parked cars. He took the left turn down the hill.

He drove slowly, visibility limited by the rain. As he approached Sherborne Lane on the left, he caught movement up ahead.

Dougie frowned, slowing further. A figure had emerged from Sherborne Lane, a pedestrianised alleyway leading towards the old mill. Whoever it was, they were running, oblivious to the rain.

"Slow down, mate," Dougie muttered as the figure darted in front of his car. It took a sharp turn right and headed up Pound Street.

Great. Some drunken idiot who'd decided to keep as dry as possible by running home from the pub. And they were taking the same route he was.

He stopped at the junction, peering up and down the road leading up from the seafront, and took the sharp right turn up Pound Street. He scanned the street as he drove, alert for the runner.

There you are.

The figure was up ahead, to his right. Trudging up the hill, now, defeated by the slope.

Dougie allowed himself a smile. *No one can run up there, mate.*

As he drew level with the figure, it swerved suddenly and darted out into the road.

He slammed on his brakes.

The figure stopped in the middle of the road, a hand on Dougie's bonnet. The person turned and looked at him.

Dougie felt his breathing grow shallow. It was a man, wearing a hoodie utterly unsuitable for the weather.

No wonder he was running.

Dougie waved a hand. "Get home, you idiot!" he shouted. It was a good job he was impatient to get home himself, or he might have stopped and had a word.

The figure gave him a final startled look and continued running, disappearing into Holmbush car park. Dougie allowed himself to breathe.

Bloody idiot, he thought, as he made for home.

CHAPTER THREE

ANNIE KNEW FIRST AID. She'd certainly attended enough first aid courses when she'd been working for the local council. But she was still grateful the operator was telling her what to do.

"You said you can't find a pulse?" said the woman, who'd introduced herself as Jayda.

"I've tried. Twice." Annie knew she was panicking. "I can't feel one."

"OK. You've tried her wrist, right?"

"Yes." Annie gritted her teeth.

"In that case, I need you to try her neck. Use your index and middle fingers, not your thumb."

I know that. Annie said nothing, just grunted as she moved her hand up to Peg's neck.

"Can you see where the large muscle in the centre of the front of her neck meets the Adam's apple?"

Peg was wearing an open-necked shirt under a woollen cardigan. Annie could make out the spot. "Yes."

"Place your fingers so they are on that, but slightly to one side. I'm going to stop talking now so you can focus."

Annie put her fingers where she'd been told. She frowned.

Was that...?

It was.

"Yes!" she cried. "I can feel something!" It was faint, but it had rhythm.

Peg was alive.

"Well done," said Jayda. "Now, is she breathing? Place your ear as close as you can to her lips and see if you can hear anything."

Annie bent down. The faintest of breaths brushed her skin as she drew closer to Peg's lips.

"It's faint, but yes. Yes, she's breathing."

"That's great news. Thank you. Now, I need you to stay on the line while I call for an ambulance. I'll be here the whole time. You just watch your friend and tell me if anything changes."

"OK." Annie blinked back tears of relief as she looked down at Peg. *Thank God.*

There was a moment of silence before the operator's voice returned.

"The ambulance will be with you in twenty minutes."

"That long?"

"It's not the most accessible of locations. But they're going as fast as they can."

"OK." There wasn't much Annie could do to speed things up. All she could do was look after Peg while she waited, and hope that her friend carried on breathing.

"She's injured," she said. "She's been hit by a jug." She leaned in closer. "There's a bruise on her forehead."

"Is the skin broken?"

"Not... not as far as I can see. It is dark in here."

"OK. Keep her still and watch over her. The paramedics will deal with the wound when they arrive."

Annie grunted. She shifted from the squatting position she'd been in, easing herself down to sit on the cold concrete floor. The wind blew in through the open door, chilling her back.

"Oh, Peg," she said.

"Is everything OK?" asked Jayda. "Has something changed?"

"No. Sorry."

"That's OK. You're doing great. Just fifteen minutes to wait now."

Annie looked down, at the broken jug. She blinked and looked up, towards the open door. A paint tin had been spilled, and footprints led from it to the door.

Had she done that? If she had, she certainly didn't remember doing it.

The prints were red, made with what looked like heavy boots. Annie was wearing crocs over thick winter socks. Perfect for pulling on after her swim, but not great as protection from the storm.

And Peg... Peg was wearing slippers.

That crash she'd heard...

She licked her lips. "Is it just an ambulance coming, or police?"

"An ambulance. Why? Are you in danger?"

"I'm not, but Peg... I think she was attacked."

"OK. I'll call for police to attend as well. They'll need to take a statement from you."

I know that. "My daughter's a detective. I've done this before."

"That'll help. Please wait a moment while I contact the police."

Annie drew in a long breath. The wind was filtering through her clothes now, chilling her right through. Even in her cosy dry robe she was freezing.

Get your bum off the ground. She shifted back to a squatting position but soon sat back down when her back started grumbling. *The joys of ageing.*

"The police are ten minutes away," Jayda said. "The ambulance isn't far behind."

Annie allowed herself a small smile. "It'll probably be my son-in-law."

"Sorry? Is your son-in-law there?"

"No. He's a police constable." Annie looked up. How far was she from Hill Road and the police station?

No. She needed to stay here. She'd made the call. She should leave the rest to the professionals.

She heard a car engine from somewhere not too far off. Police?

She craned her neck to see out of the door. Faint blue lights reflected off the stone walls of the courtyard outside.

At last. She felt her body slump in relief.

"I think they're here," she said.

"Good. I'll leave you with them now, Annie. You've done brilliantly. You might just have saved your friend's life."

CHAPTER FOUR

DOUGIE PUSHED OPEN the door to the house. The air inside was warm and cosy, a welcome relief from the gale outside. He shrugged off his heavy police-issue coat and hung it on the row of pegs next to the mirror.

"Hi, love," he called. "Sorry I'm so late."

Naomi appeared in the kitchen doorway, arms folded across her chest. "You said you'd be home hours ago."

He closed his eyes. "I'm sorry, Nai. I really am. I got... I got engrossed in some paperwork. Lost track of time."

She laughed, approaching him. "Only you could get engrossed in paperwork, Douglas Anderson."

He smiled and bent to kiss her on the lips. She wrapped her arms around him and deepened the kiss.

He hadn't been expecting that.

Naomi pulled away. "I've had a terrible day."

He frowned. "I'm sorry. Poppy?"

She shook her head. She was fine. Mum took all the kids for tea and cake at the Town Mill Bakery this afternoon, they loved it."

"That's a bit fancy, for those three."

"You know what she's like."

Dougie did indeed know what his mother-in-law Annie was like. She adored her grandchildren and loved to spoil them. More than once, Naomi and her sister Tina had been forced to tell her to stop.

"So what happened?" he asked.

She shook her head, turning back into the kitchen. "Long story. Make me a cuppa, will you?"

He followed her through and switched on the kettle. "Is Poppy in bed?"

She nodded. "You missed bedtime."

Dougie grimaced. "I'm sorry. I really am."

She grunted. "Anyway. My day. It was that awful Fenella woman again."

Dougie had heard this story before. He forced back a sigh. "What did she do this time?"

"She has no idea how difficult my job is. She thinks I'm just a glorified dogsbody, there to clean up messes and wipe away tears."

Naomi was a teaching assistant at St Michael's Primary School, near where her mum lived. Fenella was the teacher she shared a class of six-year-olds with. Fenella had only joined the school two months earlier, and in the short time she'd been there, she hadn't made herself popular.

"I'm sorry," he said, pulling two mugs from a cupboard and lifting the kettle to fill them.

She gave him a *you don't understand* look. "I can't stand it. I've half a mind to resign."

Dougie almost dropped the kettle. He turned to his wife. "You can't do that."

Her eyes widened. "Can't I?"

"No. Well, I don't mean you *can't*. But what about money? We can't afford this house just on my salary."

She slumped against the wall. "You're right. And it's not as if Lyme Regis has a bunch of primary schools for me to choose from. But God, she is awful."

He passed her a cup of tea. She took it and drank, then gave him a smile. "Sorry. I harp on about it too much."

"You don't," he said. "I'm spoiled, with Jim Connors as my boss."

She stepped across to him and poked his waist. "You're going to stay working in that police station until the day they give you a gold clock, aren't you?"

"A gold clock?"

"A gold clock. Retirement gift."

He laughed. "I don't think they do that anymore." He cocked his head. "But yes. I can't see why I wouldn't stay there."

She gave him a long look. Naomi had asked him why he didn't want to become a sergeant on more than one occasion. The truth was, he just didn't. Her sister Tina was a DC, and he knew she wanted to progress. But he didn't feel the same way.

"Give me a cuddle," she said. "Cheer me up."

He wrapped his arms around her just as his phone began to ring in his back pocket. *Damn.*

"Sorry, love." He pulled it out. "It's Wendy."

She sighed. "Answer it, then."

He gave her a *sorry* smile as he picked up the call. "Wendy? Everything OK?"

"Sorry to call you at night, mate." PC Wendy Sharman was his partner. They'd known each other since childhood and worked together for years.

"That's OK." Wendy wouldn't call unless it was important. "What is it?"

"I'm at the pottery, near the old mill," she said. "There's been a break-in. A woman in her seventies attacked, by the looks of it."

He frowned. "Is there an ambulance there?"

"They're attending to her now. I wouldn't call you about this kind of thing Dougie, only..."

Naomi was watching him, her expression puzzled.

"Only what?" he asked Wendy.

"Only Annie Abbott is here. Your mother-in-law. It seems she found the victim."

Oh, hell. He looked at Naomi, shaking his head. "Your mum," he whispered.

She raised her eyebrows.

Annie had a knack for getting into trouble. For finding herself at the centre of crimes.

"I'm on my way," he said into the phone. "I won't be long."

CHAPTER FIVE

HELEN ARRIVED home from the Pilot Boat a little tipsier than she'd intended.

She let herself in through the back door of her art gallery and strolled through it, fingers brushing against her favourite pieces. This was a routine of hers, her favourite way to end each day. She knew that tonight, her touches were probably more heavy-handed than was wise.

"Oh. It's you."

Helen turned to see a human shape illuminated in the doorway leading to the first-floor flat. She put a hand on her chest.

"You gave me a shock."

"So did you. I thought you'd drowned."

Helen walked towards her girlfriend, trying to keep her footsteps even. It wasn't working.

"Why would you think that?"

"It's the last bloody day of November and you and your mates insisted on going for a swim. And then you didn't come home for hours. I've been calling you."

"Have you?" Helen frowned. She removed her hand from her own chest and placed it on Harper's. Harper didn't react.

"I'm sorry, my love," she said. "Sally suggested going to the Pilot Boat afterwards for a warming brandy."

"Brandy? Since when was the Pilot Boat a gentleman's club?"

Helen fought to keep down a hiccup. "You'd be surprised at the range they stock." She smiled, then giggled.

Harper shook her head. "Looks like you sampled a fair selection of that range."

Helen leaned forwards, placing her head where her hand had been. Harper's chest was warm. She sighed and nuzzled her girlfriend, working her way closer in.

Harper stepped back. "Don't."

Helen put out a hand to stop herself falling, almost sending a tacky sculpture of the Cobb – one she hated but which would be guaranteed to sell – spinning off its shelf.

"Don't what?" she asked.

"I've been sitting upstairs watching old *Star Trek: Voyager* episodes, unable to focus. I even watched the one where they find Seven of Nine." Harper pursed her lips. "Can't remember a word of it."

"But you love that episode."

"I do. That's how worried you got me."

Helen sighed. "I'm sorry. Let me..." She pulled her phone out.

Ah.

She'd forgotten to charge it earlier. It stared up from her hand, the screen blank.

She waved it towards Harper, showing her. "Phone dead. Sorry."

Harper's nostrils flared. She stared at Helen for a moment, then turned away. "I'm probably overreacting. You swim in that bay almost every day."

She turned and walked up the stairs.

Helen followed her up and into the kitchen, where Harper clattered around with a mug and the kettle.

"You're making tea?" she said, aware that her voice sounded pathetic. Wheedling, even.

Harper looked at her. "Coffee. For me."

"Is that wise, so late at night?"

"I'm not as old as you, Helen. My body can still handle caffeine after lunchtime."

"That was low."

Harper shrugged. "Next time, tell me you've finished your swim." She waved a hand. "Not in the mornings, I know you're fine in the mornings. But at night, like this." She rubbed her brow. "I worry."

"And I love that you worry about me." Helen stepped towards her girlfriend and put a hand on her arm. "I do, really."

"Not enough."

Helen felt like she'd been punched in the stomach. She watched Harper, who had turned her back to her and was pouring hot water into a mug. Only one mug.

"What do you mean, not enough?"

Harper didn't turn. "You *know* what I mean."

Helen slumped against the worktop. In the summer, Harper had proposed. Helen had turned her down – she'd had no choice – and she thought she'd reassured Harper that marriage wasn't all that important. After all, neither of them was the conventional type.

It seemed she'd been wrong.

"How long has this been brewing?" Helen asked.

Harper sighed. "I don't know. A while, I guess. I just..." She turned. "I was imagining you out there, in the sea. Drowned. If you died, would they even let me see you, in the hospital?"

"Probably the mortuary, darling."

"That's not the point. I'm not your next of kin. We have no formal bond."

Helen stepped forward. "We have our love for each other."

"I need more than that." Harper met her gaze, her eyes piercing.

Oh, bloody hell. This was serious.

"You want rights," Helen said. "And we can sort that out. I can add you to the deed, for the shop and the flat. And your workshop, out the back."

Harper shook her head. "This isn't about property. It isn't about money. It's about you and me. I told you in July, Helen. I want to stand up in public and tell the world I love Helen Cruickshank."

Helen realised she'd been biting her lip so hard she'd drawn blood. She rubbed it. "And we can do that, my love. We don't need the bureaucracy that comes with—"

Harper pulled away, her back sliding along the edge of the kitchen units. "You just don't get it."

"I do. I made you that tea towel, didn't I? *Helen Cruickshank loves Harper McCoppin?* Embroidered into a hundred towels, all around the kitchens of Lyme Regis. And beyond."

Harper grunted. "It's just a tea towel."

"I thought you loved it."

Harper softened. "I did. I do. I'm... I don't know. I need some time to think. To get my head together." She made for the door, brushing Helen's proffered hand aside.

"Harper..." Helen said.

"Not now. I'm going to sleep in the workshop tonight. I need to be alone."

CHAPTER SIX

DOUGIE WAS BLASTED in the face by a squall of rain as he climbed out of his car. Mill Lane, narrow for most of its length, widened here into a courtyard surrounded by artisan shops, a café and, of course, the old mill. The ambulance had been reversed in; some impressive manoeuvring. And Wendy's panda car was beside it. Both were empty.

He grabbed his torch; there were lights here, but they weren't enough. Taking a moment to get his bearings while the wind pounded against his coat, he headed for the pottery. Round the back, Wendy had said.

Lights were on and there was movement inside, although the rain on the windows obscured his view. The back door was open.

Dougie walked in to see his mother-in-law standing to one side, two paramedics hunched over a woman on the floor. Wendy watched over them, her expression tense.

She turned. "Dougie." She glanced at Annie. "Glad you're here."

He nodded towards the woman on the floor. Peg Johnson, Wendy had told him on the phone on his journey here. "How is she?"

One of the paramedics turned. She groaned, pulling herself upright. "Alright, Dougie."

"Becca." He gave her a tight smile. Becca Novak had been two years above him at school, where she'd had a mass of frizzy hair and a passion for Pokémon. She hadn't changed much, apart from the tattoos running up both of her arms. "You haven't moved her yet."

"We're just getting her ready. No sign of concussion, but you can't be too sure."

Dougie looked past her to see that Becca's colleague, Nick Rogers, had put a neck brace on the woman. He didn't know Nick as well as Becca – he was from Yeovil, which seemed a world away to Dougie – but knew he and Becca were a good team.

Annie's friend was in excellent hands.

"I'm gonna need your help, Bec," Nick said. Becca gave Dougie a glance then bent back down.

"OK," she said. "It would be helpful if you could clear the room."

Dougie raised an eyebrow at Annie. "Let's go outside."

She nodded and followed him. The two of them stood out of the way while Peg was stretchered into the ambulance.

He looked at Annie. His mother-in-law was a force of nature, one who cared about people, but a force, nonetheless. Right now, she looked soggy and defeated.

"What happened?" he asked her.

Wendy was leaving the workshop, coming out behind the paramedics. She stopped next to Dougie, listening in.

Annie shivered. "Peg's sister, Sally, told me she was ill. I wanted to check on her. She didn't answer her phone. When she didn't answer the door either..." Another shudder. "I got worried. So I came round the back." She closed her eyes. "I found her on the floor."

Wendy patted her back. "You've had a shock. We need to get you inside."

The rain had eased a little but was still coming down. Dougie gestured for Annie to follow him to his car. The workshop was a crime scene; she didn't need to go back in there.

"Wendy, can you...?" he asked.

She nodded. "I'll secure the scene. We'll need Forensics in."

"No way they'll get here tonight."

"No." Wendy gave Annie a smile. "Look after yourself, Annie. Don't go overdoing it, yeah?"

Annie grunted. Dougie wondered if his mother-in-law was capable of not overdoing it.

He led her to his car and let her in the passenger seat. Once inside, he turned the heating on. It was good to get out of the rain.

"So you went into the workshop," he said.

She nodded. "I found her in there."

She pointed back towards the door. Five of them there'd been in there, plus poor Peg. Forensics would not be impressed.

"Well, it's good that you did," he said. "She's in good hands now."

A sniff. "Yes."

"Best thing you can do now is to get yourself home and dry off before you make yourself ill. I can come over tomorrow to get your statement."

Annie started at the sound of someone knocking on the

window. Dougie looked past her, but whoever it was, they were obscured.

Wendy, probably. Checking in before sending him home.

"Wait a minute," he said, pushing the door open.

He grimaced as the wind hit him again, forcing the door back towards him as he climbed out of the car. Lyme in November might be pretty – the Christmas lights, the lack of crowds – but it could be bleak.

It wasn't Wendy. In fact, the woman standing by his passenger door looked remarkably like the woman who'd just been driven away in the back of the ambulance.

"Can I help you?" he asked.

She looked at him, her wrinkled face pale. "What's happened? I saw an ambulance."

Annie had got out of the car. "Sally," she said. "You're back."

Sally looked at her. "I went for a drink with Helen. What's happened?"

Dougie remembered hearing something about the people who ran the pottery and the attached shop. Twins. This must be the other one.

"Let's go inside the shop," he said. He gestured towards the front entrance; no way was he letting Sally go round the back.

Sally nodded, her eyes wide. She turned away from him and walked towards the shop, her back hunched. After she'd unlocked the door and let them in, she turned to Annie.

"What's going on? Why are you here?"

"I wanted to check on Peg," Annie said. "After you told me she was ill."

Sally frowned. "I told you it was nothing."

"Sally..." Annie put a hand on the other woman's shoulder. "That was Peg who just went off in the ambulance."

Sally's face fell. "She was... No. It was just a cold. She's fine. What...?"

Dougie stepped in. "I'm afraid your sister's suffered a head injury. She isn't fully responsive right now and she needs to be checked for concussion. But the paramedics will take good care of her."

Sally looked at him. "Where have they taken her?"

"Probably Dorset County, in Dorchester," he said. "I can check for you."

"That's miles away."

He shrugged. Sally was looking at Annie's hands. Dougie hadn't noticed before, but there was what looked like blood on them.

"Annie?" he said. "Have you been hurt?"

She looked down. "No. At least, I don't think so." She rubbed her hand. The red came off in flakes. She looked up. "It's paint," she said. "I remember now. Seeing a trail of footprints. In paint."

"Peg's footprints?" Sally asked.

Annie shook her head. "No. Too big. And I heard a noise." She gasped and looked at Dougie. "And there was that jug. The broken one, on the floor."

Dougie nodded. For the first time in many years, Annie Abbott seemed vulnerable.

She stared at him, her eyes wet.

"Peg... She was attacked," she said.

CHAPTER SEVEN

"THIS IS NICE," Rosamund said.

Her twenty-year-old son Cameron rolled his eyes. "Don't be like that."

Rosamund looked down at her plate: chicken katsu curry, Cameron's favourite. A deliberate choice.

"Like what?" she asked.

"Just..." He waggled his hand. "Like that."

She sighed. "OK." She ate a few more bites, trying to ignore the tension in her stomach.

"Sorry," Cameron said. "That was unfair."

She looked at him. Yes, it was. But she wasn't going to make a thing of it. He had his own reasons to be on edge.

"Thank you," she said.

Ever since her husband David had left, she'd been trying to make this austere modern house feel more like her own. Cushions, candles, rugs. She still wasn't sure if it was her, or simply *not David*. Maybe she should ask Cameron what he'd like the place to look like.

But then, Cameron had been talking about moving out.

She smiled, nodding over at the red candle holders on the sideboard. "I very nearly lit the candles."

He laughed. "Ooh, steady now. Nearly making it a special occasion."

"The way this storm's going, I wouldn't be surprised if we end up with a power cut. But I decided it would be a bit too weird."

"Candles are always fun."

"You know what?" She put down her fork. "You're right. Let's light them, just for fun. And just in case the lights do go out."

Rosamund went to the sideboard and yanked open a drawer. She pulled out a box of matches with a *ta-dah* flourish and lit the candles. Cameron went to the light switch and turned off the overhead light.

Rosamund smiled as she sat down. Yes, she couldn't see her curry very well. But the candles cast a pleasant glow.

"This whole thing with Dad," Cameron said.

Rosamund looked up, surprised. Cameron never talked about his father.

Was it the candlelight? The curry? The combination of the two?

"It's a bit weird, isn't it?" he continued.

Weird didn't begin to describe what David had done, as far as Rosamund was concerned. But she bit back her reflexive response.

"Weird? In what way?" She tried to keep her voice level.

"Well..." Cameron looked down at his plate. "In the way you're behaving, for one." He frowned. "It's just... urgh." He looked up at her. "Can I trash-talk Dad for a bit?"

She resisted the urge to laugh. "You just say what you need to say."

He took a deep breath, putting down his fork and picking up a napkin – one of the new paisley ones she'd bought in Dorchester. He clenched it in his fist.

"He ghosted me for months," he said. "Literally, months." He squeezed tighter. "I guess he ghosted you, too?"

She nodded and shrugged, not wanting him to know how hurt she'd been. How angry she still was.

Cameron's relationship with his father was separate from her own. That was important.

"And now he's back," Cameron continued.

She swallowed. "He is."

"Like... back in touch, like nothing's happened. He wants to meet up. He wants to be all pally."

Rosamund looked at her son. He'd placed the napkin on the table, where he was smoothing it out like his life depended on it.

"You're angry," she said.

He sighed. "Maybe."

"You don't have to be ashamed of that." She hesitated. "I'm angry, too. But your father will want a chance to explain his actions to you, I'm sure."

"He doesn't." Cameron shook his head.

"He does."

His jaw was clenched. "His messages are all about me meeting his new girlfriend. Shari." He looked at her. "He sounds properly excited, like me meeting her suddenly makes everything fine. Like..." He stopped smoothing. "Oh, I don't know."

Rosamund reached a hand across the tablecloth. They were sitting at right angles, her at the head of the dining table and him to one side. Where she now sat had been David's customary place. No way was she going to leave it empty as if he were some kind of ghost.

She looked at him, searching for the right words. After months of ignoring his son, David didn't know how to talk to Cameron anymore. She wasn't sure if he ever had. She wasn't going to leap to David's defence, but neither was she going to 'trash-talk' him.

"He hasn't even mentioned the fact that he just went dark for months," Cameron said. "It's like he wants to pretend it never happened."

Rosamund came from a family who had plenty of expertise when it came to glossing over difficult conversations. Her mother, Joanna, preferred to hide them under mountains of trivia and fluff.

But Cameron deserved better.

"How do you plan to handle it?" she asked.

He frowned. "What d'you mean?"

"You don't have to go along with the pretence, if you don't want to."

He pulled in a breath. "I could call him out."

Rosamund shrugged. "Up to you." She forced a neutral expression onto her face.

Cameron pushed his plate away. "I see how he's playing this. He's said nothing about me and him meeting up, just the two of us. It's all about me meeting this Shari." He looked at Rosamund. "Either he's showing off..."

"...the newer, younger model." She forced a smile.

He shook his head. "I don't think it's that. I just think he's scared to be alone with me."

Rosamund eyed her son. How had he become so much more perceptive than his father, in so few years? How had he become so much more courageous than her?

"You don't have to play along," she said.

"It would be super-awkward if I called him out over what he's done, with his new girlfriend sitting right there."

Rosamund imagined it. Oh, she'd love to see that conversation. Cameron giving his irresponsible dad what for with the undoubtedly glamorous Shari looking on, wishing she'd never got involved.

But if it did happen, Rosamund wouldn't be there. And in reality, it wouldn't make her feel better. Even if Shari did decide to run a mile.

"Darling," she said. "I know you'll do what you think's best. But make sure you do what's best for you, not just what's best for everybody else."

He grunted. "Yeah."

Rosamund put her hand out further and was shocked when he actually took it.

She smiled at her son. "And remember," she said, "a little bit of social embarrassment never killed anyone."

CHAPTER EIGHT

DC Tina Abbott knew her mum could be calling her after ten at night for any of a number of reasons.

A moan about the roadworks on the corner of Anning Road and Church Street and the way they stopped the buses getting past. A chat about her latest swim and how bracing it had been, as if that was news. A simple enquiry about what her grandchildren were up to.

She knew that for most people, a call at this time of night probably meant an emergency. But not for Annie.

Even so, Tina's heart picked up pace as she answered the call. She was sitting in the living room of the house she shared with her husband Mike Legg, a fellow detective at Dorset Police HQ. The kids were safely tucked up in bed and she'd just poured herself a glass of wine. Mike was out having a drink with Johnny, and she had no idea when he'd be back. His turn, for once.

"Mum," she said. "Don't tell me. You want to know if Daisy's added anything else to her Christmas list. She's not even one year old, you know. She really doesn't need much. And she certainly can't write a list."

"No. It's not that."

Annie's voice sounded thin. Tina sat up straight and placed her glass down on the coffee table.

"Mum? You OK?"

"I'm OK. I'm fine, love. Please, don't panic. It's Peg."

"Peg?"

Tina ran through her mum's friends in her head. There was Rosamund, the snooty one whose husband had run off with his PA. Figgy, the young geek who was slowly emerging from her shell and had a not-so-secret crush on Rosamund's son. And Helen, the bohemian gallery owner.

She couldn't recall a Peg.

"Who's Peg, Mum?"

"Peg's my swimming friend, Tina. Surely you remember."

Tina looked up at the ceiling. Best to lie.

"Ah, Peg," she said. "Of course. She's the one who..."

"She's one half of the twins. Peg and Sally. The ladies in their seventies who run the pottery."

It still didn't ring any bells with Tina, but at least now Annie had filled her in on the basics.

"Of course. I remember. What's up with her?"

"She's been attacked."

Tina frowned. "Sorry? Attacked? When? Mum, I need you to hang up right now and call 999. If you're in the middle of something—"

"Don't be ridiculous, you silly girl. I called 999 hours ago. Two very nice paramedics came, along with Wendy and Dougie."

"Oh. Good." Tina hesitated. "Well done."

"Don't patronise me, Tina Abbott. I'm not calling you because I expect you to act as emergency responder. I'm calling you because you're a detective."

"Ah." *Now* it was making sense.

"Is she OK?" Tina asked. "Peg? How badly hurt was she?"

"I don't know." Annie's voice broke. "They took her off in an ambulance. Oh, love, I don't know what to..."

Annie started to cry. Tina listened, helplessness mixing with bewilderment.

"Do you want me to come over, Mum? When Mike gets back, I can—"

"No. I'm alright. But Peg will need you."

"Mum," Tina said. "I can't just come rushing over there and take over an investigation. It doesn't—"

"You did the last two times."

Tina swallowed. Annie was right. Previously, when Marco Calllington and then Clifford Muldoon had been killed, she'd got involved without being asked. But in the case of Marco, the police hadn't even been aware of a body. And besides, she'd been on maternity leave. And bored.

"I need to play by the rules now, Mum," she said. "I'm thinking of applying to do the sergeant's exam, and—"

"Sergeant's exam? My daughter, a detective sergeant?" Annie's voice had picked up. "Oh, my!"

"I'm only thinking about it. Don't tell Dougie, please. Or Naomi."

"Why ever not?"

"Because I don't want to make a thing of it. If I decide to go for it – and I might not – then I don't want to tell anyone until it's done."

"You think you'll fail."

The truth was, Tina had no idea what the answer to that statement was.

"I don't know, Mum. Anyway, tell me about your friend. Peg. Tell me she isn't dead."

"No. Although when I found her... oh, Tina love, I did think she was dead! There was no pulse, and I couldn't see her chest moving, and then Jayda helped me find her pulse and listen to her breathing and told me I might just have saved her life, and the paramedics arrived, old friend of yours one of them was, and—"

"Mum. Slow down. Peg's alive, and she's been taken to hospital. Dougie and Wendy are on the case, so they'll prosecute whoever attacked her." A thought struck Tina, and she felt her blood turn cold. "Were you there when it happened? Were you attacked, too?"

"No. I already told you I found her."

Of course. Annie had been talking so fast that Tina had missed it.

"Yes," she said. "Of course. What happened? Where was she?"

"In the workshop, at the back of the pottery. The one by the old mill, you know the one."

"I do."

"Someone broke in, I'm sure of it. I heard them."

Tina pulled in a shallow breath. Why did her mum have such a knack for attracting danger? "I hope you didn't do anything silly."

"Of course not, love. Besides, whoever it was, they were gone by the time I turned up. They left prints, though. Boot prints, in paint. And a jug. A broken jug." Her voice wobbled. "They must have hit her with it."

"It sounds like a burglary," Tina said. "Maybe Peg

disturbed them. Was anything stolen?"

"How am I supposed to know?"

She was right. "Well, Dougie will ask the right questions, I'm sure." Tina knew this wasn't over, no matter how much she wished it to be. "Mum, why don't you get yourself a stiff drink, to calm your nerves? Either that or a strong cup of tea."

"I already got the whisky out of the cupboard. I'm staring at it right now."

Tina's dad had been a whisky drinker. She knew how desperate Annie must be feeling to contemplate breaking into his supply.

"I'll come over, as soon as Mike's back," she said. It would mean a long drive to Lyme, and then a long drive back in time to get Louis to preschool the next morning, but she was used to long drives.

"That would be good. You can stay here for a bit and help me find out who attacked Peg."

Tina sighed. "No, Mum. You can't do that again."

"Still. You're a detective. Dougie and Wendy are good police officers. But they don't have your skills. And neither of them is a sergeant."

"I'm not a sergeant either, Mum. Not yet."

"Ah, but you will be. How about you come over in the morning, bring the little ones. I can have them for a few days, take them to the Christmas Fayre at St Michael's on Saturday. They'll love it."

Saturday meant more than a couple of days. But Louis and Daisy often stayed over at Granny's. And Lyme Regis at Christmas was special.

"They do enjoy that kind of thing," Tina admitted. And she did have a day off scheduled, the next day.

"There," said Annie. "That's settled then. And it'll give

you a break, too. I'm sure you need it. Prepare for the exam, and all that."

"The exam isn't for weeks."

"Still. It does no harm to start early."

Tina was already wishing she hadn't said anything. "I'll come over in the morning. I want to check you're OK. But I'm not storming in there and taking over this case."

"Of course."

"I mean it," Tina said. She knew that tone in her mum's voice.

"You do. You mean it, and so do I. I'll see you in the morning. I'm looking forward to it."

Annie hung up. Tina stared at the phone, wondering if she'd just been run over by a steamroller.

CHAPTER NINE

DOUGIE RETURNED TO THE STOREROOM. Wendy was in the doorway, taping it up.

"It's a mess in there," he said, looking at the broken jug on the floor and the paint marks. The boot prints had become smudged by the movement of the paramedics as they'd taken Peg out. Frustrating, but getting her to hospital was the priority.

Wendy nodded. "I didn't think to check her pockets for a key. I'll have to tape this up, close the door and hope for the best."

Dougie eyed the door. In this weather, that was risky.

"I think we should nail it shut," he said. "Have you got anything in the car?"

She raised an eyebrow. "Luckily, I come prepared." She handed him the roll of tape. "Can you finish off this, while I fetch it?"

He nodded and yawned. "Just the door?"

"No. Look over there."

He turned. "What am I looking at?"

"Use your torch, silly."

Dougie shone his torch into the courtyard. "Oh, hell. Did I just trample all over those?"

There were red footprints heading away from the store-room door.

"Probably," said Wendy. "But then, so did I, and so did the paramedics. Not to mention your mother-in-law in her crocs."

Dougie grimaced. "She really does get everywhere, doesn't she?"

"She certainly has a knack for attracting trouble."

He sighed. "Give me the tape. I'll do the footpaths, too." They didn't want people accessing this spot from the alleyway into town, or from the low footbridges that spanned the River Lyme.

"Thanks." She handed him a roll. "Take some photos while you're at it. I'm worried the storm will get up again and destroy all our evidence."

Dougie didn't have a proper camera with him, unlike the forensic investigators who'd arrive in the morning. But he did have his phone. He made his way methodically across the courtyard, relieved that the wind had subsided.

The boot prints faded as they got further from the pottery, until they petered out in the centre of the courtyard. He stood over the final footprint, photographing it from a variety of distances and wondering where Peg's attacker had gone from here.

He crouched down, waving the light from his phone across the ground. This was definitely the last print.

He stood and groaned at his cracking knees. *Where did you go, you bugger?*

He walked to the far end of the courtyard, firing off more

photographs as he went. He placed a hand against the wall of the old mill and yawned.

It was late, and his brain was fuzzy. He'd been on a week of night shifts until the day before yesterday, and he was knackered from being up all day today.

And he was supposed to be off duty. Not that that ever stopped him.

He made his way back to the pottery, photographing the prints from the other side. Beside a wall was a pair of dust-bins. One had been knocked over.

Dougie pushed back his natural urge to set it upright – he liked to do his bit to keep Lyme tidy – and photographed it instead. He edged in closer, looking for traces of paint.

Nothing. But that didn't mean it wouldn't have the attacker's prints on it. Especially if they'd knocked it over.

Wendy was back at the entrance to the pottery, the door now secure. "You need your sleep, mate. I saw you almost fall asleep leaning on that wall."

He yawned. "Yeah. See you in the morning, yes?"

"See you in the morning, Dougie. We've got a case to solve."

CHAPTER TEN

THE SWIMMERS DREW two tables together in the café, forming a protective huddle around Sally. No swimming today: it was too cold, and they were all in shock.

Helen and Rosamund were both quiet. Annie had expected Helen to be full of ostentatious concern for Sally, clucking over her and voicing her sympathy for all to hear. But instead, she sat away from Sally, her face pinched. Had she been crying?

And Rosamund... Rosamund was at the other end of the table, looking just as moody. Mind you, Annie knew the reason for that.

David was back in town. She'd spotted him and the outline of his girlfriend driving up Broad Street in a swanky electric hire car on her way to the Town Bakery café.

Surprisingly, it was Figgy who sat at Sally's other side, squeezing her hand with a maturity which made Annie proud of the progress her young friend had made.

"You must be devastated," Figgy said.

Sally sniffed and nodded.

"I'm so sorry," Annie said. "If I'd got there a few minutes earlier..."

Sally turned to her. "Then he might have attacked you both."

"He?" Helen asked, perking up.

Sally shook her head. "It must have been a man. Would a woman have done that?"

They all sat quietly for a moment. The police had said nothing so far about a suspect, but Annie had seen that smashed jug. Anyone could have wielded that. And Peg was elderly...

"How is Peg now?" Annie asked.

"Still unconscious. She's had so many tests. CT, MRI, you name it. Being in hospital with her was a whirlwind. I thought it would be a relief to come home. But I just want to go back." She turned to Figgy, her eyes wet. "What if she wakes up and I'm not there?"

"We could take you back?" Figgy suggested. She looked around the group. She didn't have a car, but she knew that Helen, Rosamund and Annie all did.

Annie kept quiet. Tina was due to arrive in an hour with the little ones. Once they were here, she would be happy to help. But she knew Tina didn't always approve of her getting Louis and Daisy involved in this sort of thing.

"Of course," said Rosamund. "I'll drive you, just say the word."

Helen gave Rosamund a look that seemed to hold a mixture of relief and gratitude. What was up with her?

"Have you been home yet?" Figgy asked.

Sally shook her head. "I can't face it. And besides, it's a crime scene." A shudder ran through her shoulders. Annie gave them a squeeze.

"I'm sure we can get it all tidied up for you," Rosamund said.

"Rosamund's very good at tidying up," Helen added. "Are you still cleaning those cottages?"

"I am. Although I'm very glad David didn't decide to hire one of them."

"He's back?" Figgy looked across the table at her.

Rosamund nodded. "Apparently. He messaged Cameron, but he hasn't made contact with me." She shrugged. "Why would he?"

"So if he isn't staying in one of the Clappentail Cottages..." Annie said.

Rosamund raised an eyebrow. "Wisteria Cottage. The big old house as you drive into Charmouth."

"I know that," Helen said. "Fancy."

Rosamund wrinkled her nose. "Three thousand pounds a week. Nothing but the best, for Shari."

"Shari?" Helen asked. It seemed whatever was bothering her, it was no match for her natural curiosity.

"His girlfriend. Younger, she was his PA." Rosamund looked around the group. "A cliché, I know."

"It can't be easy," Annie said. She reached across to put a hand on top of Rosamund's, finding herself twisting to keep her other arm around Sally's shoulders.

Rosamund shrugged. "It's not me I'm worried about. It's Cameron. He's angry that his dad won't be alone with him."

"They've seen each other?" Annie asked.

"Not yet. David wants to introduce him to Shari. He doesn't want to explain why he didn't bother contacting him for months on end."

"Poor Cam," Figgy muttered. Rosamund looked at her but said nothing.

"Maybe he wants to make up with Cameron," Annie suggested. "Christmas goodwill, and all that." She smiled. "Has anyone opened the first window of their advent calendar?" She was saving hers for when the grandkids arrived.

"Oh, yes," said Helen. "I did that... back in 1978, when I was ten."

Annie frowned. *No need to be like that.*

Sally looked around her friends. "It's our busiest season," she said. "But I just can't face running the shop." She sobbed.

They all sat in silence for a moment, sipping their drinks. Then Annie had an idea.

"I can help," she said.

"You can?" asked Sally. Helen rolled her eyes.

Annie nodded. "You need someone to run the shop for you. Just until Peg's better." There was no need to voice the possibility that Peg might not get better. "And you're ready to come back."

"I can see where this is going," muttered Helen.

Annie ignored her. She puffed up her chest. "You need a shop manager, Sally. And I'm happy to step in."

"What do you know about running a shop?" Helen asked.

Annie looked at her. "I worked on the front desk at Dorchester Town Hall for years. I know plenty about customer service. And I know everyone in Lyme. I'm sure I can find a way to convince each and every one of them to buy a piece of pottery."

"You think you can?" Sally asked. "You really think you can help?"

Annie forced back the worry that was already niggling at her. Had she really meant to become a volunteer shop manager? Had she been secretly hoping Sally would say no?

"Of course," she replied. She pushed on a smile. "It'll be fun."

She'd have to find a way to get the grandkids involved. That might be tricky, but she was sure she could manage.

"If you really don't mind..." Sally said.

"I don't. I promise." Was Annie lying, both to Sally and to herself?

Sally smiled. "I'm so grateful, Annie. I can go back to Dorchester, be by Peg's side."

"You can't be in the ward twenty-four seven," Helen pointed out.

"Peg and I have a friend in the town. She's already offered to put me up." Sally took Annie's hand. "Thank you, Annie. You're a lifesaver."

"It's nothing," Annie said, unconvinced.

She could do this. Just how hard could it be to sell pottery?

They all stood up.

"I'll need to talk you through some of the practicalities," Sally said.

"Of course," Annie replied, hoping she had time before Tina arrived.

"I'll meet you there in five minutes." Sally headed out of the bakery, suddenly energised.

Annie stood with her friends, watching Sally go. What had she done?

"Do you really have retail experience?" Figgy asked.

"I can guarantee you'll be knocking on my door asking for help within five minutes," Helen added.

Annie turned to her. "I can do this, Helen. Why do you insist on doubting me? And what's got into you this morning? You seem..." *Grumpy. Combative.* "... low."

Helen's expression dropped. "Harper's left me."

Annie gasped. "She did *what*?"

"Don't make me say it again."

"What happened?"

"Oh, Helen." Figgy rubbed Helen's arm.

Helen pulled it free. "We had a row, last night. About the... you don't need to know what about. She told me she'd sleep in the workshop."

"So she's just gone to the workshop," Rosamund said. "Not *left you*, left you."

Helen gave her a harsh look. "I'm not stupid, Rosamund. I know what being left looks like."

Rosamund shrank back.

"That was mean," said Figgy.

Helen looked from her to Rosamund. "You're right. I'm sorry. But she has left. I went to the workshop this morning, and she wasn't there."

"Maybe she—" began Annie.

Helen held up a hand. "Her things were gone, Annie. Not just Harper, but all her clothes, her equipment. Somehow, she even got the steel reindeer she's working on out, too."

She looked between her friends and sniffed.

"Harper's left me, ladies. And it's all my fault."

CHAPTER ELEVEN

"Bit less spooky today," Dougie said as he entered the workshop at the back of the pottery for the second time in the last twelve hours.

Wendy, who was already inside, turned to him. "I heard from the hospital. Peg Casey's not doing well."

He pulled a face. "That's not good."

"The doctors thought she was improving last night, didn't think she had concussion. She was even lucid first thing this morning. But then an hour ago, she suddenly fainted."

"In her hospital bed, I hope?"

"I think so. She hasn't regained consciousness yet. I don't know if it's a coma or something less severe, but..."

Douglas felt the hairs on the back of his neck prickle. "If she doesn't make it, this is a murder investigation."

"Let's not get ahead of ourselves."

"So why aren't the Major Crime team here?" Dougie's sister-in-law Tina was a member of that team, based at the Dorset Police HQ in Winfrith.

"First off, they probably don't know about Peg losing consciousness. Secondly, she's not dead yet."

"But it's not just murders they investigate."

"This could just be a burglary gone wrong, mate," Wendy said. "We can solve this one."

"With the sarge's help."

"With Sergeant Connors's help. Of course. I briefed him before coming here."

Dougie looked past her towards the two forensics investigators crouched on the floor. One was taking impressions from the paint footprints. The other was dusting the shelves and pieces of pottery for prints.

He'd been feeling cheerful on his way here, optimistic about their chances of turning this one around quickly. Now, he just felt empty. And then there was the dream he'd had...

He shivered.

"I remembered something, when I woke up this morning," he told Wendy. "In the storm, when I was on my way home."

"Remembered something?"

He nodded. "I was driving up Pound Street. There was a figure, wearing a hoodie, running from this direction. He'd come out of Sherborne Lane and was running up the hill." He grimaced. "Well, walking, mostly."

"No one in their right mind runs up Pound Street."

"And Sherborne Lane leads directly here."

Wendy's brow furrowed. "You think it's got something to do with this?"

He shrugged. "I don't know. I mean, he wasn't exactly dressed for the weather. But it was the kind of storm that catches you by surprise."

"It bloody was. I had a load of washing out on the line."

"You were hanging washing out, in November?"

"It was windy but dry earlier on," she reminded him. "Perfect drying conditions. Or so I thought."

"Where's your washing now?"

She blew out her cheeks. "Half of it went over the fence into Mrs Donaldson's. Her dog came in from its morning you-know-what with a pair of my pink knickers in its mouth."

Dougie laughed, then put his hand over his mouth. "Sorry. Not appropriate." A woman was in hospital, unconscious.

Wendy shook her head. "If you don't laugh in this job—"

"You'll cry. I know." He put a hand on her shoulder and gripped it, not knowing if it was for reassurance or support.

One of the FSIs stood up, a process that seemed to take at least half an hour. He was possibly the tallest man Dougie had ever seen.

"Who's in charge?" he asked.

Dougie and Wendy exchanged glances. "Neither of us," Wendy said.

"Both of us," Dougie corrected her.

The FSI shook his head. "I'm Gavin Larcomb. I've been looking at these boot prints and they're quite distinctive. The pattern on the sole isn't your run-of-the-mill Doc Martens.".

"That's encouraging," Wendy said. She turned to Dougie. "The bloke you saw, I don't suppose you happened to notice what he had on his feet?"

"No chance." When Dougie had got the clearest view of the man, he'd been right up against the bonnet of his car.

They'd locked eyes, just for a moment. But water had been streaming down the windscreen. Dougie wouldn't be able to pick him out from a line-up if he was up against the Cookie Monster and all four of the Teletubbies.

"Well, we can match them up to the brand, hopefully," Gavin said. "They're size nine, I can tell you that much. So it's very unlikely these prints are from a woman. He attacked an elderly woman, is that right?"

"Peg Casey," Wendy said. "She owns the shop with her sister Sally."

"Right," Gavin said. "So hopefully we can find the person who attacked her using these prints. Or at least narrow it down."

"I've got something else," said the second investigator, standing up. He was shorter and managed to reach an upright position significantly faster than his colleague.

"This is Brett," Gavin said. "You don't often get the two of us together, but our boss Gail's got a week off. Christmas shopping in London with her mum, she is."

"Sounds nice," Wendy said. Dougie couldn't think of anything worse.

"Come over here," Brett said. He gestured for Dougie and Wendy to follow him. They'd both been given forensic suits when they entered the room, not that there seemed much point after all the contamination last night.

"Under there," Brett told them.

Gavin stood behind Dougie, getting an easy vantage point over his head.

"What are we looking at?" Wendy asked.

"Blood," Brett said.

Dougie frowned. "Where?"

"Under this shelf." Brett twisted to duck down under a shelf which was about five feet from the ground. He shone a torch downwards.

"You look," Dougie told Wendy. "You're littler than me."

"Oi." She gave him a dig in the ribs.

A moment later, Wendy, too, was bending, holding onto Brett's arm to keep herself from falling over.

"I see it," she said.

"It's not immediately apparent," Brett said. "And there isn't much of it. What kind of wound did the victim sustain?"

Dougie thought back. "Head wound. She was on the floor when—"

Wendy put up a hand. "I got here first. She was lying on the floor. The only visible wound was to her forehead. But I didn't see any blood."

"Not on her fingertips?" Brett asked.

Wendy shook her head.

"What about you?" Brett asked Dougie.

"I can't remember any blood. But it was dark."

"Not in here, it wasn't." Wendy pointed at the ceiling. "That strip light's like Abbotsbury Subtropical Gardens at Christmas time." She grimaced. "And I should know, I've been twice."

"You're right," Dougie said. "It was bright."

"Only one way to find out," said Gavin. "You'll need to speak to the hospital. The paramedics, maybe. Find out if she was bleeding."

"Because if she wasn't," Brett added, "this here could be her attacker's blood."

CHAPTER TWELVE

Annie hurried to the Millside Pottery, conscious that Sally would be eager to get back to the hospital and her sister.

"Oh," she said as she turned into the courtyard.

The area around the pottery was cordoned off with police tape. Both bridges crossing the river beyond it were blocked off, too.

Sally stood next to the cordon, talking with Dougie. Annie approached, her arms out wide.

"Dougie," she said. "Surely you're going to let Sally into her own home."

He tightened his jaw. "It's a crime scene, I'm afraid. We have to wait until—"

"It's alright," Sally said. "I didn't want to go back in anyway." She rubbed her cheek.

Annie looped a hand under her arm. "You'll be needing to fetch some clothes. For Peg. And for yourself."

Sally shook her head. "I'll be fine. Please, I don't want a fuss."

Dougie smiled at her. "Give me a minute and I'll see

what I can do." He turned away, approaching a ridiculously tall man in a white forensics suit.

"Maybe I'll just leave it closed until Peg's better," Sally said. "I mean, it's only money."

"It's your livelihood," Annie said. "You just told me it was your busiest time of year."

Sally sighed. "It is. But all this..." She swept her arm around to take in the scene. It was certainly anything but homely. Mind you, it was far less forbidding than it had been last night.

Dougie was back. "Mrs Casey," he said.

"Miss," Annie corrected.

He nodded. "Miss Casey. I can let you into the shop at the front of the building. It looks like there's nothing in there we need to examine, now."

"That means you can get to the stairs, and your flat," Annie said.

Sally looked at her. "And the shop can be reopened."

Annie cocked her head. It hadn't taken long for Sally to change her mind on that score. But then, the woman had gone through a hell of a night.

"Of course," she said. "Just show me what I need to know, and I'll crack on." She glanced at her watch. Tina would be here in twenty minutes.

Sally approached the shop door, her steps hesitant, and brought up her key. She turned to Dougie.

"You're certain it's alright?"

"Certain," he replied.

She unlocked the door and stepped inside. Annie followed, her heart racing.

In daylight, the space looked far more welcoming than it had when she'd peered through the windows last night. The shelves held colourful pottery items, many with a Christmas theme. And on the table in the centre was a box full of plain mugs and craft supplies. They looked perfect for creating Christmas-themed mugs.

Annie examined the items, rubbing her hands together. She'd speak to her girls, get them to bring the other mums down. This was going to be a breeze.

She heard a footstep, and she looked up. Sally was in the door to the stairs leading up to the flat. She had a small suitcase in one hand and a shopping bag in the other.

"That was quick," Annie said.

Sally shrugged. "I made a list. Sitting by the bedside of someone who's unconscious gives you a lot of free time."

"Oh, Sally. You poor thing."

Sally shook her head. "Please. You'll make me cry. I just need to tell you how it all works, and leave."

There was a knock on the door, and the very tall forensics investigator opened it.

"Er, ladies..." he said.

"Yes?" Annie replied.

"I'm sorry, but we can't let you in here just yet, after all. We need to be absolutely sure that whoever attacked the other Miss Casey didn't come through this way."

"I was here," Annie told him. "Standing right by that door. I'd have seen him."

"Still. Please?"

Sally walked past Annie, past the man. "Come on, Annie. I'll buy you a cup of tea in the café across the way. We can talk in there."

Annie looked around the shop. "But don't we need to be on the spot, so you can demonstrate things to me?"

"Looks like we've got no choice. I've written it all down. You'll be fine." Sally smiled. "Come on."

Annie followed her friend out of the shop, giving the forensics tech a disgruntled look as she did so. She really did wish they'd make their minds up. Sally was already across the courtyard and entering the Tuck Shop café.

For a septuagenarian, Sally really did move fast. It must be all the swimming. Annie followed her inside.

The Tuck Shop Café was more shed than café, leaning against the largest mill building. Two small tables with gingham tablecloths filled the dingy space. A sad tinfoil star hanging over an empty display cabinet was the only nod to Christmas.

Annie shivered as she followed Sally to the counter, where a woman finished serving a family and turned to them.

"We're closed," she said.

Annie pointed at the family, who'd bought hot drinks and chocolate bars.

The woman, whose badge read *Millie-Jo*, folded her arms across her chest. "Oven's not working."

"Well, we only want tea," Annie said. "I hope your kettle's working."

The woman gave them a weary look. She had pale skin and deep bags under her eyes.

"I can do tea," she conceded.

"Thanks," Sally said, her voice almost as weary as Millie-Jo's.

"Can you do a coffee for me instead?" Annie asked. "One sugar."

Millie-Jo scowled but nodded, then turned towards the kettle on the counter behind her. Lyme Regis boasted more than its share of artisan coffee shops with proper espresso machines, and Annie wondered how this place did any trade. Maybe there was a market for this kind of thing amongst the more nostalgically inclined.

They sat down at the furthest table, eager not to be too close to Millie-Jo, who was now moving around the kitchen area with a brusqueness that suggested she'd regretted agreeing to their drinks. Annie looked around the café.

"I haven't been here before," she said.

Sally smiled. "I don't blame you. It's a dive. But it's convenient."

"Surely you can do better simply by using your own kettle?"

"I can. But you know how sometimes you just need a change of scenery?"

Annie nodded. If she was in need of a change from the Millside Pottery, she'd head further into town, to the Old Mill Bakery or even as far as the Kiosk. But Sally was older than Annie, no matter how fast she walked.

She stood up. "I just had a thought." She left the café and stood outside it, looking up at its front.

She'd been right.

Back inside, she sat next to Sally and leaned in to whisper. "They've got a camera."

Sally frowned. "Sorry?"

"CCTV. It might have caught whoever attacked Peg."

Sally's shoulders dropped. "Oh. Yes."

Annie sniffed. "What *is* that smell?"

There was a musty, watery smell in the air, just on the edge of unpleasant.

"Damp," she said, answering herself with a grimace. How was anyone tempted to linger in this place?

"The waterways converge under this area," Sally told

her. "Tunnels and drains. Seeps up through the stonework. You learn to ignore it after a while."

Annie wrinkled her nose. She hoped the pottery didn't smell like this. But she'd been in there enough times and didn't remember a smell.

Millie-Jo arrived with their drinks in polystyrene cups. She placed them down on the table, spilling some of Annie's coffee.

"Closing in ten minutes," she said. "Drink up."

Very welcoming. Annie gave her a smile. "Can I ask you about the camera outside your shop?"

Millie-Jo glanced towards the door. "What camera?"

"There's a camera on the front corner of the building. As I'm sure you've noticed, a crime was committed near here last night." Annie gestured at Sally. "My friend's sister was brutally attacked."

"I heard about that." Millie-Jo looked at Sally. "Sorry about your sister." Her voice was flat.

"Thanks," muttered Sally.

"So I was thinking," Annie continued. "Your camera might have caught some footage."

Millie-Jo gave her an irritated look. Then she shook her head. "No."

"No?"

"No."

"I don't get you," Annie said. "No, it won't have caught any footage, or no... what?"

"No, it won't have caught any footage. 'Cos it isn't working."

"You're sure?"

"What do you think I am, an idiot?"

"OK, OK." Annie put up her hands. Sally was already more than halfway through her tea. "I'm sorry I asked."

Millie-Jo grunted. She turned back towards the counter, giving the clock on the wall behind it an ostentatious stare.

"Such a rude woman," Annie said.

"I try to steer clear of her," Sally replied.

"I don't blame you."

Sally smoothed a sheet of paper on the sticky tablecloth. "I wrote it all down, while I was sitting with Peg. I can talk you through it. The till, the stock system, the workshops." She looked up. "If you're happy running workshops."

"Happy? I can't wait."

Sally gave her a sad smile and started reading from the paper.

Annie listened, occasionally glancing up at the ever-grumpy Millie-Jo.

Such a shame about the CCTV. She sighed. *Ah well, hopefully the police will find something soon.*

CHAPTER THIRTEEN

Tina had no intention of getting dragged into an investigation into a burglary gone wrong, no matter how much her mum pleaded.

But she had a day off – one without the kids, no less – and Tina wasn't very good at days off. When she'd been on maternity leave with Louis, she'd taken him to the Chipperies in Wareham and uncovered a clue that had helped solve a murder investigation her husband Mike was working on.

Half an hour in the police station on Hill Road, having a cuppa and a catch-up, wouldn't do any harm.

Sergeant Jim Connors was in the kitchen, about to pour two mugs of tea. Tina stood in the doorway, smiling.

"Hey, Sarge."

He started. "Tina. You gave me a fright. Don't tell me, they've sent you here for a murder case no one's told me about."

She shook her head. "I've got a day off and my mum's got the kids. I thought I'd pop in and say hello."

He gave her a look. "Have you ever considered using your days off for something other than police work, Tina Abbott?"

She laughed. "I took the kids to the tank museum last month."

"That's not a day off. It doesn't count unless you spend it doing what *you* want to do. When was the last time you had a day off, and no kids to look after?"

Tina wrinkled up her nose, thinking. "2021?"

He laughed. "That's before Louis was born."

"Exactly. Humour me, Sarge. I want to find out what's happening on the Peg Casey case."

"That one? Looks like she disturbed a burglar, poor woman. She's still unconscious at County, but they say she's stable. Doesn't look like we'll be bringing the MCIT in."

The MCIT was the Major Crime Investigations Team, Tina's unit at Dorset Police HQ in Winfrith. It was where she'd met Mike, although he now worked in the Cold Cases team.

"Give me half an hour of your time, and I'll be out of your hair. Who knows, I might even go and look at the Christmas lights. Or do some Christmas shopping." Her heart sank as she heard her own words. "My mum's done all hers already, and I've barely started."

"Oh, you'll get there in good time." Jim held out a mug of tea. "Come on. Let's see what news Wendy has."

There was an open packet of biscuits on the counter, so Tina helped herself to one, realising she'd not eaten since leaving the house at seven that morning. She shoved the first of three custard creams in her mouth and followed the sarge.

Wendy Sharman was at her desk. Dougie's was empty.

"Dougie out at the crime scene?" Tina asked.

Wendy turned, beaming. "Tina." She stood up to give Tina a hug. "How are those gorgeous kids of yours?"

"Currently getting up to no good with my mum, I've no doubt."

"As long as she doesn't start dragging them into her amateur sleuthing again."

Tina rolled her eyes. "She rang me last night, told me it was her who found the victim at the Millside Pottery. I hope she's not sticking her oar in."

When she'd dropped the kids off, Annie had been eager to send her on her way, insisting that Tina had better things to do than chat with her old mum. It had made her suspicious.

"She's been down to the crime scene this morning," Wendy said. "It looks like she's going to be running the shop at the pottery, while the victim's sister is with her in Dorchester."

"Oh, Lord." Tina put her mug down on Dougie's desk and slumped into his chair. "When will she learn?"

"In fairness to your mum, I think this time she's just helping a friend out," Jim said.

Tina raised an eyebrow. "That, and giving herself an excuse to spend all her time on the scene. And besides, she's supposed to be looking after Louis and Daisy."

She gritted her teeth. She'd have to have a word with her mum later.

She sighed. "Go on, then. Forget about Annie Abbott, and tell me what you know so far about the case."

Jim walked to the centre of the room, where a projector stood on a small table. He switched it on and fiddled with it for a moment before a photo of a woman in her seventies appeared.

"This is all very high-tech," Tina said.

"Don't mock," Jim muttered.

"Sorry." Tina mimed zipping her mouth shut.

Jim pointed to the screen. "Peg Casey. Seventy-nine years old. She lives and works in the Millside Pottery, with her twin sister, Sally." He looked up. "Right now, Peg is in Dorset County Hospital in Dorchester with a serious head injury. She was rallying last night but then lost consciousness in the early hours. She's stable, but still unconscious. There's talk of moving her to Exeter for more specialised care if her condition deteriorates."

"You spoke with the doctors at County?" Tina asked.

He nodded. "She's suffered significant trauma to the head. A single blow, consistent with her being hit by the broken jug we found beside her in the workshop at the back of the pottery."

"Prints on the jug?"

"FSIs are still there. They've been dusting the whole area, and of course they've taken the jug in as evidence. And they found this."

He nodded at Wendy, who clicked her mouse. The photo shifted to a close-up of a fingerprint on a wooden surface.

"Is that blood?" Tina stood and approached the screen.

"It is," said Wendy. "FSIs found it under one of the shelves."

"Whose blood?"

"We don't know that yet," said Jim. "But what's odd is that it's the only print, or the only one made in blood, anyway."

"If someone had blood on their hands, you'd think there'd be prints everywhere," Wendy said.

"Even on one finger, you'd touch more than one surface," Tina agreed. She cocked her head, examining the print. "So there can't have been much blood."

"Or not much that found its way onto this person's finger," added Jim.

Tina nodded. "Does the print match the victim?"

"Nope," said Wendy. "We've run it through the database, but not found a match yet."

"I've put a call in to Devon Police," Jim said.

Tina sucked her teeth. Until recently, her boss had been a DI who'd joined them from the Devon force. The experience hadn't been a positive one.

But that didn't mean the entire county was like that.

Jim clicked his fingers. Wendy grimaced and flicked on to the next photo, which showed an overturned paint can and boot prints leading away from it, in paint.

"They look large," Tina said. "What footwear was Peg wearing?"

"Slippers," Wendy replied.

Tina pursed her lips. "And they're definitely not my mum's."

"Your mum was wearing crocs," Wendy told her. "Much smaller than these. The FSIs say these aren't a common pattern, so they're hopeful we can narrow it down."

"Good," Tina said. "Any witnesses?" She closed her eyes, knowing what was coming next.

"I think you know the answer to this one," Jim said. "The key witness is Annie Abbott, your mum. Dougie's gone to her house to get a statement. She was too shocked to be coherent last night."

"He won't find her there," said Tina. "Not if she's running that shop."

Wendy shook her head. "They're not letting anyone in yet."

"Oh." Well, that was a relief. "So what's she told you so far?" Tina thought back to the phone call she'd had with her mum the night before. Annie hadn't made a lot of sense at the time.

"She'd been out for a swim, with her swimming club group," Wendy said. "She told me she'd been trying to call Peg 'cos Peg was sick and couldn't make the swim. When Peg didn't answer, she went round to the pottery. She heard a noise round the back, went into the storeroom, and found her lying there. She thought she was dead at first but managed to find a pulse thanks to guidance from emergency services."

"She heard a noise?" Tina asked.

"We don't know much about that yet," Wendy replied. "Like I say, Dougie will find out more when—"

"I get it," said Tina. "So we don't have much from Annie yet. Anyone else? Any CCTV?"

"There's a camera on the café opposite," said Wendy. She checked her notebook. "The Tuck Shop Café. But it's not working, unfortunately."

"That's annoying. Anything else? On the Old Mill? The other shops?"

"Nothing pointing in the right direction," said Jim.

Typical. So they were reliant on the word of Tina's mum. And the forensics. Which did look promising.

"Have the FSIs said how many sets of prints they found?" Tina asked. The storeroom wouldn't be used by many people, unlike the shop which would be awash with fingerprints.

"Four, so far," Wendy replied. "One set is Sally's, the other is Peg's. The other prints are around where Peg was found and we're assuming they're Annie's but we'll need to get her to—"

"She'll be only too eager to help," Tina said. "What about the fourth set?"

Wendy smiled. "They're on the jug, and the walls. And that shelf, the single fingerprint in blood. Like I say, we don't have a match yet, but we're hopeful."

"And you have the blood. If the prints don't turn anything up, the DNA might."

"We're assuming that's Peg's blood," Jim said.

Tina turned to him. "It pays not to assume."

He grunted. "True. Do you want us to keep you updated as more information comes in?"

Tina eyed the screen, which now displayed an aerial view of the courtyard outside the pottery. She sighed.

She couldn't resist.

"Yes," she said. "If you don't mind. But don't worry. I'm going to head into town. Do some Christmas shopping. I've got a day off to enjoy."

CHAPTER FOURTEEN

FIGGY EDMUNDS LIVED in a static caravan on Monmouth Beach, where she'd grown up with her grandparents. But her grandfather had died in a trawler accident, and then her grandma of cancer, and now it was just her.

Well... her, and her occasional tormentor Kevin. But she preferred not to think about Kevin.

Today she was engrossed in a freelance project she'd been working on, something she was supposed to finish in time for Christmas. She was contributing code to a game, one that its creator claimed would be the next *Angry Birds*. She wasn't so sure. But it paid well, and that was what counted.

At lunchtime she closed her laptop, stood up and stretched her arms above her head, fingertips grazing the low ceiling. She'd been slowly making this caravan her own since her grandmother had died. Removing some of the kitsch but keeping just enough to allow the memory of her nan to linger.

But today was the first day of December. And something

Figgy's nan had absolutely loved had been decorating the caravan for Christmas.

Figgy knew her decorations were dated. She knew they were a bit rough around the edges. But she also knew that dated could sometimes mean retro, and that rough around the edges didn't matter when the decorations held memories that ran all the way back to her childhood.

She lifted the base of her bed, revealing the storage area underneath, and propped it up with a piece of wood. She reached inside and pulled out the long box with the Christmas tree in – silver tinsel, dating back to the late eighties – and the larger rectangular box that contained the ornaments and tinsel.

Figgy allowed herself a squeal. Doing this without her nan might be hard, but as long as she focused on the positive, it was something she loved.

She shifted the boxes into the living room and opened up the larger one. There was a cardboard and glitter angel to go on top of the tree. Plastic tree ornaments – Santa, snowmen, elves, Rudolph – the paint almost entirely faded.

She pulled out the tree and sorted through its branches, laying them out on the table arranged by size. Just as she was about to erect the tripod stand, there was a knock at her door.

"Only me!"

She smiled and straightened up. *Cameron.*

She opened the door, the tatty plastic Rudolph still in her hand. "Hey."

Cameron stepped into the caravan and shut the outer door. "Hey." He rubbed his hands together. "That seagull of yours was giving me evil looks."

"Kevin is *not* my seagull."

Figgy stood on tiptoes to plant a kiss on Cameron's cheek. "This is nice."

"Flying visit," he said, frowning. "Gotta build a double wardrobe for a holiday cottage this afternoon. I needed to ask you something."

"Sounds ominous," she said.

"Ugh. Not ominous. Just… ugh." He blew out his cheeks and sat down at the table, gazing at the sections of the tinsel tree. "What's all this?"

"What does it look like?"

"Well, it looks like the eighties are asking for Christmas back."

She gave him a playful punch on the arm. "That's my nan's stuff. I happen to like it."

His smile dropped. "Oh, I'm sorry, Fig. I know how much this means to you. How could I be so tactless?" He looked at the decorations, still frowning.

"It's OK," she said. "You were going to ask me something. Something ominous."

"Oh. Yes, that. How do you feel about double dates?"

"Isn't that something…" She considered. "Isn't it something old people do?"

He barked out a laugh, making her flinch. "Oh, it gets worse." He picked up a tinsel branch and peered at it, then put it down again. "It's my dad. You know he's back in town. He wants us – you and me – to have dinner with him and this Shari person."

"This Shari person," Figgy repeated. "Are you going to pretend to like her?"

He screwed up his face. "I don't even know her. And it's not her I'm angry with."

"*Are* you angry?"

He pulled in a breath, about to speak, then stopped himself. He closed his mouth and picked up a plastic angel, turning it over in his hands.

"I'm sure a therapist could spend a dozen sessions unpicking that," he said.

Figgy spread her hands. "I can only speak of the benefits of therapy."

Cameron was a few years younger than Figgy. If his mum had had her way, he'd be off at university right now, expanding his mind instead of doing odd jobs in Lyme and hanging round with the weirdo who lived in her grandma's caravan on Monmouth Beach. Figgy was sure Rosamund would have preferred that.

"Therapy will not get us out of this double date with your dad and his girlfriend," she said. "But you could say no."

He looked at her. "I know I could."

"But you haven't."

He shook his head.

Figgy sat down next to him and put a hand on his knee. She put the plastic reindeer down on the seat between them. "It's OK to be conflicted. He's your dad."

"He's an arsehole."

"He's your dad, *and* he's an arsehole. It's more common than you might think."

Figgy couldn't remember her own dad. He and her mum had died in a car accident when she'd been little. Her nan had made sure to show her photos as she was growing up, but it wasn't the same.

Would she rather have an arsehole dad than no dad at all? She wasn't sure.

"So where are we going?" she asked.

"He says he's cooking at their holiday home." Cameron snorted.

"He's not a good cook?"

"He's *never* cooked."

A double date. Being presented as Cameron's girlfriend, like a prize cow for inspection. The awkwardness between David Winters's new girlfriend and his abandoned son. All that, and the possibility of bad food.

But Figgy was curious.

"I'm happy to support you," she said.

He raised an eyebrow. "Are you just being polite?"

She shrugged. "Maybe. But I'm curious."

He snorted. "You want to see the car crash as it happens."

She wrapped an arm around him. "It won't be a car crash. I'll be your wing woman."

"Ouch." He reached down between them and brought up the Rudolph Christmas ornament. He flicked its nose.

Figgy resisted the urge to tell him to be careful.

"Yeah," he said. "You wanna see the car crash."

She gave him a wry smile. "I mean, if it's gonna happen anyway, I might as well see it first-hand."

There was a caw from outside and a sharp tap of beak on glass. Kevin the herring gull flapped his wings to keep balance on the window edge.

"Ugh," said Cameron. "That seagull's giving evil villain energy."

Figgy laughed. "Kevin doesn't mean any harm."

"No? I thought you hated him?"

"Well... at least he doesn't try to cook."

Cameron pulled away, smiling. "Don't you compare my dad to your monstrous seagull."

"Like I said, he's not mine."

"I beg to differ." He eyed her. "So does that mean you're joining me for the double date from hell?"

She rested her head on his shoulder. "Of course I am. You can't go through that on your own."

CHAPTER FIFTEEN

"Oh no, Daisy, you can't eat that." Annie pulled the leaf out of her granddaughter's hand and threw it in the bin. Daisy was in her highchair, leaning back and grabbing things from the windowsill.

When had she become so flexible? And so long-armed?

"You're a proper Mr Tickle, you are," she said as she tickled Daisy's tummy and moved the peace lily further away. It looked like she was going to need to do some rearranging.

"Granny got biscuits," Louis said. It wasn't a question.

"Indeed I do," she replied, bending to bring her face closer to his. Four years old and getting more articulate every time she saw him.

Her journey to the high cupboard where she hid the biscuits was interrupted by a knock on the door.

She eyed her granddaughter. "Granny has to go answer the door. Daisy, don't you go grabbing anything nasty while I'm gone."

Daisy blew a raspberry and giggled.

"Louis, you can come with me." Annie grabbed his hand.

"Who is it?" he asked as they made their way through Annie's narrow hallway to the front door. "Police ofasa?"

She smiled down at him. "Not everyone is a police officer, you know. Although I can see why you might think that." With both parents and his uncle, the poor lad was surrounded by coppers and their irregular hours.

She opened the door. Standing outside, stamping his feet on the steps for warmth, was Dougie. He wore his full police uniform, even the hat.

"Police ofasa!" Louis cried.

"Well," Annie said. "I have to admit you were right this time. But not everyone who knocks on the door is from the police."

"Salesman! Poltishan!" Louis cried.

She laughed. "How many politicians do you get knocking on your door in Sandford?"

Louis giggled. "Lot."

"I bet," said Dougie. He stepped inside and reached down to pick his nephew up. "How's the big fella?"

Louis grabbed Dougie's hat and slapped it onto his own head. "Louis police ofasa!"

Annie raised an eyebrow. "You knew they were going to be here, didn't you?"

Dougie winked at Louis. "Somebody's mum might just have popped into the police station and told everyone she'd left Louis and Poppy with their granny."

Annie rolled her eyes. "She's supposed to be having a day off. That girl. Mind you, having the MCIT involved will help you—"

"They're not involved, Annie," Douglas said. "Tina's just

a workaholic who couldn't resist finding out what was going on. And I'm—"

"... here to take my statement. I know." Annie closed the front door and followed Douglas and Louis into the kitchen, where Daisy sat beaming from her highchair.

"Daisy-doo," said Dougie. He put Louis down and gave the baby a kiss on the top of the head. "How is my favourite niece?"

Daisy squealed. Louis ran around the kitchen table, clutching Dougie's hat to his head and making *nee-narr* noises.

Annie smiled. It was chaos when her grandchildren came to stay. Even more so when she had all three. But she wouldn't have it any other way.

Douglas sat down at the table. He fished in his bag and brought out a large notepad and an iPad. He passed the notepad to Louis, who'd taken the seat next to him.

He looked up. "Please tell me Granny has crayons. We need a distraction."

She nodded and pulled her largest pencil case out of the cutlery drawer. She had another one which she kept by the front door for outings. It never hurt to be prepared.

"Why don't you draw one of your police officers?" Dougie suggested. Louis nodded, his expression grave, and set to work.

Dougie looked at the baby, then at Annie, a question in his eyes.

"I have just the thing," she said. She opened up the bread bin and pulled out the last of the crusty loaf she'd bought at the Town Mill Bakery last week. "This'll keep her busy."

She handed the bread to Daisy. The baby grabbed it and

plunged it into her mouth. Realising how crusty it was, she frowned and began to gnaw.

Annie had switched the kettle on when she'd heard Dougie's knock. She poured a coffee for him and a tea for herself and set them down on the table.

"Right," she said as she finally sat down. "You're going to want to know what happened. And I'm going to have to tell you in terms suitable for the ears of two small people."

She could leave them in here and take Dougie into the living room. But she wouldn't be able to see her grandchildren from there, and besides, Louis would only follow her.

"OK," Dougie said. He fired up the iPad and started tapping at it. "Start at the beginning. What made you decide to go to the pottery?"

"Well, that's easy. Peg wasn't well."

"Peg Casey."

"Is there another Peg?"

"I have to be sure."

She tutted. "Very well. So Peg wasn't well. She had a virus of some sort, according to Sally. That's her sister, Sally Casey."

He nodded. "You were with Sally when you went to the pottery?"

"Oh no. She was in the Pilot Boat with Helen." Annie realised she hadn't checked in on Helen, asked her if Harper was back. A task for later. "Helen and Sally went to the Pilot Boat after our swim. Figgy and Rosamund each went home. I decided to—"

"Hang on a minute," he said. "What time was this?"

She pursed her lips, thinking. Louis looked up.

"Dinnertime!" he shouted.

She rubbed his arm. "Shush now, sweetie. You do your drawing." *And stop listening.*

She nodded. "Seven-thirty, we finished. I remember, because the clock at—"

"You were swimming at seven thirty in the evening? In November?" Dougie shook his head. "Wow."

"Don't you judge, Douglas Anderson. Have you not noticed how hardy the ladies of the Lyme Regis Women's Swimming Club are?"

He smiled. "I heard you've been calling it that. I'm impressed." He typed some more. "So you decided to go to the pottery, alone, to check on your friend. Peg Casey."

"Yes."

"Which route did you take?"

That was easy. "I left Rosamund at the Cobb Gate car park. I crossed Bridge Street there, then made my way up Coombe Street. From there I turned left into Mill Lane and crossed the courtyard to the pottery."

"And did you see anybody, while you were walking from the seafront to the pottery? Apart from your swimming club friends?"

She shook her head. "It was raining cats and dogs."

Louis gasped. "Dogs? Where?"

She rubbed his hand. "It's just an expression, kiddo. Not a real dog."

"Cat?"

"No cats, neither."

"Oh." He scowled and went back to his drawing. Annie glanced across at the baby, who was using her tiny sharp finger-nails to pick fragments of crust off the bread. The highchair tray was already half-covered in a mix of crumbs and dribble.

"It was blowing a gale," she said. "And the rain was..." she paused, eyeing the children. "It was very heavy. Lyme Regis was deserted."

"Right. So you went to the pottery, and—"

"Wait," she said. "I did see someone. Not on foot, but in a car."

"Where?"

"In Mill Lane. I had to tuck right into the wall for it to get past me."

"Did you make a note of the registration plate?"

She eyed her son-in-law. "Dougie, I'm a retired local authority admin assistant, not a cop. No, I did not make a note of the registration plate."

"Did you see what kind of car it was, at least?"

"I did." Annie beamed, proud of herself. "It was a BMW. Quite a swanky one, in some shade of grey or silver."

"Which?"

"Sorry?"

"Grey or silver?"

"Is there a difference?"

He sighed. She shrugged. "Silver, I suppose. But I wouldn't put money on it."

"Silver car," Louis said. "Brrum, brrum."

He mimed pushing a car across the table.

"That's a good idea, Louis." Annie stood up and went to the cupboard under the stairs, one of the many places where she kept toys. She returned with a shoebox full of toy cars.

"Look at this!" she proclaimed, placing the box on the table. Louis leaned over and delved through it. Annie gave Daisy a smooth plastic one, purchased last Christmas. Safer to gnaw on.

"Those bring back memories," Dougie said. "How old are they?"

Annie watched her grandson play with the cars. He seemed to be enjoying making them collide.

"It varies," she said. "Some are new, some go back to when Tina was little." She nodded towards a toy panda car. "There are a couple that date from Ted's childhood."

"You're happy to let the kids play with those?"

"Of course I am. They're toys, aren't they? They're for playing with." She waggled her eyebrows. "And they've given me an idea."

"They have?" Dougie asked.

Annie pulled the box towards her and rummaged through it. After a few moments, she pulled out a car.

"This one," she said.

"Sorry?"

Louis made a grab for the car, but Annie held it firm.

"This was the colour of the car I saw," she said. "I haven't got the right make or model in my collection, but..." She turned it from side to side. "Yes. That's the colour."

The car was silver, with a hint of blue. Quite distinctive. Annie smiled and handed it to Dougie. "You can take that."

Louis yelled. Annie turned to him, her expression firm.

"Now, now, Louis. Uncle Dougie needs that car to help him with his police work."

"Solve mudda," Louis said.

"Not a murder," Annie corrected. "But a crime, yes. Somebody hurt my friend and Uncle Dougie is going to find out who."

Dougie pocketed the car. "So that's the car," he said. "What about the driver?"

"Did I see him, you mean?"

"Him?" Dougie paused, his fingertips poised above the iPad.

She nodded. "Him. At least, I'm pretty sure it was a him. And before you ask, no I did not see his face. It was obscured. But I did see that he had grey hair." She clapped a hand to her mouth. "Oh my goodness, I didn't register it at the time. He was holding a towel against his face."

"Did he look as if he'd been out in the rain?"

"No idea." Annie shrugged. "I can only assume so, if he had to towel himself off. But I didn't catch his face at all. Sorry."

Douglas looked at her. "There were footprints, in paint."

She nodded. "I remember those. In..." She glanced at the children. *Choose your words.* "In the storeroom. With Peg."

"Did you see any paint on the car?"

She tapped her fingers on the table. "I don't think so. But then, it was dark. And raining. And blowing a gale."

Dougie drew in a breath. Annie looked across the table. Daisy was slumped in her highchair, dozing off. The plastic car and what remained of the hunk of bread lay on the floor.

"My, my," Annie whispered. "Are we really that dull?" She looked at Dougie. "Give me five minutes to take her up for a nap. Once that's done, I'll brew us another cuppa and we can chat in the living room while Louis continues to create a smash car derby here."

"Smash!" shouted Louis, ramming two cars together.

Dougie nodded. "You can tell me what you saw in the workshop. Without an" – he put his hand up so Louis couldn't see his mouth – "audience."

Annie smiled. She already had the dozing baby in her arms. "Exactly. Be right back."

CHAPTER SIXTEEN

LYME REGIS WASN'T where Tina would do all of her Christmas shopping, but she knew she could make a good start there. She'd already been in one of the many fossil shops and bought a bead necklace for Naomi, and she'd found a fleece for Mike in Salt Rock. Now she was in the Lyme Regis Bookshop, searching for books for Louis and Daisy.

She was disturbed by the sound of a man's raised voice.

"Well, this really isn't good enough, you know," he said, just a decibel or so below shouting. "Three times I've been in, and three times you haven't been able to help me."

"I'm very sorry, sir," replied the woman behind the counter. "Perhaps if you could give me more information about what you're looking for, I can help you narrow it down?"

"Good God, woman! I've already told you. It's a history book – actual history, mind you, none of this historical fiction nonsense. It's published by Faber, and it has a photograph of a castle on the cover. A Norman one, motte and bailey. You know the thing."

Tina tried to watch as surreptitiously as she could. If this escalated, would she need to step in? Around her, people were openly staring.

"Perhaps," the bookseller offered, "if you can give me an idea of the author, I can help—"

"If I'd known who the author was, I'd have bloody told you, wouldn't I?" He looked around the shop. People shifted their gazes and turned away. But he'd spotted the stares.

"Annabel," he said, leaning in closer than was polite to read the woman's name badge. He'd pulled on a thin smile and looked nervous, now he knew he'd made himself the centre of attention.

"Arabella," she corrected.

"Really? Annabel's a much nicer name."

Arabella's jaw tightened. "If you can't give me more to work with, then I'm afraid I can't help you. Maybe if you give it some thought, then—"

"I shall. And I shall go to Waterstones in Bridport to make my purchase. I'm sure they're far more knowledgeable."

He turned away from the till and stopped, registering the people still very obviously staring-but-not-staring at him. He cleared his throat and broadened his smile.

"Nothing to worry about, everybody." He drew his arm around in an expansive gesture. "Just attempting to purchase a book. I wish you all the very best of luck with your shopping."

He turned again, taking a circuitous route around the displays to avoid slamming into the queue which had been building behind him. As he passed Tina, she spotted a yellowing bruise on his temple, and she wondered if a previous shopping trip had resulted in a punch to the face.

I wouldn't blame them. She smiled, then put her hand to her mouth. *Not the way a copper should think.*

She turned back to the display. The shop had gone fully festive, but in a way that mirrored the tasteful white Christmas lights strung over Broad Street. The shelves were festooned with sparkly white lights and pots of poinsettia were dotted in amongst the displays.

At last, she had what she needed. She turned towards the till just as her mum bustled into the shop, struggling to get Daisy's pushchair through the door.

Tina's heart sank. The kids would find it confusing bumping into her like this, and she'd been enjoying some peace and quiet. Although she wasn't sure if it was Daisy and Louis who would shatter that peace, or Annie.

"Mum." She stepped forward.

Annie was bending over to pick up a sock that Daisy had jettisoned from the pushchair. She stood slowly, a hand on the small of her back.

"Tina, love." Her eyes brightened. "How lovely to see you. Look, kids, it's Mummy."

Daisy looked up at Tina and started crying. Tina bent over the pushchair, unbuckled her and picked her up.

"Shush," she said as she jiggled her daughter in her arms. "Mummy's not that scary, is she?"

Daisy gave a loud, juddering sob and plunged a thumb into her mouth. Tina turned to Annie.

"Has she had a nap?" she asked.

Annie gave a firm nod. "She's not long woken up from it."

Tina pulled Daisy closer. "She's probably still groggy." She put the girl back in her pushchair. "Hang on." She reached into her bag and pulled out a box of carrot sticks. Daisy reached out to grab one.

"That girl does love to gnaw things," Annie said.

Tina felt movement behind her. She turned to see Louis with a book in his hands.

Damn. It was the one she'd been about to buy him for Christmas.

"Sam-Sam," he said. It was how he referred to Fireman Sam, one of his favourite TV characters.

She smiled. It looked like she'd be buying another Christmas present.

"Sam-Sam," she confirmed.

"You leave it with me," Annie said. "I'll buy it for him. I can see you've got other things to pay for." She raised an eyebrow at the stack of books under Tina's arm.

Tina shifted the pile to her side. One of them was a Christmas-themed mystery novel for her mum. "Don't go peeking."

Annie winked. "I saw nothing. Now you pay for your books and get out of here while he's engrossed." She looked down at Louis, who'd sat on the floor to leaf through his new book. Arabella behind the counter was watching him, no doubt hoping they were actually going to buy the book now he'd got his sticky fingers on it.

"Thanks, Mum." Tina squeezed Annie's arm.

"My pleasure, love. You get home. We're here for the storyteller at four, aren't we kids?"

"Stories!" Louis cried. Daisy waved what remained of her carrot stick.

Tina planted a kiss on each of her children's cheeks and hurried to the till. She was looking forward to a night alone with Mike.

CHAPTER SEVENTEEN

"Hey, Sarge."

Dougie shivered as he took off his thick coat and draped it on the chair. The cheer of Lyme's Christmas lights had helped distract him from the drizzle and the freezing cold. But somehow coming inside the warm police station made him aware of what he'd left behind.

Sergeant Connors swivelled in his chair and gestured at his phone, held against his ear.

"Right." Dougie mimed drinking from a mug.

The sarge used his free hand to give Dougie a thumbs up. Dougie grabbed the used cup from his desk and headed for the kitchen.

He was surprised to find Wendy in there, wearing her coat.

"Alright, Wendy. Fancy a brew?"

"Sorry. I've just come off my lunch break and I'm heading straight out. Accident on Sidmouth Road."

He winced. "Nothing nasty, I hope."

"Doesn't sound like anyone's hurt, from what 999 have

told me. But there's a tractor straddling the road. I need to see if it can be moved or if it'll need a diversion."

Diverting traffic coming into and out of Lyme on Sidmouth Road wouldn't be easy. For larger vehicles, it would mean a fifteen-mile detour via Axminster.

"I'll come with you." He put his mug down.

Wendy shook her head. "You haven't had a break yet today. I'll call if I need you." She put a hand on his arm. "Bloody hell, you're freezing. You need that cup of tea."

He shivered. She was right.

"More layers tomorrow, I think," he said. He was only wearing a thin shirt under his uniform fleece.

"That's the secret," she replied, lifting her own fleece. "Two T-shirts, one thermal and a vest under here. And woolly tights under my trousers. I'm toasty."

"You must be sweltering when you come inside."

She laughed. "Yeah. But it's totally worth it." She made for the door. "You warm up. I'll call if I need you."

"Ta." Dougie filled the kettle and waited for it to boil. Should he go home, fetch more layers?

No. He had too much to do. Writing up Annie's statement, for one. And going back to the Millside Pottery to see if the FSIs had found anything more.

Five minutes later he was back in the office he shared with Wendy and the sarge.

"Coffee, two sugars." He put a mug down on the sarge's desk.

"Perfect," said Connors. He indicated his phone, which was now lying on his desk. "Just had a call from Devon."

"About the prints from the pottery?"

"Yup. Spoke to a woman called DI Patterson. Jesus, she was rough around the edges."

Dougie nodded. He was pretty sure DI Patterson was the woman who'd been Tina's boss until recently, before moving back to Devon. He'd heard the stories, but he wasn't about to go badmouthing a DI.

"Did she have the prints on file?" he asked between sips of tea.

"She did." Connors glanced at his notes. "A Reece Lumbard. Ring any bells?"

Dougie shook his head. "It's Devon, I suppose."

"He only lives in Seaton. I don't think criminals respect county borders."

"Probably not." Dougie still hadn't heard of him. Either he'd restricted his activities to Seaton until now, or this was his first offence.

But then, if Devon had his prints...

"So how does Devon know him?" he asked.

"Habitual low-level criminal. A few arrests for burglary, two for possession, and one for dealing meth."

"Meth?"

The sarge grunted. "It seems they're looking for him right now."

Dougie remembered the man he'd almost driven into on Sunday night. "Have they sent any mugshots over?"

"They have." Connors brought the images up on his screen.

"Oh." Dougie felt his body slump.

"Not what you were expecting?"

"No." The man Dougie had seen running in the rain... it had been dark, of course, and raining. And the man had been wearing a hoodie.

But he was pretty sure the man had been white. And Reece Lumbard was Black.

"Damn," he said. "It's not him."

"Well, it *is* him. In the sense that it's our guy. Prints all over the storeroom. Including on the jug that was used to assault Peg Casey. And the bloody fingerprint under the shelf."

"Presumably his blood."

"We'll be able to check that. Devon took a DNA sample when he was arrested for dealing. He got two months in HMP Exeter."

"Only two months?"

"I know," said the sarge. "But I'm prepared to bet he's part of a larger operation, if Devon are looking for him."

"If we arrest him, will we have Devon's Organised Crime division on our backs?"

The sarge snorted. "Probably, but he attacked a member of the public, so..."

Dougie smiled. This was why he liked working for Jim Connors. He stood up and drained his mug.

"I'll check his home address now," he said. "Strike while the iron's hot."

A grunt. "Fat chance of him being there."

"Doesn't do any harm to try, Sarge."

"Hmm. Be careful though. Take Wendy with you."

"Will do." She was bound to have the traffic incident under control soon enough, and Sidmouth Road was on the way to Seaton.

"Good luck," said the sarge. "Let's hope he's there. And be careful, yes? He might not be alone."

"Will do, Sarge." Dougie gave a mock salute and pulled on his coat.

CHAPTER EIGHTEEN

"THIS IS NICE." Tina raised her glass and clinked it against Mike's.

"It's also some kind of miracle," he replied. "Both kids with your mum and neither of us working late on a case."

She sighed. "We're just working on dotting the i's and crossing the t's with the Musketeers right now. It's deathly dull."

The so-called Musketeers were three men the MCIT had arrested a month earlier for two murders. It was the kind of investigation that would never result in a conviction unless the evidence was as tight as the swimming trunks Mike had bought last summer. The latest fashion, he'd claimed, then never worn them.

"Court date set yet?" Mike asked.

"Let's not talk about work."

"OK." Mike looked up as the waitress arrived with their food. Sea bass for Tina, steak for Mike. They were in the Bear, a cosy pub with a restaurant on Wareham's North Street.

After a few moments' silence, Mike put down his knife and fork.

"I don't know what else to talk about," he said.

Tina swallowed a mouthful of potato. "The kids?"

"Really? You want to be those parents? The ones who finally get a night off and can't talk about anything except parenting?"

She considered. "No. OK. So that's work and kids banned from the conversation. What else is there?"

He cocked his head. "You were in Lyme Regis today. What's going on there?"

"Really? Surely that combines work *and* family."

"Not necessarily. Maybe there's some gossip."

Tina ran her day through her mind. "Well, there was an older gentleman in the bookshop shouting his mouth off at the poor assistant. He had a nasty bruise, too."

"Administered by the shop assistant?"

Tina laughed. "From the look on her face, I don't think that was far from her mind."

"Maybe he'd had a fall. Old people do that. Don't you worry about your mum, with all those steep hills and alleyways?"

"My mum's fit as a fiddle. Swims every day. And besides, 'old people do that'? Isn't that a bit of a cliché?"

He gave his shoulders something between a shrug and a shake. "Let's not talk about the older generation."

"No," she agreed. Mike's dad had come to Dorset for a visit during the summer. It hadn't gone well.

He sniffed and attacked his steak, with more gusto than Tina suspected he really felt.

"OK," she said. "My mum's friend Helen. She's not old."

"Depends what you mean by old."

"She must be at least ten years younger than my mum."

He raised an eyebrow. "You reckon? I'm not so sure. All those kaftans and the fancy attitude make it difficult to tell."

"Helen's not fancy." Tina lowered her voice. "And we shouldn't be mean about her. It looks like her partner's left her."

"The one who makes the monstrous sculptures?"

"Harper. Yes."

"That can't be fun at Christmas." Mike reached out and grabbed her hand. "Don't you go leaving me ever, yeah?"

She laughed. "Don't be daft."

"I mean it, T. You're the best thing that ever happened to me. I know I was a bit shit when you told me you were pregnant with Louis. But I love our little family. And I love you."

"I love you, too." She grasped his hand. "And I'm not going anywhere."

"Good. So d'you think the sculptor will come back?"

"I'm not sure. Mum says Helen's being tight-lipped about it."

"Helen?" he replied. "Tight-lipped?"

"I know. They had a row, but Helen won't say what it's about."

"Sounds serious."

Tina nodded, enjoying her fish.

"I'm not sure if talking about your mum's mates' love lives is more or less boring than talking about work," Mike said.

Tina laughed, then clapped her hand over her mouth as she almost spat out a mouthful of fish.

"You're right," she said. "Do you think the kids are OK?"

"They're with Granny. They love it at your mum's. Let's face it, she does stuff with them we'd never have the time for."

"You're right. She took them to a storyteller session this afternoon, and tomorrow they're decorating ceramic Christmas decorations at the Millside Pottery."

Mike eyed her. "That's open already? I thought it was broken into."

"It is. They've... oh, hell." Tina dropped her fork, making the man at the next table flinch.

"What is it?" Mike asked.

"The pottery. The craft session. She's dragging them over there so she can do her damn amateur sleuthing again, isn't she?"

Mike frowned. "It might just be an innocent craft session."

Tina laughed. "Really? This is Annie Abbott we're talking about."

"You're right." Mike put down his cutlery. "She'd better not put Louis and Daisy at risk."

"She won't. Because I'm going to stop her."

The man at the next table tutted. Tina glanced at him. Had she raised her voice?

"Good luck with that," Mike said.

"No, Mike. She's interfering with the activities of the local policing team, and she's dragging our kids into something totally unsuitable for a toddler and a baby."

"It's just a break-in. I thought you said they'd reopened."

Tina shook her head. "Not just a break-in. A woman was assaulted. A friend of my mum's, which gives her all the more reason to go poking her nose in."

"Oh, hell."

Tina gritted her teeth. *Bloody Annie Abbott.* She meant well, but sometimes...

"I'll have a word with Dougie," she said. "I'll find an opportunity to call him, and I'll give him a warning."

"Good," said Mike. "I just hope it works."

CHAPTER NINETEEN

JUST AS ANTICIPATED, Wendy had the accident under control, and the tractor was no longer blocking traffic.

"See?" she said as Dougie pulled up beside her. "I told you I could handle this on my own."

"Nice one," he said. "So d'you want to join me for something a bit more interesting?"

"Always. What's up?"

"Get in."

She looked across the road. "What about my car?"

"We'll come back this way. You can pick your car up."

She eyed the car for a moment then nodded. It was safely tucked away in a field, nowhere it might cause an obstruction.

"I assume that gate won't be locked while we're gone?" Dougie asked.

"The tractor driver's had to go to A&E for a broken wrist. He won't be closing any gates for a while."

"Ouch. How did that happen?"

"He hit a car as he was coming out of the gate. Rammed his arm into the steering wheel."

Dougie grimaced.

Wendy walked around his car and got in the passenger side. "So," she said. "What's this exciting job you've got for me?"

"Devon have given us a match for the prints in the pottery workshop. He lives in Seaton."

"And we're going to pay him a visit. Nice." She buckled in and listened as he filled her in en route.

Reece Lumbard lived in a neat semi in a mid-century housing estate on the edge of town. The garden was well tended and the car outside looked like it had recently been washed.

"Nice," said Wendy.

"Not what I was expecting," replied Dougie.

They walked to the house, where a plastic wreath hung on the door.

"Even nicer," said Wendy.

Dougie raised an eyebrow, pressing the doorbell. Thankfully, it worked. "Let's not jump to any conclusions," he said.

The door was opened by a tall woman in her fifties with brown skin and a shock of highlighted hair. "Yes?" She glanced at her watch. It was getting late, and Dougie knew she'd immediately assume the worst.

Dougie held up his ID. "I'm PC Anderson, this is PC Sharman. We're looking for Reece Lumbard."

"Reece?" The woman pulled a face. "No, I've not seen Reece for a few days." She was well-spoken, with just a hint of a Devon accent.

"Are you related to Reece?"

"I'm his mum. Alison," said the woman. "Reece lives

with me here. Well, he's meant to. I hardly see him some weeks. Can you tell me why you're here?"

Wendy smiled. "Mind if we come in?"

She grunted and stood aside. The three of them walked into a living room that stretched from the front to the back of the house.

If Douglas had expected serial offender Reece Lumbard to be living in a grubby flat, he'd been mistaken. This house was well decorated and clean. It was busy, almost cluttered, with books, jigsaws and shelves of pottery animals.

"When did you last see him?" he asked.

She waved a hand at the sofa, gesturing for Douglas and Wendy to sit. "I should think it was Saturday morning. He helped me with the shopping. Gave me a lift and then went off somewhere. Not seen him since."

"And you don't have any idea where he was going?"

She shook her head.

Wendy leaned forward. "Could we take a look at Reece's room, do you think?"

"What is it you're looking for?" Alison asked. She sounded more puzzled than defensive. Did she know about his record?

She must do. He'd done time.

"We really need to speak with him," Wendy said. "He was present at an incident where someone was badly hurt."

"And you've got evidence of that?"

Dougie frowned. *Defensive, all of a sudden.* "We just want to talk to him."

She turned up her lip. "Top of the stairs, turn right. Reece isn't the physical sort. People really aren't his thing at all. Never could tell the good ones from the bad. You know that's how he got into trouble in the first place."

"The burglary charges," said Dougie. "The drugs."

"He just fell in with the wrong crowd. Made some bad decisions."

"Right," said Wendy. This wasn't the time to debate the rights and wrongs of Reece's life choices. "We'll just take a look then."

Dougie and Wendy left Alison downstairs.

Reece's room was sparse. There was a bed, a bedside table, a chest of drawers and a small wardrobe. It took them moments to search the lot.

No drugs. No money, apart from a tenner and a few coins on the bedside table.

"So, he only turned to burglary because he fell in with a bad crowd," noted Wendy, eyebrow raised.

Dougie shrugged. "Can't be fun, having your kid turn out to be a criminal. I guess she's trying to make sense of it all."

"I guess."

"There's nothing here except some clothes." Douglas straightened up from examining the chest of drawers. "No paperwork, no laptop."

"Nothing." Wendy sighed.

They went back downstairs.

"Thank you, Alison," said Dougie. "So you're sure Reece hasn't been in touch since Saturday?"

Her face still looked pinched. "He never phones. Doesn't text me unless he needs something."

Dougie nodded. "Right. We'll be off now. But please, let us know if you hear from Reece."

Alison made no comment but nodded at the card Douglas handed her.

"Can I ask about the car?" Wendy said.

"Car?" Alison raised her eyebrows.

"You said Reece gave you a lift. Was he driving his own car?"

You're right, Dougie thought. That silver-blue BMW, the one Annie had mentioned...

"The car is registered to me," said Alison with a shrug. "Better for the insurance." She turned towards the front window. "That out there is a hire car. I've got a work trip tomorrow; I need to go to Bristol."

Dougie nodded. "The car Reece was driving, he hasn't returned it?"

"Not yet."

"What make and model is it?"

"It's a VW Golf. Red."

Damn. Not a silver-blue BMW.

"What's the registration number?" Wendy asked.

Alison told her and she made a note in her pad. "Thanks. We'll let you know if we find it."

"And you'll let me know if you find Reece, I assume."

"Of course."

"Good. He's not a bad boy. Not really."

Dougie and Wendy gave Alison the same sympathetic smile. But they'd both heard plenty of other mothers say exactly the same thing.

"Thanks for your help," Wendy said.

As the door closed behind them, Dougie and Wendy shared a look.

"That didn't get us very far," he said.

"Uh-uh. We know what he was driving now. Find that, maybe we'll find him."

"You reckon he's sleeping in it?"

"I reckon there's a fair chance."

CHAPTER TWENTY

Annie sat outside the Kiosk early next morning, watching Louis stack pebbles on the beach. Daisy sat in her pushchair, breakfasting on a croissant.

Annie leaned back and took in the sun's thin rays. The weather had improved, and she wasn't the only one enjoying the morning on one of the Kiosk's distinctive orange deckchairs.

"Annie!"

She turned to see Figgy walking from the direction of her caravan. She wore her dry robe over jeans and a thick black sweater.

"Figglington. How's things?"

"Oh. A bit odd."

Annie raised an eyebrow. "Odd?"

Figgy nodded. "Give me a minute to get a hot chocolate and I'll fill you in."

Annie waited while her friend queued for a drink then brought it over, dragging a deckchair with her.

"I'm glad the storm's gone," Figgy said. "My caravan was rattling like a tin can."

"I didn't think of that. Is it unpleasant, being in a caravan at this time of year?"

Figgy smiled. "Oh no, it's wonderful. The beach is deserted, and I get to see the sunrise without having to wake up at silly o'clock." She sipped her hot chocolate and briefly closed her eyes. "I love it. And I've decorated now. All Grandma's Christmas kitsch is in its proper home."

"That's good to hear." Annie knew how comforting this would be for Figgy.

"Anyway, I wanted to ask your advice about something."

"You did?"

Figgy nodded, placing her cup carefully on the pebbles. Annie noted that she'd brought her own; a pink one with unicorns.

"Cameron's invited me on a double date with his dad and his dad's new girlfriend. Is that weird?"

"Hmmm." Annie tried to find the right words. "Well, it's not something you'd expect, but I guess if Cameron needs moral support, then..."

"That's what I thought. But what if they look down their noses at me? David Winters is loaded, you can tell from the way Rosamund talks about him. And I live in a caravan."

Annie put a hand on her friend's knee. "Figgy Edmunds, there is absolutely nothing wrong with living in a caravan. And don't you forget it."

Figgy shrugged. "I suppose so."

"I'm right, Figgy. Don't you let anyone tell you you're inferior because you live in... Because you own a piece of prime real estate right on the seafront." She winked.

"Well, I don't own it. Just the lease. But yes. I suppose it is a prime spot." Figgy sighed. "What d'you think she'll be like?"

"The young girlfriend? I've no idea."

Figgy pursed her lips. "I hope Rosamund won't think I'm being disloyal if I go along."

"She won't if she's got any sense. Look, here she is. You can ask her yourself."

Figgy paled. Annie turned to watch Rosamund making her way along the prom from her habitual parking spot at Cobb Gate. She was dressed for the weather, too, but more elegantly than Annie and Figgy; a grey wool coat with a mustard scarf that set off her complexion.

"You look very smart," Annie said.

Rosamund gave an *oh, this* shrug. "Thank you. I'm off into Dorchester to do some shopping."

"You are?" Annie had imagined Rosamund would be spending the day in Lyme Regis. She looked like she was dressed for the possibility of bumping into her husband's new girlfriend.

"I am. There's a new artisan coffee roasters opened up. Cameron has asked for a selection."

"They sell artisan coffee at And Giants & Idiots," Figgy pointed out.

Annie snorted. She had no idea where the name of the coffee roasters' came from, and she couldn't decide if it was memorable or not.

Rosamund shrugged. "It's what he's asked for."

Figgy grunted.

"Figgy's got something to ask you," Annie said.

Rosamund cast a smile in Figgy's direction. "You have?"

"Have I?" Figgy was blushing. "No, I don't think so."

Annie turned to her. "But you—" She felt a kick from

Figgy under the deckchairs. "Oh." She frowned. "Oh look, here comes our fourth member."

Helen was walking along the same stretch of prom Rosamund had just covered, her head low and her feet dragging.

So Harper isn't back, Annie thought and pulled on a sympathetic smile.

"Morning, Helen. How's things?"

Helen slumped down onto the pebbles in front of them, not caring that her green knitted coat would get damp. "Bad. Very, very bad."

"Harper's not back yet?" Figgy asked.

"No." Helen sniffed. "I've been an idiot, ladies."

Annie rubbed the back of her shoulder. "Oh, I'm sure you haven't."

Helen turned to her. Her eyes were red-rimmed. "I have. I really have."

"What did you do?" Rosamund asked. There was an edge to her voice; the tone of a woman who was still recovering from abandonment herself.

"I don't want to talk about it." Helen looked over at Louis, who was gathering more stones. He loved building little piles of them and would compete with himself to build them as tall as possible. "Louis, my small friend," she said, scooting over towards him. "Do you want some help with that?"

He grinned and nodded. Helen sat beside him and started what looked like a deep discussion about which were the most suitable stones for adding to a pile.

"She's looking for distraction," Rosamund said.

"No harm in that," Annie said. "I know I sought out plenty of distraction when my Ted died."

Rosamund grunted. Figgy put a hand on Annie's knee. Annie gave her a grateful smile.

"So have the police taken your statement yet?" Rosamund asked. "About you finding Peg?"

Annie nodded. "Our Dougie came round yesterday afternoon. I told him how I was trying to get into the shop and heard a bang, then went to investigate." She grimaced. "I'm bloody glad I did."

Rosamund and Figgy nodded. Annie slumped into her chair. *Poor Peg.* Was she still lying in hospital, unconscious?

"I also told him about the man I saw. Driving past me when I was on my way there."

"Her attacker?" Figgy asked.

"No idea. He didn't look much like a burglar. But then, I couldn't see his face."

"'Cos he was inside the car?"

Annie shook her head. "No. 'Cos he was holding a towel up to his face."

"Maybe he'd been injured," Rosamund suggested. "What kind of car was it?"

"A silver BMW. Silver-blue, actually. I found a car exactly the same colour in the children's toys and gave it to Dougie."

Rosamund had paled. "What did you say?"

"I found a car exactly the same—"

"No, not that. The car. Describe it again."

"A silver-blue BMW."

"You're sure?"

"Pretty sure." Annie considered. It had been raining, and dark, but there were some lights, and the colour had been distinctive. "Yes. I'm sure."

"That's what David drives," Rosamund said, her voice low. "A silver-blue BMW."

Figgy's jaw dropped open.

Annie looked up at Rosamund, frowning. "Surely you're not suggesting..."

Rosamund pulled herself upright. "With David Winters, I have no idea what I'm suggesting. That man has proven to be full of surprises."

Annie exchanged a look with Figgy. Surely Rosamund didn't think her ex-husband had attacked Peg?

"He wasn't in Lyme then, was he?" she said.

"He was. Arrived on Saturday."

"Oh." Annie frowned. "But what possible motive could David have to attack Peg?"

Rosamund shrugged. "No idea. It's probably just a coincidence."

"It probably is. Figgy, are you alright?"

Figgy had gone very still. She remained motionless even at the mention of her name.

Annie rubbed her knee. "Figgy?"

Figgy started. "Oh. Oh, yes. Yes. I'm fine." She gave Rosamund an uneasy glance. "Fine." She stood up. "Time to get moving, I suppose."

Annie nodded and pushed herself up from the deckchair. "You're right. I need to open up the shop."

"Peg and Sally's pottery?" Rosamund asked. She still looked pensive.

"The very same."

"The police have let you in now?"

"They have. It's time for the Mill Pottery to reopen its doors. Anyone want to witness the grand opening?"

"I can do better than that," said Rosamund. "I can help."

Annie raised an eyebrow. "Really? Aren't you going into Dorchester?"

"That can wait."

Figgy's face was still strange, like she'd been hit on the head but hadn't yet realised it.

"Figgy, are you sure you're alright?" Annie asked.

Figgy swallowed and looked at Annie. She pulled on a smile. "Yes. I'll help, too."

"I thought you had work to do."

Figgy glanced at Rosamund. "I can do it this evening. Let me help, too."

"Very well. Thank you." Annie walked over the pebbles to Helen and Louis. "Come on, handsome boy. We need to run a pottery."

Helen stood up. "You sure you're going to be alright doing this?"

Annie pushed back irritation. "I'll be fine. Promise."

Helen nodded. Her face was pale, and she wasn't wearing her customary mascara and blusher. Annie rubbed her hand.

"She'll come back. She loves you."

Helen sniffed. "I'm not so sure."

CHAPTER TWENTY-ONE

"Right," said Jim Connors as he, Dougie and Wendy took their seats in the team room. Dougie was feeling agitated, frustrated by the fact that Reece Lumbard hadn't been at home last night.

"Right," Wendy muttered. She was looking at her phone, scrolling through something.

"Will you stop that and pay attention?" the sarge said.

Wendy looked up. "I'm not on TikTok, Sarge. I've got an email from Forensics."

"You have?"

She gave a thumbs-up gesture with her free hand. "Hang on while I read it all the way through."

Dougie picked up his cup of tea, anxious to distract himself while they waited. The sarge folded his arms across his chest.

Hurry up, Wendy.

"OK." She looked up and placed her phone face-up on her desk. "So, the blood on that fingerprint. The one under the shelf in the storeroom. It's not Reece Lumbard's."

"No?" Dougie said.

"No. Devon gave us his DNA profile, and it doesn't match."

"What about the victim?" the sarge asked.

"Not hers either."

Dougie pulled in a breath. He didn't want to have to ask the next question. *What about my mother-in-law?*

"I don't suppose it might be Annie Abbott's blood?" he asked.

Wendy looked at him. "Did she say she'd been injured?"

"No." He swallowed. "But she went swimming, just beforehand." He spotted their expressions. "Yes, I know. She's crazy. But maybe she cut her foot on a rock or something."

"That wouldn't fit," Wendy said. "When Annie arrived, Reece had already left. So how could he end up with his prints in her blood?"

Dougie nodded. "Could there be a chance Reece came back, after Annie left? Maybe if he was trying to steal something..."

"We secured the scene," Wendy reminded him. "Nailed the door shut, remember?"

The sarge leaned forward. "There's a chance Reece might still have been inside. Did you search the rest of the building?"

"I did," Wendy told him. "But not thoroughly." Her face fell. "My God. What if he was there all along, and I missed him?"

"Don't beat yourself up," Connors said. "You'd been called out to the scene of a violent crime, in one heck of a storm. You had the victim, the witness and the paramedics to deal with."

"Still," Wendy muttered. "I could kick myself."

"There's one easy way to find out if that print was left in Annie's blood after she left," the sarge said. "And that's to get her DNA profile. Dougie, can you take a kit to her at home?"

Dougie's heart sank. "I think she's working at the pottery," he said. "Now it's open again."

"Really?" said Wendy.

Dougie nodded. "Peg Casey's sister is in Dorchester, keeping an eye on her. Annie stepped in to run the shop."

Connors rolled his eyes. "If she tries some amateur sleuthing..."

"I'll have a chat with her," Dougie said. "Tell her that if she has any information, she's to give it to us."

"Good."

"And she did tell me about the car she saw."

Wendy grunted. "The silver-blue BMW we haven't been able to track down."

"Well, we've got two cars to look for now," Dougie reminded her.

"Of course." She turned to Connors. "Sarge, we think Reece Lumbard might have been driving a red Golf belonging to his mother."

"He wasn't at home?" the sarge asked.

"She hadn't seen him since Saturday."

The sarge tapped his chin. "So he knows he's in trouble." He stretched out his arms. "Right then, we've got two cars to track down and a DNA test to administer. How hard can that be?"

CHAPTER TWENTY-TWO

OPENING up the pottery shop had been fun. Helen and Figgy had joined in, helping Annie to arrange displays, check how the till worked and make the shop itself look tidy. Now it was spick and span, ready for the Christmas ceramics workshop later on.

But now her friends had left – they had their own lives to live, after all – and she was alone. Well, alone except for her grandchildren, but much as she loved them, they weren't exactly the company she needed right now.

She stood in the doorway to the storeroom, her heart heavy. The police had done a reasonable job of cleaning up, but there were still shards of that terracotta jug on the floor, not to mention stock out of place.

And the whole place smelled of chemicals. Whatever it was the police used to check for blood residue and the other things they checked for. And the patches of fingerprint dust made the place look dirty and tired.

She sighed, went into the kitchen and found a bucket

and some cleaning products. Under the sink were cloths and rubber gloves. She'd need those.

She returned to the storeroom, pausing momentarily at the door, and went inside.

Don't think about it. If she remembered the sight of Peg's unconscious body lying right where she was standing, she'd never be able to do this.

Daisy was in the shop, snoozing in her pushchair. Louis was in the living room of Peg and Sally's flat, watching CBeebies. Annie knew that leaving him up there was risky, but the flat was spartan and she didn't think there was anything he could break.

Not like down here.

The shelves were lined with pots and ceramics, some elegant and plain – the kind of thing she imagined Rosamund owning – and others painted in cute designs, more Annie's style. She made her way around the room in an anticlockwise direction, dusting, wiping and spraying. At last, she was making progress.

As she reached the last shelf, a brightly coloured piece of pottery caught her eye. A gaudy reindeer, painted in bright colours with swirls of green and pink.

She picked it up, examining it from all angles. It was unlike anything else in the room. Its antlers stuck out at a weird angle, branching from its head in a way that didn't seem anything close to natural. About twelve inches high, it stood on a stand painted in swirls of red and purple.

She stared at it for a few moments. Would this work, in the shop? Maybe it had started life as a tasteful white reindeer and someone had come along to a workshop and painted it. Maybe Peg and Sally were experimenting with a new line of Christmas ornaments.

If it was going to sell at any time, it would sell now. Only one way to find out.

She carried it through to the shop and placed it on a shelf, next to two polar bears wearing green and red hats. She stood back and smiled. It brightened the place up... and kitsch was in fashion, wasn't it?

She turned at the sound of a knock on the shop door. A slender woman with long dark hair was pressed up to it, peering through the glass.

Annie opened the door, about to explain that the shop wasn't open yet. But the woman wafted in as though propelled by the wind.

"Oh, you are open," she said.

Annie frowned, then shrugged. The only way to sell Peg and Sally's pottery was to open the shop.

"We weren't," she said. "But I suppose we are now."

"Granny!" came a voice from upstairs. She looked towards the door leading to the twins' flat. *Louis.*

She looked at the woman, trying to assess how trustworthy she was. Her coat was cream cashmere, and her hair looked expertly blow-dried. She didn't seem like the kind of person who'd steal pottery.

"I'll be right back," she said. She darted up the stairs, scooped Louis up from the sofa and brought him back down.

He yelled, leaning over her shoulder and reaching upwards. "Noo!"

"Yes, kiddo. We've got a shop to run. Pottery to sell."

He frowned at her, then plunged a finger into his nose and brought out a huge bogey. She grabbed a hanky from her pocket and wiped it away.

At the bottom of the stairs, the woman was perusing the

items on the shelves. Daisy had woken up and was watching her with wide eyes.

"Your kids are cute," the woman said. She had an American accent.

"Grandkids. And yes, they are." Annie gave Louis a wink.

"I love this stuff," the woman said. "It's so rustic."

Annie felt her hackles rise on behalf of her friends. "It's fine craftsmanship," she said. "Most of it made by Peg, who runs the pottery."

The woman flashed Annie a smile. "You're not Peg."

"Peg's in hospital. I'm just minding the shop."

"I love your accent," said the American. "What is it?"

Annie didn't know how to answer that. "A bit of this, a bit of that. A whole lot of Dorset."

"Hmm. I thought everyone in England talked like they do in *Downton Abbey*. Although this area... it's a bit more *Pride and Prejudice*. Did they film that round here?"

"Film it?"

"*Pride and Prejudice*. Keira Knightley. Have you seen it?"

"I've read it," said Annie. "And *Persuasion*, also by Jane Austen. Some of that takes place in Lyme Regis."

"Hmm." The woman gave her a blank look. "Tell me about this piece."

The woman's elegant finger came to rest on the reindeer Annie had brought through from the storeroom.

"It's a reindeer," Annie said.

The woman gave her a quizzical look. "Of course it is." She picked it up and smiled into its face. "What does it symbolise?"

"Er... symbolise?"

"Does it have any local cultural significance? You see, I'm

searching for a gift, something with meaning. I want my gifts to have meaning... what's your name?"

"Annie."

"Shari Temple-Newhart," said the woman, putting splayed fingers on her chest.

"Nice to meet you, er, Shari," said Annie. "It's very Christmassy but, no, not locally significant. We don't get many reindeer in Dorset. Deer, here and there. Red deer, roe deer, sika deer. Not reindeer."

"No. Of course," said Shari Temple-Newhart. "Back home you can't drive up out of Toronto without seeing deer or moose. Majestic creatures."

"You're Canadian," said Annie, mentally correcting her assumptions.

"Yes. Not American." Shari laughed. "Thank God. Yes!" She held her hands up in mock surrender. "I should put it on a T-shirt. I *constantly* find myself being told I'm American. Oh, teapots."

She slid over to a display of teapots.

"Er, yes," said Annie. "Very traditional. Always time for a cup of tea."

"Is a teapot a good gift, though? I want something for my boyfriend's ex."

"Oh."

The woman turned to her. "Does teapot scream old lady? If I give it to her, will she be insulted? But this one is so beautiful." Her fingers traced over a tea set with four cups and saucers on the centre table, all painted with a sea and fishing boat motifs around the lower half. The saucers were rimmed with little blue fish.

"I couldn't say," Annie said.

The woman wrinkled her pretty nose. "It screams old

lady, but I love it." She moved on to a pottery lamp with a warm earthy glaze and a simple fabric shade. "Oh, but this is beautiful. And all wired up, too. Can't resist this. And how much is the reindeer?"

Annie picked up the reindeer and turned it over. It was heavier than it looked; maybe not hollow. There was a price tag taped to the reindeer's rump.

"Three hundred?" read Annie. *Three hundred?*

"It's charming," said Shari.

Annie wasn't sure *charming* was the right word. *Expensive* certainly was. But she wasn't going to argue.

Shari pulled a credit card out of her bag. "You can wrap it, yes?" she said. "The reindeer. Just a bag for the lamp."

Annie went to the counter and looked for bubble wrap and paper.

The shop door opened again. Her daughter Naomi entered, with six-year-old Poppy following close behind. "Hey, Mum. Can Poppy join in the ceramic painting workshop? She's off school with a cold."

Annie smiled. It was good to have someone familiar in here.

Was all shopkeeping going to be like this? Glamorous strangers buying vastly overpriced goods?

"Of course," she said. "Do you want to leave my big girl and get some time to yourself?"

Naomi rolled her eyes; she hated it when Annie said that.

"You're sure?" she said. "You've got Tina's two."

"In for a penny, in for a pound," Annie replied.

"Thanks," said Naomi. "I've got a hair appointment."

Poppy ran to the central table and inspected the plain Christmas decorations, ready for painting.

"Don't touch, sweetie," said Naomi. "Not until the workshop." Poppy pulled her hand back.

"I'll be right with you, Naomi," Annie said. "If you can wait five minutes?"

Naomi nodded. "Appointment's not till eleven," she said.

"These are your family?" Shari asked.

"They are."

"I think children are a gift."

"So do I. You have any?"

"Oh no. But I hope to be gaining a stepson soon."

Annie looked at her, eyes narrowed. Shari, the new girlfriend...

She wasn't sure how Cameron would feel about her installing herself as his new mother. He already had one, for starters. And she couldn't be more than ten years older than he was.

She shuddered, then pulled on the best smile she could muster for the woman as she wrapped the awkwardly shaped reindeer.

Poor Rosamund.

CHAPTER TWENTY-THREE

HELEN DRAGGED her feet as she closed the front door to her shop. Christmas was normally a busy time in the gallery, but she'd barely sold a thing today. Maybe the customers had been put off by her glum expression and sludgy body language.

As she was about to turn back into the shop she spotted somebody outside, running towards her. Waving.

Helen sighed. It would be Annie, with her relentless positivity. The woman meant well, but sometimes she was a bit much.

As the figure drew closer, she realised it wasn't Annie; it was Figgy, wrapped up against the elements in her dry robe and a brightly coloured scarf. She unlocked the door, surprised.

"Figgy," she said. "Aren't you busy working?"

Figgy shook her head. "Just hit a deadline. Early." She held up an orange Kiosk cup. "I brought you a hot chocolate, to cheer you up."

Helen wasn't sure how she felt about being cheered up,

but she took the cup anyway and let Figgy in. She closed the door again and put her cup down to help the younger woman shrug off her dry robe.

"Brrr!" Figgy exclaimed, shaking her shoulders. "My, but it's cold!"

"Your caravan must be difficult to keep warm at this time of year."

Figgy frowned. "Everyone thinks that. But no, it's really quite snug. I've got my gas heater, and lots of blankets. Not to mention my view of the roiling waves."

"Roiling? That's a good word." Helen picked up her cup. She looked at it and huffed out a sigh. "I'm afraid if this is going to cheer me up, it'll need something stronger added to it." She turned towards the doorway to her and Harper's – *still* her and Harper's, whatever the title deed said – flat upstairs.

"Aha!" said Figgy. She rummaged in the pockets of her dry robe, which she'd slung over her arm. "I can help you with that."

"You can?"

Figgy grinned at Helen. She held up a half-bottle of brandy that looked like it dated back to 1973.

Helen peered at it. "Um... does it have a sell-by date?"

Figgy held it up to her face. "Brandy doesn't have a sell-by date, does it? I thought it kept for decades." She shrugged and held it out to Helen.

"Thank you," Helen said. It did no harm to be gracious. "That's very kind of you."

"I found it in the box where my nan kept the Christmas decorations." Figgy's eyes narrowed. "I'm still trying to work out why it was there."

"Maybe she found Christmas stressful."

Figgy shook her head. "Nan adored Christmas. She *created* Christmas." She hesitated. "I don't mean literally created Christmas, that was... I'm not sure who that was. But she was the one who made Christmas happen, in my family."

"All the more reason to find it stressful."

Helen opened the bottle and poured a tot into each of her and Figgy's cups, then a second for herself. All this talk of Figgy's dead grandmother was making her melancholy.

They sat on the rickety wooden chairs Helen kept behind the counter for those times when there were no customers to see her taking the weight off. She gulped hers down while Figgy sipped gingerly.

Figgy eyed Helen over the rim of her cup. "I don't suppose Harper has come back yet?"

Helen felt her muscles constrict. But the *yet* was kind. Figgy was being kind, she had to remember that. Not nosey.

She took a final gulp and put down her cup. "Thank you, Figgy. I enjoyed that. And no, she's not back."

"It's such a difficult time of year, for... for something like this to happen."

"For Harper to leave me, you mean?" Helen sighed. "I'm afraid there's no good time for something like that."

"No." Figgy took another sip. "I suppose not. Well, if you don't have plans for Christmas, you're very welcome at my caravan."

Helen tensed. It hadn't occurred to her that Harper might not be back by then. Not that Christmas was really a thing, in their household. Helen preferred the winter solstice.

"That's very kind of you," she said. "But I assumed you'd be spending Christmas with Cameron?"

Figgy's eyes widened. "Did you? I hadn't considered it."

"You seem pretty tight."

"Yes." Figgy drank the last of her brandy-infused hot chocolate and hugged her arms around herself. "I guess we are."

"Good for you."

Figgy wriggled on her chair. "I'm sorry. You don't want to hear about me and Cam. Not with…"

Helen shook her head. "It doesn't work like that. I'm happy for you."

"I don't think Rosamund is."

"Oh, she'll come round. Believe me, you have less of a challenge with our Rosamund than I did with Harper's parents."

"You think so?"

Helen laughed. "God, yes. When I met her, they were trying to marry her off to some bloke. I mean, have you *seen* Harper?"

Figgy giggled, then caught herself. "I'm sorry. It's not funny."

"Oh, but it is." Helen's thoughts flew back twelve years, to when she'd met Harper at an artists' retreat. Harper had been the only one to refuse to join in with the morning sun-worship.

She sighed. "I just don't understand why she didn't leave a note. I mean, I know why she left. She was angry with me. But not to communicate anything…"

"Maybe she left clues," Figgy said.

"Clues?"

A nod. "She knows about our little swimming club, and our reputation for solving mysteries. Maybe she left clues for you to decipher."

"Being tangential to other people solving two murders does not exactly make me Miss Marple," Helen said.

Figgy shrugged. "OK. But what if she left clues without meaning to?"

"Harper doesn't think like that." Helen had a mental image of Harper's face as she told her she was going to sleep in the workshop, the night she left.

If she'd known, would she have told her the truth?

"OK. So what was she working on?" Figgy asked. "Is there anything in her workshop that might give you a clue as to what she was thinking?"

Helen sighed. "I've already looked."

"Maybe a fresh pair of eyes will help." Figgy rose from her chair, hesitant.

"I suppose it can't do any harm."

Helen led her friend out of the back of the shop, through the courtyard and into Harper's workshop. Being in here made her want to cry.

Or scream blue murder. One of the two.

"Right," said Figgy. "Has anything changed?"

"Everything's changed. She even managed to take her current project. A steel reindeer."

"Her projects are big."

"Mm-hmm."

Figgy looked around. "Was there anything else? Sometimes she works on smaller projects. Ones that are easier to sell."

"As if I don't know that. It's me who sells them."

Figgy's eyes widened. "Have you got anything of Harper's in your gallery? Right now?"

Helen pulled in a shaky breath. She did. A driftwood

Christmas wreath. She'd put it in the gallery's storeroom, unable to look at it.

"Show me," Figgy said.

Helen took her back through the courtyard and into the narrow hallway behind the shop. She opened the door to the storeroom and switched on the light.

Honestly, this was all a waste of time.

"This is very tidy," Figgy said.

Helen raised an eyebrow. "You sound surprised."

"No." Figgy blushed. "But it is."

Helen grunted. Figgy was right; the shelves were clearly labelled, the racks for stacking paintings and prints alphabetised.

"Is that it?" Figgy pointed to an object on the floor, leaning against the shelves.

Helen hadn't been able to store it properly. She'd just wanted to hide it away.

"Yes," she said.

Figgy regarded it. She sucked her lips together. Helen watched. Why had she let the young woman in? Why had she accepted that hot chocolate?

If she'd ignored the figure running towards the shop just as she was closing up, she could be upstairs now. Wrapped in a blanket. Working her way through a bottle of wine.

"Where does the wood come from?" Figgy asked.

"The wood." Helen forced herself to look at the wreath. It had a vulgar beauty. "The wood."

"Where did Harper get it from? You don't get all that much driftwood along this stretch of coast."

Helen let out a small cry. She grasped her friend's shoulder.

"Figgy," she said. "Figgy, I think you might have solved the mystery."

Figgy smiled. "Really?"

"Yes." Helen loosened her grip. "I think I might know where she is."

CHAPTER TWENTY-FOUR

"There," Annie said. "Both tucked in and fast asleep." She planted herself down on the sofa and snuggled in next to Tim.

"This is nice," he said. "You and me and a quiet house."

She turned to him, suspicious. "You're joking, right?"

They had been intending to go to the seventies karaoke night at Breaststrokes café-bar on the seafront, but small children and karaoke nights out didn't mix.

He rubbed her shoulder. "I do. Things always seem to get so busy around you, Annie Abbott. It's nice to have you to myself."

She felt herself beaming inside and out. "Well, you know how to make a woman happy, Tim Cromwell."

He waggled his eyebrows. "I think I can make you even happier."

She tensed. She was growing fond of Tim and enjoyed being close to him like this. But that was all, for now.

He bent over and reached into the carrier bag he'd brought with him. He pulled out a bottle of red wine.

"Ta-dah! Happier?"

She laughed. "Wine! Perfect. I'll get glasses."

Annie went into the kitchen and clattered around in the cupboards. She knew exactly where the wine glasses were; there was a set in the sideboard right behind the sofa, in fact.

But she needed a moment.

Tim's comment about making her happy, and the conclusions she'd leapt to... It had made her scared, but excited at the same time.

On the wall above the kettle was a photo of her and Ted, taken on the Cobb when the girls were teenagers. She brushed it with her fingers.

"I hope you don't mind, love."

She cleared her throat and straightened up before heading back into the living room. Tim was standing up, rifling through the collection of records she still kept in the sideboard.

She wondered if he'd noticed the glasses.

"Those go back years," she said. "I don't even have anything to play them on."

Sentimental value, she thought. like so many of the things in this house.

"I thought you did," he said. "In the summer..."

She shook her head. "That wasn't my turntable, it was Dante's. My temporary and somewhat chaotic lodger."

Dante was her son-in-law Mike's dad. He'd visited the area briefly. When Mike had refused to take him in – lingering family tensions she'd never quite got to the bottom of – she'd offered him a room.

Tim pursed his lips. "There was a time when I thought you and Mr Legg were an item."

She made a sound of derision. "Goodness, no. I might

give the impression of being a mad old lady, but I like my men sensible. Dignified."

He turned to her. "I hope that's how a person would describe me."

"I think it is."

"And I don't think you're mad," he added. "Neither do I think you're old."

She put a hand on his arm. "It's all relative, I suppose."

He held up an album from the vinyl collection. "I wish you had a turntable, so we could play this."

She laughed. "*Pinky and Perky Have a Party*? My God, how old is that?" She reached for it and turned it over. "1976. Our Tina wasn't born until 1996."

"Which means you bought it for personal use."

She sniggered. "It must have been a charity shop find, when the girls were little."

"Nothing but the best for your girls."

"Nothing but the best, indeed." She passed it back for him to return to the stack. "So are you going to pour this wine then?"

His cheeks flushed. It made him look even more outdoorsy. "You must think me very rude."

"Oh, I understand. You were distracted by the musical charms of Pinky and Perky. Who on earth came up with the idea of singing pigs?"

"Those voices, too." He picked up the bottle and poured wine into the glasses she'd placed on the sideboard.

"You remember?" She gave him a grave look. "You were clearly a fan."

"Oh, clearly." He handed her a glass and raised his. She clinked it with her own.

"Merry Christmas," she said.

"Merry Christmas, Annie Abbott. Closet Pinky and Perky fan."

She almost spat out her wine. "That's me."

They sat down on the sofa. He put a hand on her knee, and she felt a shiver run through her.

Annie Abbott, you're behaving like a silly young girl. She smiled to herself.

"Talking of Christmas," Tim said, "I've been meaning to ask you a favour."

She put her glass down. "Ask away."

"The Christmas Fayre, on Saturday. Like an idiot, I've volunteered to run the tombola."

"That's very community-spirited of you."

He shrugged. "You make it sound like I'm rescuing puppies."

"Rescuing puppies isn't as community-spirited as running a tombola. And it's kind of your job, isn't it?"

"I run the lifeboat building and the shop," he reminded her. "I very rarely actually go out in the boat these days. And I don't recall ever rescuing a shipwrecked puppy."

"It would be cute, though." She raised an eyebrow over her glass. "Are you telling me you need a helper?"

"No." He shook his head. "Although, if you're volunteering..."

"Tim, I'd be very happy to help."

"Thank you." He clinked her glass again. "And I'd be very happy to be helped."

"That settles it then."

"Actually, that wasn't the favour I was about to ask you."

Annie was bent forwards, about to pick up the wine bottle. How had she got through her glass so fast? She paused. "It wasn't?"

"I need items to sell. Well, to give the people with winning tickets. You know how it works. I've donated some bits and bobs from the shop, paid for by myself of course. But I need more. And more variety."

"You need donations?"

"I do. Any help would be gratefully appreciated."

Annie nodded. She had a shopping habit, a serious one when it came to buying presents for her grandkids. Her spare room was full of toys she knew Tina and Naomi would roll their eyes at.

"I think I can help," she said.

"I knew you'd come through for me."

"And I can ask my friends. Between us, we'll give you the best-stocked tombola Lyme Regis has ever seen."

He raised his glass. "I'll drink to that."

CHAPTER TWENTY-FIVE

FIGGY STOOD in the poky bathroom of her caravan, regarding herself in the mirror. She had no idea what a person was supposed to wear to go on a double date with their boyfriend's dad and his girlfriend. Let alone a double date at someone's house.

As far as she could tell, David was loaded. So why *had* he invited them to his rented cottage instead of taking them to a swanky restaurant?

Her eyes widened in the mirror. *Oh, my God.* Was this one of those dinners that would be catered, with lackeys in black dresses and white aprons? Or the even more sophisticated kind of event she'd seen in American TV shows, with handsome waiters dressed entirely in black?

If that was the case, she'd probably have more in common with the staff than the people on the other side of the table. Closer in age, closer in social class, and likely to be the only other people of colour in the room.

She sat down on the toilet lid. This was going to be awful. Why had she agreed to it?

Because Cameron needed her support, that was why. And her feelings for Cameron... well, they were deepening. Enough for her to tolerate his frankly neglectful father and the new girlfriend.

She was pulled from her worries by a knock on the caravan door. It was firm, so firm it made the whole van reverberate.

She stood, gave her reflection a final check, and walked to the door. She squared her shoulders and threw on her bravest smile before opening it.

Cameron was wearing a linen jacket over a white T-shirt and pressed jeans. It suited him.

"Wow," he said. "You look gorgeous."

She blushed and patted her hair. "Really?"

"Yes. That dress is amazing."

She smoothed down the skirt. "Are you sure it's not too much?"

The dress was a 1950s-style number she'd bought from an online vintage shop. It was black, with purple detailing on the bodice and a lace underskirt that made the skirt stick out. She'd taken it off, replaced it with jeans and a blouse, and put it back on again. Seven times.

"Who cares if it's too much?" he said. "You look amazing." He leaned in and kissed her. Figgy melted into it, allowing her nerves to dissipate for a moment.

"Right." He clapped his hands together. "I've borrowed my mum's car. Madam, your carriage awaits." He gave her a lopsided grin.

Figgy put her hand in his. The jacket, and the formality, and the intensity of that kiss. He was nervous.

"It'll be OK, you know," she said as they drove away from

the caravan site and through Lyme Regis. "I won't let him upset you."

He glanced at her. "It doesn't work like that."

"No?"

He shook his head. "If my dad pisses me off, it's because of what he *doesn't* do, not what he does. Never being around when I was growing up. Never showing any interest in the way I like to build things. Not to mention ghosting me for months."

She reached out in the darkness and squeezed his knee. "I'm sorry. Tell me what I can do to make this easier."

He clutched her hand, briefly, then put his hand back on the steering wheel. Figgy suddenly had a memory of the first time she'd been in this car. Rosamund had injured her foot, and there'd been a dead man sitting in the front seat.

"You're a good human being, Figgy Edmunds," Cameron said. "Do you know that?"

Figgy shrugged. She'd lied to the police about the dead man in her friend's car. What sort of human being did that make her?

"You just being here with me makes this easier," he continued. "I'm grateful."

She gave him what she hoped was an optimistic smile. "I'm sure we'll have a lovely evening," she lied. "You'll see."

Cameron grunted. They were out of Lyme Regis now, on the Charmouth Road. He reached the roundabout where it met the main road and took the right turn for Charmouth. Figgy wondered if David had chosen to stay in Charmouth to avoid awkward encounters with Rosamund, or simply because he liked it more.

Probably because he liked it more.

"You want some music?" Cameron asked. "My phone connects to Mum's car. I think it'll help my nerves." He handed her his phone.

She scrolled through Spotify and chose some tracks; calming but not dull. She fiddled with the controls on the central console and at last the sound of 'Wildflower' filled the space.

"Your mum's car's very... complicated," she said.

Cameron laughed. "My dad chose it for her. I'm not entirely sure she really knows how to work it." He indicated a row of controls on the steering wheel. "This button's for sports mode, this one's eco mode. Then there's driver assist, whatever that means."

"No idea."

"I just get in the thing and drive. I think my mum does, too." He glanced at her. "Do you drive?"

"Do I, or can I?"

"Either. Both."

"I don't, obviously. No car, and I rarely leave Lyme. And I kind of can, but not legally."

"What do you mean, kind of?"

"My grandad gave me some rudimentary lessons, in Charmouth Road car park. Not exactly road experience."

"No." He wrinkled his nose. "My mum seemed to think it was a mandatory rite of passage. First lesson on the morning of my seventeenth birthday." He slowed the car. "Here we are."

Wisteria Cottage was no cottage. It was a broad, red-brick building set back from the road with – Figgy counted – thirteen windows and a broad front door. And that was only the front.

"Surely they should call it Wisteria Mansion," she said as they pulled onto the wide gravel driveway.

Cameron raised an eyebrow. "Nothing but the best for my dad."

Figgy gave him a *you've got this* smile as they walked towards the front door. The bare branches of a climbing plant she could only assume was wisteria surrounded it. All thirteen windows twinkled with fairy lights and behind two of the downstairs windows were fully lit Christmas trees.

"Ow." Figgy reached down for her foot. Her heel had caught in the gravel, and she'd twisted her ankle. "Ow."

"You OK?" Cameron had taken a few steps back and was standing over her, shifting from foot to foot. Behind him, that broad front door was opening.

Figgy closed her eyes. *How humiliating*. She yanked her shoe free and let Cameron take her weight as she stood upright.

"You hurt?" he muttered.

She shook her head. "I'm fine. Come on."

They continued walking to the front door, past two expensive-looking cars: a white SUV and the silver-blue BMW Rosamund had mentioned down at the beach.

She looked at it. It couldn't be the one Annie saw. Could it?

A slim man with greying hair wearing chinos and a linen shirt was stepping out of the front door.

"Cam," he said. "Welcome. It's so good to see you. And you must be Figgy."

A slender woman with bright white teeth and a perfect blow-dry stood in the doorway. She couldn't be more than four years older than Figgy, ten years older than Cameron.

She gave them a grin and a little wave.

David turned back towards her. "And this is Shari," he said. "My gorgeous Shari."

Cameron made an involuntary noise. Figgy squeezed his hand.

Here goes.

CHAPTER TWENTY-SIX

"THANKS, LOVE," Naomi said to Dougie from across their tiny kitchen table. "I know how busy you are with everything going on at the Mill."

He swallowed a mouthful of the curry he'd made and wiped his mouth. "You know I enjoy cooking." He picked up his empty plate, grabbed Naomi's, and headed to the sink.

Naomi shuddered. "And I hate it. Fortunately, Poppy had her tea at Granny's today, after a stint helping her out at the pottery."

He ran the tap, wafting his hand in the stream of water to check when it was hot enough. "Helping out, or getting in the way?" He turned to Naomi. "Please tell me nothing got broken."

Naomi laughed. "You underestimate our daughter." She patted her hair. "Anyway, have you noticed anything?"

He frowned. *No.* Then... *oh.* He nodded. "You've had your hair cut. It looks lovely. You always look lovely."

"Well done, Dougie. You've covered all the bases." She stood and joined him at the sink, where she grabbed a tea towel. She'd been trying to work out how to fit a dishwasher into this tiny kitchen since they'd moved in, but the space was just too small.

He turned to her, arms still in the soapy water, and kissed her cheek. "I mean it. It suits you. You look hot."

She raised an eyebrow. "Really?"

He gave her a serious look. "Yes. Really. I fancy you, Naomi Anderson. Would you like to go on a date with me?"

She snorted and gave him a playful slap with the tea towel. "I wish." She sighed. "Anyway, I don't know why I bother. All this effort to make myself look good, and tomorrow all I've got to look forward to is the bloody science fair."

He finished washing the pot he'd cooked the curry in and placed it on the draining board. "Part of the school Christmas celebrations?" he asked.

"Something like that." Naomi grabbed the pan to dry it. "I can't see how a science fair is Christmassy, but Fenella suggested it to the head, and he pounced on the idea like a cat on a mouse."

"How did I know Fenella would be behind this?"

"If something's making my job harder, you can be sure Fenella is behind it."

He rubbed her arm. "I'm sorry, love."

The washing up was done and everything put away. Dougie filled the kettle.

"Tea and telly?" he suggested.

She smiled. "Tea and telly. What glamorous lives we lead."

"It won't be forever." His gaze went upwards to where their daughter slept above their heads.

"Did we lead glamorous lives before we became

parents?" Naomi asked as she took her cup of tea from him. "We live in Lyme Regis, after all. Hardly a bustling metropolis."

He cocked his head. "I like living here. We've got the bay and the views. Plenty of pubs if we want to go out, and all our friends are here."

She sighed. "I know. I love Lyme, too." She stroked his cheek. "Don't worry about me, I'm just grumpy because of this science fair."

"Maybe it'll go better than you think. Maybe tomorrow will be a surprise for both of us. Your fair will go without a hitch, and I'll find the bloke who attacked Peg Casey."

She held up her mug to clunk against his.

"I can drink to that," she said.

CHAPTER TWENTY-SEVEN

F<small>IGGY WAS DETERMINED NOT</small> to be nervous. Sure, these people were all wealthier than her; even Cameron, not that he cared. And yes, this house was ten times the size of her caravan, at least.

But it was going OK. David was polite, if a little distant. Shari, who it turned out was Canadian, was bending over backwards to be friendly. And – thank God – there were no staff. It looked like David and Shari had done the cooking themselves. And it was much better than Cameron had led her to expect. A paella, followed by the lemon tart they were eating right now.

"I'm so sorry I didn't check if you had any dietary requirements, Figgy." Shari leaned across the table. "It was incredibly rude of me."

Figgy shrugged, her mouth full of the delicious tart. Dietary requirements were for people who could afford them, as far as she was concerned. Back in her caravan, she'd probably be eating tinned tomato and 'end of shelf-life' sausages with pasta. This was a vast improvement. There had been seafood in the paella that she hadn't eaten since her grandfather used to fish for it.

"It's all delicious," she said, putting down her fork as she realised that she was eating faster than everyone else. "And I don't have any dietary requirements, so it's fine."

Shari frowned. "Surely you must do. Everyone has dietary requirements, even if it's just one item they struggle with. David, for example, is lactose intolerant."

Cameron looked up. "Since when?" He'd been pushing his tart around his plate, letting Figgy do the talking. It didn't come easily to her, but she supposed that was why she was here.

David met his son's gaze. "It's probably been a couple of years. But it was Shari who noticed."

"How? I mean, how would she know if you didn't?"

David put down his dessert fork. "Cam."

"Don't *Cam* me like I'm five years old."

David's jaw tightened. "And don't be aggressive towards Shari. Please."

"Aggressive?" Cameron frowned at Shari. "I wasn't being aggressive, was I?"

Shari looked from Cameron to David, then back to Cameron. She gave him a weak smile. "I don't—"

"You don't know if I'm being aggressive because you don't know me." Cameron grabbed the napkin from his lap, balled it up, and threw it onto his plate. "I'm a very calm person, normally."

"Cameron," Figgy whispered. She put a hand on his arm.

He shook it off and looked into her eyes. "I am a calm person, aren't I? You know I am."

She nodded.

He returned the nod then looked at his dad. "See? I'm

chill. I'm easy-going. But then when someone pretends I don't exist for over half a year—"

"I'm sorry," David said. His voice was hard. "I know you're pissed off with me. Christ knows, your mother is, too. But it was her I left, Cam. Not you."

"That's not how it felt." Cameron stood up. "Come on, Figgy. We shouldn't have come."

She swallowed and stood up, careful not to drop her napkin and wishing she'd finished her slice of tart. Cameron had managed to sit all through dinner, making polite conversation. He'd even told the story of how they'd tried to fool the scavenging Kevin and his seagull friends by painting stones to look like food.

So what had made him snap?

Shari stood and followed them out of the room. David remained on his chair, his face thunderous. Figgy looked back at him, wondering if he'd been so unresponsive with Rosamund.

At the front door, Shari caught up with them. "It was lovely to meet you both," she said. "I'm sorry about David. He can be... stubborn."

"I know that," Cameron grunted. "I spent the first nineteen years of my life living with him."

"Of course. Yes, of course."

"Thank you for the lovely food," Figgy said, unsure of what else to say.

Shari gave her a sad smile. "I bought the most delicious chocolates. From an artisan chocolatier in Lyme." She made the word *chocolatier* sound far more natural than Figgy could have. "I'm sorry we couldn't have continued the evening longer, shared them with you."

Cameron grunted. Figgy gave an awkward shrug.

"Oh." Shari put a hand to her mouth. "I almost forgot."

She reached down and picked up a box from beside the console table by the front door. It was about twelve centimetres cubed and wrapped in pretty seaside paper.

She held it out towards Cameron. "This is for your mother." She smiled nervously. "A peace offering, I guess. I think it has local significance."

Cameron's hands remained at his sides. Figgy took the parcel.

"I'll pass it on to her," she said.

"Really? I think it's best that Cameron—"

"Rosamund and I are friends," Figgy said. She hoped that was still true. "I'll make sure she gets it."

Whether Rosamund would accept the gift was another matter entirely.

"Thank you," Shari said. "And please tell her I'm sorry for any pain I've caused her."

Figgy nodded. Cameron was already out of the door and striding towards the car. She hurried to catch up and got in next to him.

He revved the engine. "That was a shitshow."

"I'm sorry."

She looked back at the house. Shari stood in the brightly lit doorway, waving hesitantly. There was still no sign of David.

He eyed the parcel on her lap as they drove back towards Lyme. "That'll be maple syrup," he said. "Isn't that what Canadians always give people?"

"It's the wrong shape for maple syrup." She gave it the smallest of rattles. Something inside shifted.

"I want you to look at it," he said. "I don't want to see it."

"Are you sure? It's for your mum."

"Please. Just tell me what that woman's decided to give her."

"OK." Figgy found the edge of the Sellotape and prised it unstuck with a fingernail. She pulled open the wrapping, careful not to tear it, then opened the lid of the box.

"Oh," she said.

Cameron blipped the brakes. "Oh?"

She nodded. "Just... oh. It wasn't what I was expecting. Oh no... wait. Yes, it's a moose." She pulled out her phone and shone the torch at the object. "No, it isn't."

"You're making no sense."

Figgy turned the object around. She didn't want to pull it out of the box – that was for Rosamund to do – but she wanted to work out what it was.

"It's a reindeer," she said. "A pottery reindeer, decorated for Christmas."

Cameron grunted. "Sounds awful."

"Hmm." One thing was certain: Rosamund would hate it. Figgy quite liked it, not that she'd admit to that.

She closed it up and resealed the wrapping. "I hope your mum likes it," she said.

Cameron snorted. "She won't. She really bloody won't."

CHAPTER TWENTY-EIGHT

HELEN'S HEART was in her chest as she drove out of Lyme Regis. She'd tried calling Harper's mobile to confirm that she was right, but it had just rung out. As it had the previous twenty or more times.

The sun was setting as she sped along Sidmouth Road, disappearing behind hedges and reappearing again in that annoying way that meant she kept taking her sunglasses off and then putting them back on. She was going too fast for this winding road, she knew. More than once, she had to slam on her brakes and squeeze into the hedge at the side of the road.

She was probably scratching the paintwork. She didn't care.

As she rounded another bend, twin headlights came at her.

"Shit!" She threw up an arm to shield her eyes and then threw it back down to grab the wheel. The car squeezed past her, barely slowing.

Helen's ancient Skoda, on the other hand, had ground to

a halt. The offside front wheel was in a ditch, and the hedge had hit the wing mirror so hard it had snapped into the closed position.

"You bloody idiot!" She turned around and saw the car driving away. A silver-blue BMW, 2023 reg.

Helen's eyes narrowed. Wasn't it a silver-blue BMW that had almost mown down Annie before she found Peg unconscious on Sunday night? And hadn't Rosamund said that her ex drove a silver-blue BMW?

Was the car that had now disappeared from view one of those cars? Maybe even both of them?

She shook her head. There was nowhere to turn along here, and she'd never manage to chase the car down, even if she could go back.

And she had more important things to worry about. A more important person.

She reversed out of the ditch, muttering curses under her breath the whole time. At last, she was on the move again.

Slow down, she told herself. She took the last few miles at a steady pace. If Harper was where Helen thought she was, she wasn't going anywhere.

Finally, she arrived at the turn-off: a narrow left-hand turn immediately before the bridge that led into Axmouth. In the daytime, cars would be parked all along here. But tonight, it was quiet.

She parked as close to the beach as she could get and climbed out of the car. The wind hit her instantly and she winced.

"Bloody hell." She took a deep breath. *Harper, please be here.*

She fought her way round to the back of the car, opened the boot and yanked out her biggest winter coat. She already had a purple velvet jacket on, but this wasn't 'purple velvet jacket' weather.

After a few moments of struggling she had the overcoat on, along with the yellow woolly hat she kept in its pocket.

If Harper was where she thought she was, she'd be feeling the brunt of this. *Just don't blow away.*

Helen trudged along the path that led towards the beach and past the harbour. Harper had a friend – Pansy – who owned a battered caravan overlooking the beach. And the beach here, the section where it retreated inland and followed the River Axe for a short distance... it was one of the few places Harper had been able to source driftwood.

More importantly, Helen knew that this was one of Harper's favourite places within a twenty-mile radius of Lyme.

She gritted her teeth as she walked, one hand pressing the hat firmly down on her head. The air rang with the clanging of ropes against masts.

At last, she was past the marina. What few lights there had been petered out. Ahead of her, the beach was in darkness.

No lights from a caravan window.

Damn.

Carry on. She'd come too far to give up now. And Harper might have closed the curtains against the storm.

Helen brought out her phone and fumbled with it until she had the torch lit. Holding her breath, she raised it in front of her.

The light glinted off something metallic.

Helen's breath caught in her throat. She held the torch up higher, walking towards the reflected light.

"Ouch."

Her foot had hit something. She shone the torch down. A boulder.

"Bastard thing." She bent down and rubbed it. That'd teach her to shine the light up and ahead, instead of down and ahead.

"Hello? Is there someone there?" a voice called from the darkness.

Helen gasped and threw the torchlight up again. "Yes. It's me, Helen."

"Helen?"

A woman stood up ahead, right next to the motorbike that had reflected the torchlight. Behind her was the dark shape of a caravan and the light of an open doorway.

"Harper?" Helen said. She raised her voice so it was more than a whisper. "Harper? Is that you?"

"You found me." Harper's voice was hesitant.

Oh, hell. Please don't be angry.

"The driftwood sculpture you left behind." Helen shone the torch up and into her own face. Harper became a shape silhouetted against the lit doorway.

"You found it," Harper said.

Helen's chest clenched: hope. "Did you want me to?"

Silence. Helen realised she'd lost her hat in the wind.

"Harper?" she said. "Did you leave the sculpture as a clue? You wanted me to find you, right?"

Silence. Helen waited, resisting the urge to fill the void.

At last, Harper spoke.

"Well done," she said. "I guess you'd better come inside."

CHAPTER TWENTY-NINE

"Here she is," Wendy muttered to Dougie, who'd been checking his phone for a message from the council.

He looked up to see his mother-in-law striding towards them. She had Louis's small fist in one hand, the lead of a worryingly bouncy Labrador in the other, and was somehow pushing Daisy along in a pushchair at the same time.

He forced a smile. She wasn't just here to pry, he told himself. She was running the pottery; she had a reason to be here.

"Annie," he said.

"Dougie, love," she replied. "You've had a breakthrough?"

He frowned.

"Nothing like that," Wendy said. "We've been called in to close off the area due to flooding."

"Flooding?" replied Annie. "What flooding?"

Wendy gestured towards the River Lyme behind them. It was running high, close to breaking its banks.

"The river's been spilling over for the last hour or so," she said. "It's at risk of bursting its banks."

"That wouldn't be good." Annie stepped past them, leaving the dog tied to the pushchair. "Now you be careful, Louis. Don't get too close."

"Fish!" Louis pointed at the river. It was lapping at the squared-off edges of its banks where it ran past the mill.

Annie wrinkled her nose. "Can't see any fish, pet." She looked back towards the pottery, which sat downhill from the riverbank. "But if that starts to overflow..." She pulled him away from the water.

"Fish!" he repeated, tugging at her hand.

"Be a good boy now, Louis. Stay with Granny."

The boy was crying. "Fish."

Dougie stepped forward to look. He smiled.

"Sorry, mate," he said to his nephew. "That isn't a fish, it's a sock."

He watched as the sock floated towards the mill and the drain leading under it. It bobbed in the water, not making any forward progress.

"Alright folks, what's happening then?"

He turned to see two council workers in high-viz climbing down from a van. Wendy approached them.

"We can't work it out," she told them. "The river looks like it's about to burst its banks, but it hasn't rained the last twenty-four hours."

"It doesn't always work like that," the shorter of the two women from the council said. She turned to her colleague. "Flo, you might need your waders."

They'll need more than waders, Dougie thought. He knew how deep the cutting that carried the river past here was.

"If you're planning on going in," he said, "you'll need diving gear."

The woman snorted. "Don't be daft."

Her colleague closed the back doors of their van. "Right, Jo. Waders ready. Where d' you want me?"

Flo and Jo, Dougie thought. You couldn't make it up.

He shrugged at Wendy, who rolled her eyes. Annie had tight hold of both Louis's hand and the dog lead, while Daisy sat in her pushchair, staring at the water as it lapped over the concrete towards them.

"Oh, bugger," Annie said. "Dex, stop it."

The dog was pulling at its lead, whimpering.

"Stop it," she repeated. "Sit."

The dog ignored her.

"You want a hand with that?" Dougie asked. It didn't look like his mother-in-law's strength would hold the lead for much longer.

"I didn't know you had a dog, Annie," Wendy said.

"Dex isn't mine." She staggered forward as the dog tugged at her. "He belongs to a neighbour. I just walk him sometimes."

"Ah." Wendy smiled.

"Dex!" Annie cried. "Bad dog!"

The dog had beaten her. It bounded across the tarmac, lead dragging out behind it.

"I'll get it." Wendy sprinted after the dog and grabbed its collar.

Dougie frowned. He'd been expecting the dog to leap in the river; that was the kind of thing dogs did, wasn't it?

But it had veered off to the right and made for a dilapidated building that sported a sign announcing it as the Tuck Shop Café but was currently shuttered. Right now, the dog was tugging against Wendy's grip and whining, claws skittering against the café's side wall.

What's up, boy? he wondered. *What's in there?* That was the café with the CCTV that didn't work.

"Dex!" shouted Annie with a firmness Dougie had never heard before. He was impressed.

"Watch out!"

He turned to see Jo – or was it Flo? – running towards them from the river. The one without the waders. Her colleague was behind her, waist-deep in the water. Those waders would be useless now.

"Everybody move!" she shouted.

Dougie exchanged glances with Wendy. *What the hell's going on?*

The dog barked.

"Dex!" Annie shouted. "Here, now!" She was dragging the pushchair away from the water. Wendy followed her, carrying Louis in her arms.

"The water's out of control," Flo called. "The drains are blocked."

What, by a sock?

Dougie rushed towards Wendy and grabbed Louis from her. The boy was crying.

"Good boy, Dex," Annie said. The dog had joined them and was now making a low whimpering sound.

"What happened?" Annie was staring at Dougie, her eyes wide.

He juggled Louis in his arms. "Shush, big fella. I've got you." He turned to his mother-in-law. "No idea," he said.

Jo was with them now. Flo followed, struggling in her waterlogged waders.

"There's something blocking the drain that runs under

here," she said. "We'll have to get a team out, see if we can clear it."

"See if you can clear it?" asked Wendy. "What, you think you might not be able to?"

Flo pushed back her hair. There was something Dougie preferred not to identify hanging from her wrist.

"They'll clear it," she said. "The question is how long it'll take."

The water was still moving towards them.

"We'll need to cordon the area off," Wendy said. Dougie nodded.

"What about the pottery?" Annie asked. "There's valuable stock in there."

The water hadn't reached the door to the pottery yet.

"You can't go in," Jo said.

Annie approached her. "My friends Sally and Peg run that pottery. Peg was attacked on Sunday, and Sally's with her in hospital. They don't need to have their stock ruined on top of all that."

"You're right," Dougie said. He looked at the council workers. "I'm authorising her to go in, just for as long as it takes to make the stock in that shop safe."

"Thanks, Dougie." Annie squeezed his arm. "I knew there was a reason I wanted you to marry Naomi."

He frowned, not wanting to unpack that statement. "Just be quick," he said.

She gave him a wink. "Come on, kids."

"No," Dougie said. "Leave the kids out here with me. I'm not taking the dog, though."

"Fair enough. We'll be quick, I promise." Annie yanked on the lead then ran towards the pottery, the dog bounding along beside her.

Dougie watched them, wondering where his mother-in-law got her energy from. He could only hope he wouldn't regret this.

CHAPTER THIRTY

HELEN HAD SPENT the night on the sofa in the caravan's living area, with Harper retreating to the bedroom almost as soon as they went inside.

"You woke me," Harper had grunted as she closed the door behind Helen.

"I found you," Helen replied. "You didn't go far." Was that a good sign?

Harper had simply shrugged. "I'm tired. You can have the couch."

And then she'd disappeared into the bedroom with no explanation of why she'd left and no indication of whether she was pleased Helen had tracked her down.

Now it was five am, and still resolutely dark outside. Helen had spent a fretful night on the sofa, barely taking her eyes off the bedroom door.

Should she be more assertive? Throw the door open and proclaim her love for Harper? Tell her she wasn't leaving until they'd sorted things out?

No. Even if Helen had the courage to do that, she knew what Harper's reaction would be.

She closed her eyes, willing herself to sleep. Harper rose at six every morning, and she wanted to be refreshed to greet her. Even an hour's sleep was better than none.

But it was no good.

At last Helen heard movement beyond the bedroom door. Had Harper gone back to sleep after Helen's arrival, or had she, too, simply lain there staring at the ceiling?

Helen forced herself up. She plumped the cushions around her and went to the kitchen sink. She splashed water on her face.

Damn. What if she'd smudged her makeup? She'd reapplied mascara and lipstick before coming out last night. It was probably halfway down her face now.

She rubbed under her eyes with a fingertip and poured herself a glass of water. She leaned against the kitchen cupboards, waiting.

After a few moments Harper emerged. She dragged a hand through her short hair and walked past Helen, not making eye contact.

Helen could hear her heart pounding in her ears.

Harper filled the kettle. She gave Helen a quick glance as she did so, eyebrows raised.

"Yes, please," Helen said. It was unlikely the caravan would have the herbal tea she preferred, but that didn't matter.

The kettle boiled. Harper made coffee for herself and tea for Helen, weak and black, Helen noted with a smile. *She hasn't forgotten.*

Harper walked to the sofa Helen had attempted to sleep

on. She sat down and slurped her coffee. She leaned back and narrowed her eyes at Helen.

"You found me."

"You left that driftwood sculpture in the storeroom of the gallery."

Harper grunted.

"But you took everything else."

A nod, and another slurp.

"Where is it all?" Helen asked.

Harper waved a hand. "In a trailer, back of the van."

"You used the caravan to tow a trailer?"

"Don't be daft. I used my bike."

Ah. Helen didn't know you could put a trailer on a motorbike. Was that even legal?

She wasn't about to ask.

She took a sip of her tea. Her heart was racing.

"I owe you an explanation," she said.

Harper's lips pursed. "You could say that."

"You owe me one, too. Taking off like that..."

Harper shook her head. "I told you I was sleeping in the workshop. You knew why I had to leave."

"I wish you'd told me."

Harper draped an arm across the back of the sofa. "I thought you were saying you owed me an explanation."

"I was. I am. I'm sorry."

"Is that it? I suppose it's an apology, but..."

"An explanation," Helen said. "I said I owe you an explanation."

"That might be more use than an apology."

"Please, Harper," Helen said. "Don't make this harder than it already is."

Harper leaned forward. "I asked you to marry me. You

wouldn't give me a reason for your refusal. I can only assume that you don't feel the same way about me as I do about you."

"I do."

Harper raised an eyebrow.

"I love you, Harper McCoppin."

A smile played at Harper's lips. Was Helen getting through to her?

"So prove it," Harper said. "Tell me why you can't, or won't, marry me. And don't give me any bullshit about tradition and heteronormativity. We've already been down that road."

"I know. And it's a can't. Not a won't. I'd love to marry you, but I can't."

"Why the hell not?" Harper's face fell. "Oh my God, are you already married?"

Helen shook her head. "Absolutely not. But I – Helen Cruickshank – cannot marry you." She took a sip from her mug; it was empty.

Here goes.

"But Genevieve Cartwright-Jones can," she said. "Or rather, she can't. But she could."

"You're making no sense. Who the hell is Genevieve Cartwright-Jones?"

Helen took a step forward. Harper frowned, and she stepped back again.

"She's me," Helen said. "My real identity."

Harper barked out a laugh. "Oh, Jesus. Don't tell me you're a spy or something."

"Not a spy. A thief."

Harper tensed. "A thief? What, like the arsehole who broke into the pottery on Sunday night?"

"Bigger."

"Bigger? What is this, *Ocean's Eleven*?"

Helen smiled. "Not as glamorous as that. I stole an artwork from... from a former employer."

"I don't get you. You buy and sell art." Harper's eyes widened. "Is the gallery a front? Money laundering? Dodgy art dealing?"

"The gallery has been legit from day one. I've never sold anything that wasn't totally legal and above board."

"Good. But... I still don't get it. Who's this Genevieve Cartwright-whatever? And who was the boss you stole from?"

"Not a boss. A client. Genevieve Cartwright-Jones is the name on my birth certificate. My legal name. When the client discovered what I'd done, they sent people after me. It was a very valuable artwork. So I changed my name and moved somewhere I thought they'd never find me."

"Lyme Regis."

"Lyme Regis," Helen confirmed. "And it worked. But if I married you, I'd have to use my real name. There'd be a record. And..."

"And they'd come after you. These must be some very powerful people."

"Wealthy. Which gives them power." Helen took a step forward again. This time, Harper didn't make her go back.

"Why didn't you just give it back? The artwork?"

"Because I'd already handed it over to the police. The artwork in question was being used as part of an insurance fraud scheme."

"So ask the police to protect you."

"It's not as simple as that."

"No." Harper stood up. She regarded Helen for a moment, then stepped towards her. "This is legit? Not some cock and bull story you've made up to wriggle out of telling me why you won't marry me?"

Helen put a hand on her heart. "I swear."

"Hmm." Harper's nostrils flared. "OK."

Helen felt her breath catch. "OK? OK what?"

"OK, I'll come home. But only so we can talk more. You're not off the hook entirely."

CHAPTER THIRTY-ONE

"Hey, Mum." Cameron yawned as he entered the kitchen.

Rosamund turned away from the stove, where she was stirring a simmering pot of porridge. "Morning, love. No work today?"

He frowned mid-yawn, his hand pausing in his hair. He'd been scratching his scalp and his stomach, almost in unison.

"Err... what day is it?"

"Wednesday."

The tension in his body eased. "No. No work. Thank God for that."

"Recovering from last night?" she asked, trying to sound casual.

"Recovering?" He walked over and peered into the pan. "Is there enough for me?"

"There is. Carbs and liquid, the perfect hangover cure."

His nose wrinkled. "I'm not hungover, Mum. I was driving. I know you Gen X-ers like to—"

"That's not true," she told him. "I never drink and drive."

"Not you, maybe. But I've seen Dad do it."

She shrugged; no longer her business. As long as David never drove intoxicated with his son in the car.

"How did it go?" she asked. "Late night?"

He shook his head. "The opposite."

So why did he look hungover?

"Right," she said. "Did everything go OK?"

He looked into the porridge pan for a few moments, then up into her eyes. She forced herself not to look away.

"I hate him," Cameron said at last.

Now that, she thought, *I can sympathise with*. But instead of agreeing with him, she cocked her head.

"I'm sorry," she said.

He grunted. "I'll come back for the porridge," he said, and eased past her towards the door.

She felt a moment's panic. *Don't let him go.* She wanted to support him, not watch him walk away.

"Cam," she said.

He stopped in the doorway, his back to her. She approached him.

"I'm always here, if you ever want to talk about it," she said.

He shrugged. She resisted the urge to take another step towards him, to wrap her arms around him. Five years ago, he'd have buried himself in her. He'd have told her what was on his mind.

Did he tell Figgy? she wondered, then slapped back the thought. There was no way she was going to start interrogating her young friend for details of her son's inner life.

He turned to her. She held her breath.

"I forgot," he said. "She gave me something. To give to you."

"She?" Rosamund frowned. "Figgy?"

"Not Figgy. Her. Shari."

"Oh." Rosamund's heart clenched at the name. "For me? Are you sure?"

"Of course I'm sure." He sniffed. "Wait here."

He bounded up the stairs, two steps at a time. Rosamund stood in the kitchen, arms hanging by her sides.

The porridge.

She hurried back to the stove and switched it off. Cameron was already back. He held a large box, wrapped and topped with a bow.

Shari had gone to some trouble... or some poor shop assistant had.

She stepped towards Cameron, reluctant to take the box.

"You're sure it's for me?" she said.

"If it was for me, I wouldn't want it."

Rosamund felt her heart dip. "Oh, Cam."

He shrugged and thrust it forward. "Go on, then."

Reluctantly she took it. "Have you seen what's inside?"

He shook his head. "Figgy has. She described it to me." His cheek twitched.

Rosamund took a deep breath and placed the parcel on the kitchen counter. She pried the wrapping open. She licked her lips and looked at her son, who was watching her.

"You're absolutely sure it's for me?"

"Just open it, Mum."

She pulled the box open, almost wishing she'd put on her rubber gloves. But that would be graceless.

"Oh," she said as she caught a glimpse of the contents.

"You sound like Figgy."

Rosamund eyed him. "Did she tell you what it was?"

He nodded. "Just look for yourself."

She pulled the object out and placed it on the countertop.

"Oh," she said again.

It was a pottery reindeer. About twelve inches tall, with swirls of paint on its antlers and strewn with moulded pottery fairy lights.

Cameron had his hand to his mouth. He was shaking.

"Are you laughing?" Rosamund said.

He spluttered. "I'm just trying to imagine what Dad told her about you, to make her buy you... this."

Her muscles hardened. "It's not funny."

She lifted the ornament. It was surprisingly heavy. Not hollow, then? She gave it a gentle shake. Something inside rattled softly.

She put it back on the worktop. "What am I supposed to do with this?"

Cameron turned to one side then the other, as if appraising the reindeer. "It's not exactly *you*."

"No. It is not." She sighed. "It was an act of kindness, though."

"A peace offering, she said."

Rosamund looked at Cameron. "She said that?"

He shrugged.

She shook her head. "Well, I'm not putting it on display."

Cameron sniffed.

"You don't mind, do you?" Rosamund said. "You'd prefer if I kept it out, for your Dad's sake?"

"Hell, no." Cameron's face darkened. "You do what you want with it."

She grabbed his hand. He yanked it away and left the room.

"I'm not hungry," he said.

"No." She eyed the hideous pottery reindeer. "Neither am I."

What on earth was she going to do with it?

CHAPTER THIRTY-TWO

ANNIE FELT UNEASY, moving the pottery items from the positions where Peg and Sally had put them.

Could she find an advantageous place to display them, while keeping them off the lower shelves? Would that even matter, if the flood kept any potential customers away? Should she just move everything from the shop into the stockroom, where she wouldn't have to space everything out so much, and keep it all safe crammed onto a high shelf?

"What do you think, Dex?" she asked her canine friend. But he was lying on the floor behind the till, sulking because she'd tied his lead to a doorknob to keep him from causing any further chaos.

"You might not be a bull in a china shop, you sulky dog," she said. "But you're the next worst thing."

She spent ten minutes moving things around, then moving them again in a fog of uncertainty. She was standing back assessing her work when there was a knock on the door.

She could tell who it was by the bulk of the uniform before she'd even opened the door.

"Wendy." Annie looked down to see that the PC was now wearing wellies. And a good job, too, given that she was splashing about in an inch of water. It wouldn't be long before it was lapping over the step up to the pottery.

"I'll be quick," Annie said. "I just want to move some things to the storeroom." She turned inside.

Wendy followed her. "Can I help?"

Annie bit back a *no thank you* and pointed to the shelves closest to the till.

"Take those, carefully please, and put them in the store-room for me."

"Anywhere specific in the storeroom?"

Annie wasn't sure. Truth was, she'd avoided going in there.

No time for that now. She unlocked the door to the store-room and untied Dex's head.

"Come on, boy. I want to keep an eye on you."

Wendy and Dex followed her through the shop and into the storeroom. Inside, Dex whimpered. Wendy, to Annie's relief, did not.

"Shush, boy. I know you want to go for your walk."

Dex responded by heading straight for the shelf behind the spot where Annie had found Peggy. He whimpered again and started pawing at the supports of the shelving unit.

"Maybe he can sense what happened there," Wendy suggested as she placed the items she'd brought through on a high shelf.

"He's got a good nose, does our Dex." Annie tugged the dog away from the shelves. "Stop it, boy, you're going to break something."

He tugged on the lead and yanked it from her hand. Wendy gasped.

"Dex!" Annie shouted. Dear God, what would Peg and Sally say if she let him create havoc in here?

But he didn't try to climb the shelves. Nor did he crash into anything, as she'd expected. Instead, he just sat staring up at the shelves. The whimpering gave way to howling.

"I think you'd better get him out of here," Wendy said. She'd gone back to the shop and returned with another armful of stock. She placed it as high as she could reach, as far from Dex as possible.

"You're right." Annie grabbed the lead, which was lying on the floor. She tugged the dog back into the main shop, and as soon as Wendy was out, she closed the door to the storeroom.

She surveyed the shop. Everything had either been removed or placed at least three feet above ground level.

"We have to get out," Wendy said. "Before the water gets in here."

"You think it will?"

"I know it will." Wendy opened the front door.

Annie's jaw fell open. "How did that happen so fast?" The water was already washing over the step.

"I don't know," Wendy replied. "But I'm asking you to leave now." She had her sternest police officer voice on.

"No argument from me." Annie pulled Dex towards the door. He tugged her to one side, towards a display shelf, and yelped.

"Stop it, boy. What's got into you?"

They were outside at last. Annie locked the door and peered in through the window.

"Poor Peg and Sally," she said.

Wendy gave her a regretful look. "You did what you could. Now I need you to get this dog away from here,

before I have to arrest him for interfering in a police investigation."

CHAPTER THIRTY-THREE

Naomi hated these things.

She'd become a teaching assistant because she loved children, especially young ones. If it were up to her, she and Dougie would have three, four, maybe even five. But Poppy's birth had been... tricky, the obstetrician had called it, in the understatement of the century. She'd been advised to stop at one.

She made up for it by spending her days surrounded by children. And around children, she felt confident. Five-year-olds told you what they thought. They didn't give you the side-eye, looks that said either *you're irrelevant* or *who the hell are you?*

Being a TA suited her perfectly. She didn't have to do parents' evening. She rarely even had to speak to parents at the end of the school day. The only adult she had to tolerate was Fenella bloody Durridge.

Fenella was in her element at the so-called science fair. How scientific a bunch of exhibits put together by five-year-olds could be, Naomi wasn't sure. But Fenella had insisted that it was educational.

Fenella was working the room, glad-handing the parents who'd made it here in the busy week before school broke up for Christmas. Naomi had noticed that she was picking off the wealthier parents first, the ones whose kids talked about waking up to sea views.

And now Naomi knew why. Fenella was making a beeline for Naomi and the children she was supervising, a man in his late sixties on her tail. He kept stopping and smiling at people, exchanging pleasantries and shaking hands in that way posh people did.

"Daddy," Fenella said. "This is Naomi. My assistant."

Naomi's jaw clenched. She forced a smile and gave the man a nod. She'd seen him before, hadn't she? Had it been at last year's Christmas lights switch-on?

"Hello, Mr Durridge," she said. "Pleased to meet you."

"You, too, my dear, you, too." He pumped her hand. "Nicola. I've heard all about you from darling Fenella here. But please, my name is Durridge-Smythe. Fenella likes to drop the Smythe, pretend she's one of the common people." He gave Naomi a wink. "Not sure she's got anyone convinced."

Naomi's jaw-clenching turned into teeth-grinding. The rictus smile remained.

"So," he said. "What have we here? The cutting edge of science, I presume?"

A small crowd was gathering around them. Mr Durridge-Smythe turned to face them, switching into performance mode.

"Good day, everyone. I'm so pleased you were all able to make it along today to our beloved school's science fair." He swept an arm to take in the decorations hanging around the school hall. Reindeer and snowmen, in varying degrees of artistic interpretation.

"Mrs Anderson has been helping me supervise an experiment involving DNA collection," Fenella said.

Helping? Naomi thought. *I set the whole bloody thing up!*

"Ah," said Mr Durridge-Smythe. "Well, that sounds marvellous." He directed another wink, this time at various members of the growing crowd. "I don't imagine it'll take a DNA test for you all to recognise me. Digby Durridge-Smythe, Chair of Governors and local councillor, at your humble service."

There was a smattering of applause. Naomi shook her head, perplexed. It was the children they should be applauding, not this pompous windbag.

"Daddy," Fenella said, "I thought it might be fun if you could get involved."

"Involved?" He looked puzzled.

She put a hand on his shoulder – he was short, Naomi realised – and directed a smile at the crowd.

"Our local councillor is going to have his DNA sampled," she announced.

Naomi narrowed her eyes. Had Fenella set this up? But her father looked as surprised as she was.

"Er... am I?" he said. His hands twisted in front of him. "What does that involve, exactly?"

"Nothing unpleasant, Daddy. We'll just give you this swab and you can scrape some cells from inside your cheek."

"Ah," he replied. "You do know I'm recovering from a cold?"

Fenella's expression dropped. "Oh. You are?"

He nodded, relief washing over him. "Why don't you ask your assistant here to do it instead?"

Naomi had done the cheek scraping before. Quite a few times, in fact. When she'd demonstrated it to the children yesterday, they'd all wanted to have a go. Without prior parental permission she couldn't let them scrape their own cheeks, so she'd let them do hers instead. Fourteen times.

"Good for you, Nai."

Naomi looked up to see Annie at the back of the crowd. She had Daisy in her arms and held Louis's hand.

"Mum," Naomi said. "What are you doing here?"

Annie shrugged. "Giving you some moral support, by the looks of it. And I thought these two would find it fun."

Naomi rolled her eyes. *Typical Mum.* But it was good to see a friendly face. She held out the stick for taking samples.

"How about you do it?" she asked her mum.

Annie grinned. "I thought you'd never ask." She shoved through the crowd, shifting Daisy higher on her hip. She held Louis's hand out to Fenella. Fenella took it, looking perplexed.

Naomi resisted a grin. She closed her eyes and regained her composure, then opened them again. "Right," she said. "Open wide."

Annie thrust her head forward and opened her mouth. Naomi took a stick and scraped the inside of her mum's cheek, ignoring Annie's flinches.

"That's all there is to it." She withdrew the stick and placed it in the test tube full of alcohol, which would separate out the strands of DNA.

"Easy," said Annie. She gave Durridge-Smythe a pointed look.

He cleared his throat. "Well, if your assistant's mother is mucking in, I suppose I should, too," he told Fenella.

There was another ripple of applause. Annie frowned at the assembled parents.

"Oi," she said. "He hasn't even done anything. Where's my applause?"

The crowd clapped. Naomi wished she could disappear into the wall behind her.

Durridge-Smythe was facing her, his mouth open. Naomi grabbed another stick and scraped the inside of his cheek, trying to hide her distaste.

When both samples were sealed up, she held them up towards their donors.

"Would you like to keep these?"

Annie waved a hand. "No thanks, love. You keep them for the kiddies."

"Thanks." Naomi placed her mum's sample on the desk containing her own samples from yesterday.

Durridge-Smythe stared at his sample, then at Annie. His nostrils flared.

"Of course, Natasha," he said to Naomi. He looked at the test tube again, his forehead flickering. "You keep it for the young ones. Let it help in their education."

"Thank you," Naomi said. She was relieved when he didn't respond but instead turned away, already deep in conversation with Fenella.

The bell rang for the end of the fair, and Naomi slumped against the wall. Was she sweating?

"Thank God that's over," she said to Annie. Fenella had left Louis behind, and he was picking up the sample tubes.

"You leave those alone, young man," Annie said. She

gave Naomi's hand a squeeze. "You did brilliant, girl. The kids will thank you for it."

CHAPTER THIRTY-FOUR

DOUGIE COULD SENSE the disapproval of the two council workers as he watched them work. They were attempting to loosen a manhole cover near the river, presumably to access the drains beneath.

"I can't do this with an audience," one of them – Flo, he thought – muttered.

Her colleague – Jo – grunted and looked up at Dougie. "I don't suppose you could stand back a bit? Your trousers are gonna get wet if it carries on like this."

He took a step back. "Tell you what," he said. "Call me if you find anything you need police help with." It was only a blocked drain, after all. And the Forensics team had finished in the pottery. "I've got something to look for."

Jo grunted and returned to her work. Dougie scanned the courtyard, going over his mental map of this part of town.

Reece Lumbard's mum's car. The red Golf. It was in the ANPR system, which meant any police car that happened to pass it would automatically pick it up.

But in this part of Lyme Regis – in lots of parts of Lyme

Regis – many of the lanes were so narrow, patrol cars rarely drove along them.

Not too narrow to get a vehicle down, though. And there were plenty of alleys and driveways someone could leave a car in.

What if Reece had left the car around here, before breaking into the pottery, and then left another way? Maybe an accomplice had picked him up. Maybe he'd heard Annie and simply run.

Dougie mapped out a route in his mind and started walking. Wendy was over at the pottery, supervising Annie. She'd call if she needed him. And he wanted to do something useful.

He started up Coombe Street. Much too narrow to leave a parked car here, but at least he could rule it out. He checked every driveway and patch of ground he passed. No sign of a red Golf.

He continued over the river and right onto Mill Green. The water wasn't as high here; maybe the flooding would subside.

Dougie turned back; he'd passed an alleyway which he knew led round the back of some houses. He stood at its mouth, hands on hips. Wide enough for a car? Maybe, if you were desperate.

He strolled round the side of the end house, aware that anyone inside might be alarmed by the appearance of a police officer in uniform sniffing around their property. He was ready with an excuse if anyone challenged him, and it was an excuse that had the virtue of being true: the drains were overflowing. The river ran right behind here.

But the house was dark, shutters closed. Probably another holiday rental, shut up for the winter. What a waste.

He rounded the back of the house. Behind it the river churned past on its way down to the mill.

There was a dilapidated garage, at the far end. One door was ajar.

Dougie glanced up at the houses and approached it. He put a hand on the garage door, and it swung open.

"Shit."

Inside was a car. More specifically, a red Golf.

Dougie delved into his pocket for his notepad, where he'd written the registration number.

It matched.

He backed away, aware that the car was evidence. Then he had a thought.

What if Reece Lumbard was inside? What if Peg Casey had fought back and injured him? They'd found his blood, after all.

He pulled on a pair of forensic gloves and stepped inside the garage, careful not to touch anything. The space was cramped, and he knew his coat was brushing up against things. But if Reece was in there, and hurt...

He shone his torch into the car and moved the beam around.

The car was empty.

Reece Lumbard, where are you?

Dougie blew out a long sigh and backed out of the garage. There was still no sign of movement in any of the three houses that backed onto the area.

He needed to call this in. He needed to talk to Wendy, get the area cordoned off.

He half-walked, half-ran back to the mill, taking a more direct route this time. When he arrived, Wendy was with the two council workers at the edge of the river. There was no sign of Annie.

"Wendy, mate," he panted. "I've found it."

She frowned. "Found what?"

"Reece's car. His mum's car. The red Golf." He pointed. "It's been stashed in a garage, round the back of Coombe Street. We need to cordon it off, get forensics in."

Wendy didn't move.

"Wendy?" he said. "I said we need to—"

She put up a hand to stop him. "I've got bigger news than that, Dougie."

Bigger? How?

"You have?" he said.

She nodded and pointed at the manhole cover a metre in front of her.

"Flo and Jo have found what's blocking the drain," she said.

"Bloody 'orrible job," Flo muttered. "I'm not going down there again."

"OK," said Dougie. "That's good. It means the risk of flooding is—"

"It's not that." Wendy was shaking her head. "The thing blocking the drains..."

"What?" he asked. "What is it?" He realised that Jo had paled.

"Human remains," Wendy said. "There's a body down there in the water. That's what's been blocking the drains."

CHAPTER THIRTY-FIVE

"Oh. Hello, Rosamund."

"Figgy." Rosamund gave one of her characteristic thin smiles. Not surprising really, given where Figgy had been last night.

"Is Cameron in?"

Rosamund raised an eyebrow. "He didn't tell me he was expecting you."

"Oh." Figgy felt lead form in her legs. She'd walked all the way up here, from her caravan to the posh end of town. A steep climb, only to have to go all the way back down again.

"He is in, though. No work today, apparently." Rosamund's smile broadened. "Come in. I'll give him a shout."

Figgy stepped inside, glad to get out of the cold.

"Nice earrings," Rosamund said as she closed the door behind Figgy.

"Thank you." Figgy raised her hands to the dangly Christmas tree earrings she'd picked out this morning. She'd hoped they'd cheer her up, after last night.

If she was really lucky, they might cheer Cam up, too. But that felt like a long shot.

"Wait here," Rosamund said. She left Figgy by the front door as she crossed the generous hall and mounted three steps of the staircase.

"Cameron!" she called. "Figgy's here to see you."

Figgy's phone pinged. A message from Cameron: *be down in 5*. She waved it at Rosamund. "He says he'll be down in a few minutes."

Rosamund eyed the phone with a grunt. Figgy began to wish she'd phoned ahead, maybe arranged to meet Cam somewhere else.

Rosamund looked at her. "I'm being rude, aren't I?"

"Well... I suppose you could say *I'm* being rude."

"You think so?" Rosamund cocked her head.

Figgy licked her lips. *Hurry up, Cam.* "Maybe I shouldn't have accepted the invitation to dinner with your ex."

Rosamund wrinkled her nose. "Why *did* you accept, Figgy? Was it because you thought it would be an enjoyable evening, or because you wanted to support Cameron?"

"The last one. Definitely the last one." Figgy lowered her voice. "It really wasn't an enjoyable evening."

Rosamund laughed. "Dinner parties with my ex-husband rarely are. Did he bore you with the minutiae of his work, or brag about how he came this close" – she held her fingers up, pinched together – "to playing cricket for Hampshire?"

"No cricket, sorry. No work stuff, either."

"Goodness." Rosamund glanced upstairs then grabbed Figgy's arm. She tugged her into the kitchen.

"Would you like a coffee, Figgy? Or... hot chocolate you have, isn't it? Hmm... I don't think I have any of that." Rosamund started banging cupboard doors.

"A cup of tea would be lovely please, if that's OK." Figgy twisted the button on the front of her winter coat, the coat that had once been her nan's. The thread was coming loose, but she couldn't resist.

"One cup of tea, coming up." Rosamund gave her another one of those smiles. "English Breakfast, I assume?"

"Er..."

"*Tea* tea," Rosamund said. "The kind you have with milk." A pause. "Unless you prefer lemon?"

Figgy frowned. As far as she was concerned, tea only came in one form. "*Tea* tea sounds lovely, thank you." Hopefully it would be what she was expecting and not have half a hedge floating in it.

"Good." Rosamund turned away to fill the kettle.

Figgy approached the vast granite-topped kitchen island. It was bigger than her bed in the caravan.

"I see Cameron's given it to you," she said, eyeing the reindeer on the worktop.

"Given it?" Rosamund didn't turn from her task.

Figgy brushed the reindeer's antlers with her fingertips. Now it was out of its box and in this brightly lit kitchen, she could see how colourful it was. She stroked the swirls of paint on its side.

"The reindeer," she said. "The gift from Shari."

Rosamund stiffened. She stood with her back to Figgy, fists clenched on the worktop.

Oh, hell. Figgy stepped away from the ornament. *I shouldn't have mentioned it.*

"Sorry," she muttered.

Rosamund turned. "Don't be ridiculous. You've nothing to be sorry for."

"Haven't I?"

"No." Rosamund gave her a smile, a real one this time. "This Shari woman is clearly eager to ingratiate herself with me. Which means she feels guilty. It's just a shame she chooses to do it in such a vulgar way."

"Vulgar?" said a voice. "What's vulgar?"

Figgy turned to see Cameron in the doorway, glaring at his mother.

Oh, hell.

"What's vulgar?" he repeated. "I hope you're not insinuating that Figgy is."

"Don't be silly." Rosamund gestured towards the reindeer. "Figgy is my friend. She was my friend before *you* noticed her. It's this... thing." She wrinkled her nose.

"You don't like Shari's gift." He strode to the kitchen island and picked it up with one hand.

"Cameron..." Figgy said.

"No," said Rosamund. "Of course I don't like it. I'm sorry, Cameron, sweetheart, but I find what it represents hard to swallow. At least for now. And..."

She gave the reindeer a disdainful look.

"It's hideous," Cameron said.

"It is," Rosamund replied, at the exact same moment as Figgy said, "it isn't."

Cameron and Rosamund both turned to Figgy.

"You like it?" Rosamund asked.

"Really?" added Cameron.

Figgy shrugged. "It's kitsch. I know that. But I like kitsch. It reminds me of my nan."

Cameron had been weighing the ornament in his hands, looking like he might throw it. "It's certainly heavy," he said.

Figgy nodded. "I don't think it's empty."

"No." Cameron put it down on the worktop, just gently enough not to smash it. Figgy let out a breath.

"Are you upset that I don't like it?" Rosamund asked Cameron.

"Why should I be upset?"

She took a step towards him. He tensed.

"Because," Rosamund replied, "I don't want to get in the way of your relationship with your father. Or with Shari."

Cameron scoffed. He gave the reindeer a flick with his finger. "I think *he's* got in the way of our relationship without any help from you." He looked at Figgy. "Come on. Let's go for a walk."

Figgy nodded. Anything to get out of this kitchen, even if it meant being bossed around by her usually gentle boyfriend.

"I'm sorry, Rosamund," she said as she followed him out, although she wasn't sure what she was sorry for.

"None of this is your fault, Figgy," Rosamund said. "I realise you're only trying to help."

Figgy nodded. *Don't say sorry again.*

Rosamund picked up the reindeer. "There is one thing you can do, however."

Figgy tensed, waiting for her to drop it to the tiled floor.

But Rosamund was holding the garish ornament out. "Take it, Figgy. You seem to like it. And I don't want to look at it."

Figgy took the reindeer from her friend. She placed it back in its box.

"If you're sure..." she said. Was it valuable?

"Yes, I'm sure. It's yours. Keep it, donate it, throw it away. Whichever you prefer. I don't mind."

Figgy tucked the box under her arm. "Thank you, Rosamund. I'll make sure you never have to look at it again."

CHAPTER THIRTY-SIX

"So HAVE they got him out yet?" Tina asked as she took the turning off the A35. She couldn't quite believe she was heading into Lyme Regis again.

"They have," Dougie replied. She'd called him after her boss, DS Nathan Strunk, had assigned her to attend the area by the mill, where council workers were pulling a body out from the drains.

"Tell them to put him somewhere secure, as close as possible to where they found him, and then wait for the forensics team."

"I do know what I'm doing, Tina."

She grimaced. "I know you do. Just being thorough, Dougie. I'm not trying to have a go."

"No."

Was he pissed off with her? It was hardly her fault that the discovery of a body meant the Major Crime Investigations Team had to be brought in.

"I'll be as quick as I can," she said. "Is the flooding too bad for me to bring my car down there?"

She was at the outskirts of Lyme Regis now. She sped past Charmouth Road Car Park then slammed on her brakes at the sight of a bus coming up the hill.

"The flooding's subsided," Dougie told her. "Now that the blockage has been removed."

Tina tapped her fingers on the steering wheel while she waited for the bus to pass. Her car's automatic windscreen wipers kicked in.

"Damn," she said. "Have you got anything you can use as a tent?"

"I don't think getting him wet is going to be an issue," Dougie replied. "They just dragged him out of the drain."

Tina frowned at her phone in its cradle. "That's not the point." *Thank God we're not leaving Uniform to handle this on their own.* "You need to get him covered up."

"It's alright, Tina. I was winding you up. Wendy and Flo-Jo have found some tarps in the back of the council van. We've covered him over and cordoned off the courtyard. It's all good."

She descended into Lyme and took the right turn in front of the museum. The traffic lights, thank God, were with her.

"Flo-Jo?" she said as she slowed for the right turn into Coombe Street.

"Flo and Jo," Dougie replied. "The council workers who found him. They've been helping us out."

"Don't let them leave," Tina told him. "We'll need to take statements."

The rain was intensifying. Tina waited as two women darted across the road in front of her. She recognised one of them as her mum's friend, the one who ran an art gallery.

At last, the narrow line widened enough for Tina to squeeze her car in against a wall. She hurried out grabbed a waterproof coat from the boot. She was pulling it on as she hurried towards the mill.

In the courtyard, she found a panda car, a Dorset Council van, and four people: Dougie, Wendy and the two women she assumed to be Flo-Jo. She nodded at them.

"My name's DC Tina Abbott," she said. "From the Major Crime Investigations Team. I gather you found the body?"

The body itself was ahead of her, just about visible from where Tina stood, but protected from the elements and the eyes of passers-by by a series of tarpaulins that had been strung between various buildings and the roof of the council van. Dougie, Wendy and the two council workers stood a good distance away from it, she was pleased to note.

"It was Flo." The smaller of the two women pointed at her colleague. "She was trying to clear the drain below the car park, clear the blockage."

"I certainly did that," Flo said.

"And it was you who removed the body from the drain and brought it here?" Tina asked.

"That was both of us." Jo looked at Flo, who gave her an encouraging smile.

"We had to," said Flo. "The river was bursting its banks, we have a responsibility to—"

"It's OK," Tina said. "You did the right thing."

"I thought you were going to accuse us of tampering with a crime scene," Flo said.

"That's not my style. And there's always a chance it isn't a crime scene."

"You reckon?" Wendy said. "Really?"

Tina shrugged. "It could be accidental death. Or suicide."

"Either way," Wendy replied, "we need to collect evidence."

Tina sighed. If she'd driven all the way to Lyme because of some idiot who'd slipped off the path...

"Yoo-hoo!"

Tina turned to see her mum standing in a gap between the buildings behind her, leaning over the police cordon.

That's all I need.

"I saw your car, Tina love! Everything OK?"

Tina gritted her teeth. "I'm working, Mum. Please, just let me do my job."

"Your job?" Annie called. "Does that mean... oh, it's not Peg, is it? Please don't tell me she's—"

Tina turned towards Annie, her movement sharp, almost violent. "It's not Peg, Mum. Please, go home. Get into the dry."

"Oh, a bit of rain never bothered me. Can I help at all?"

Tina was at the cordon now, facing her mum. "Are you a police officer, Mum?"

"Of course not."

"Are you in any way qualified to investigate the death of the man found—"

"Death? Who's died? Oh my goodness." Annie leaned around Tina.

"Mum, please. You're embarrassing me."

Annie glared at her. "I'm a concerned citizen. I very much hope that isn't somebody I know."

Tina had seen the body; a young Black man, wearing tattered jeans and the remains of a hoodie. Not a middle-aged woman in a dry robe.

"I very much doubt it, Mum." She took a breath. *Be calm.* "But if it is, we will of course inform you."

"I should bloody well hope so." Annie sniffed. "I shall leave you to it." She turned and walked up Coombe Street, towards her home in Anning Road.

Tina clenched and unclenched her fists. *Thank God for that.*

She walked back to Dougie and Wendy. They were still standing a sensible distance from the body, but both of them were leaning forward to get a better look.

"It is," said Wendy.

"Yep," replied Dougie.

"Sorry?" Tina said. "Have I missed something?"

"The body," Dougie said.

"Well, I haven't missed that." Tina looked at the young man. He seemed calm, his eyes closed and his mouth very slightly open. His skin was greying, and one arm of the hoodie had been torn off at the shoulder.

She shook her head. "Poor bloke."

Dougie and Wendy nodded and grunted.

"We know who it is," Dougie said.

Tina looked up. "You do?"

He nodded. "We do."

"Well don't keep me in suspense, then."

He exchanged a glance with Wendy. "We were so close."

"So close," Wendy echoed.

"What?" Tina said. "Who is he? And why were you so close?"

"It's Reece Lumbard," Wendy said.

Tina frowned. "Who's Reece Lumbard?"

"The person who we believe attacked Peg Casey," Dougie replied.

CHAPTER THIRTY-SEVEN

ROSAMUND STOOD IN HER KITCHEN, her fingers wrapped around a mug of coffee. She'd finally regained control of the heating and lighting systems in her so-called smart home, and the underfloor heating felt delicious through her socks. But every time she looked out of the window, she shivered.

Had she done the right thing, giving Shari's gift to Figgy?

Shari had meant well. Rosamund knew the reindeer was intended as a peace offering, although she wasn't sure Shari was the person who needed to offer one of those.

But it was hideous. Truly ghastly. Anyone who'd spent a moment in Rosamund's home would know just how she would react to it.

And David had spent plenty of moments in Rosamund's home, which meant he'd had no hand in the purchase.

She had done the right thing. She didn't owe Shari anything; she certainly didn't owe David anything. And Figgy would enjoy the Christmas ornament far more than she would.

She finished the dregs of her coffee and sighed. Standing here, feeling sorry for herself... it wouldn't do her any good.

She needed to face him.

And a walk... a good long walk *would* do her good.

Not all the way to Charmouth, though. It would be dark by the time she managed that. She'd drive to Charmouth, park at the beach, and walk up to Wisteria Cottage. She wanted to get it over with.

Twenty minutes later, she was walking away from Charmouth beach and into the centre of the village. It was cold, and the afternoon was rapidly turning to twilight, but Charmouth looked pretty, all lit up with its Christmas lights. She passed a house that had gone overboard, with a huge, illuminated snowman on the lawn and a flickering animated Santa on the roof. She stopped to gaze it for a while, trying to decide if it was hideous or actually quite fun. Maybe both, she decided, then carried on.

She mused on where she was going. "What are you doing?" she hissed to herself, not breaking stride.

Rosamund liked to think of herself as someone who had complete control of her emotions. She would maintain her composure, no matter what. It had always been her superpower.

It made her uncomfortable, knowing she was compelled to go and see this fancy so-called cottage. And why? So she could get even more angry with David?

She wanted to turn back. She was better than this. But still her feet kept going, until she was there.

Wisteria Cottage was impressive. It was more than impressive. It had been designed by a clever Georgian architect so that everything about the house was in perfect proportion. Despite its enormous scale, nothing about it seemed excessive.

There was an archway leading into the front garden beside the broad gravel driveway, on which two cars stood: a white SUV and David's BMW. She frowned; had he got himself new plates?

ON25 DDS.

Really? D for David, S for Shari. What did the other D stand for?

How vulgar.

She turned back to the path. It was decorated with fairy lights which even now, in the fading light of late afternoon, made it look magical. This wasn't the tacky ostentatiousness of the house she'd passed earlier. This was tasteful, low-key enchantment. And given Shari had bought that reindeer, it had clearly been done by the owners of the cottage, not the current tenants.

The fairy lights continued along a path that disappeared around the corner of the house.

Rosamund didn't stop to think. She let herself in through the small, latched gate and followed the path round, to check out the house from a different angle.

The windows were huge and the curtains open, which meant a good view inside. She peered into a large reception room, with a beautifully decorated Christmas tree in the corner. The room had a large oak fireplace with sofas and chairs grouped around it.

It was perfect. Exactly her own taste. Almost as if David had chosen it deliberately.

But why? To rub her nose in it? Or was she overthinking this? Was it just that in this part of Dorset, money meant taste?

And what was she planning, now she was here? She couldn't exactly slide away with her tail between her legs. But now she was looking at that idyllic Christmas scene, so perfect it made her want to cry...

Seeing the reality of it, she couldn't face him.

A woman entered the room. She was slim with long dark hair, wearing blue jeans that fit perfectly, and a cream cashmere sweater. Before Rosamund had a chance to step back, she spotted her.

"Hello?" The woman approached the door. "Who are you? Are you the new maid they said they'd send?" She shook her head. "The cleaner?"

Rosamund's cheeks burnt. Yes, she had a job as a cleaner now – housekeeper, she preferred to think of it – but the thought of her cleaning for David and his new...

"Hello?" the woman repeated. "Are you planning to speak to me, or do I have to call the police?"

She had an accent. American. No; Canadian, Cameron had said.

Rosamund opened her mouth, but nothing came out.

She shook her head and started backing away.

Speak, she told herself. *Explain yourself*. But she'd turned mute.

She turned back towards the side gate. As she rounded the rear of the house, a man came round it, heading right for her.

She cast around. Nowhere to hide.

He looked up, spotting her. "What the...?"

"Sorry," she muttered. "I'm leaving."

He frowned. "I know you."

Rosamund swallowed. She recognised the man. She'd seen him at charity fundraisers, Christmas lights switch-ons.

And they'd been introduced. By David, of course: golf acquaintances.

"I'm sorry," she repeated.

"What are you on about? And what the bloody hell are you doing here? Does David know you're here?"

CHAPTER THIRTY-EIGHT

Dougie shoved his hands under his armpits, aware that his teeth were chattering. He was in the warm and dry now, but his socks were still wet from paddling in the floodwater, and the bottom two inches of his trousers were damp.

"Should have brought wellies, mate." Wendy looked him up and down.

"I will next time."

She laughed. "Let's hope there isn't a next time." She dropped her gaze. "Sorry. That's not very respectful, is it?"

"Gallows humour," Tina said. "Don't worry, we talk like this all the time at HQ."

Wendy wrinkled her nose. "Wouldn't swap jobs with you for the world."

Tina smiled. "I get where you're coming from. But nothing beats the satisfaction of solving a big case."

"I'll take your word for it," Wendy replied. "Right now, we've got a dead suspect in a burglary, and no idea if this is a big case at all."

"Don't worry," Dougie said. "If anyone can solve this, it's our Tina. She'll be a DS before long."

"Will you stop it," Tina snapped. "I haven't even applied to do the exam yet. Has my mum been talking to you?"

Dougie smiled. "I still think you'll be a sergeant sooner than you think. And yes, Annie Abbott has been talking to me, about plenty." His smile dropped. "Which reminds me. How much did she see, when she was standing at the cordon?"

"I managed to stand in front of her for most of the time," Tina said. "Tried to block her view. But she'll know there's a body."

"That's all we need," Dougie replied. "Question is, will she work out who it is?"

"I don't see how she could," Wendy said.

Tina looked at her. "Don't underestimate her." She closed her eyes. "How many windows look out over that courtyard?"

"Not many," Wendy said. "There's the businesses, and the mill itself, but we emptied all those out. There's a couple of cottages on the other side of the river."

Tina's eyes snapped open. "Please tell me they're holiday lets."

Wendy looked at Dougie, then back at Tina. "We can knock on the doors."

"I think you should," Tina said. "Because if there are locals behind those windows, Annie will know who they are. And she'll have spoken to them already."

"She's really pissed you off, hasn't she?" asked Dougie.

Tina shook her head. "Not pissed me off. Not really. It's what she does, I should be used to it by now. But this is my job. Your job. Not an Agatha Christie novel. I just wish she'd leave the sleuthing to the professionals."

"She can be helpful, sometimes," Wendy said. "She—"

"Who can be helpful?" Sergeant Connors said, bringing a chill in through the open door. He put up a hand. "Don't tell me. I can guess."

"Annie Abbott was at the scene earlier," Dougie said. He was careful not to refer to her as his mother-in-law.

"I said don't tell me." The sarge looked at Tina. "Good to have you here, we're run off our feet what with the big Christmas fayre on Saturday."

Dougie had forgotten about that. It would mean crowds, and traffic problems, and everybody on shift.

"So is it just you," the sarge continued, "or can we expect Nathan Strunk along in a while?"

"Just me," Tina replied. "DS Strunk is busy on a robbery case in Poole."

"Poor bugger. At least we don't get much of that kind of thing in Lyme." The sarge scratched his chin. "Although we do seem to get more than our fair share of bodies. Do we know yet if this one's suspicious?"

"Forensics haven't got here yet," said Dougie, "but—"

"Correction," said Wendy, holding up her phone. "Gavin Larcomb has just arrived."

"Good," said the sarge. "You head over there, make sure the area's clear for him."

"Hang on a minute," said Tina. "Before anyone goes rushing off anywhere, we need to review what we know. And, in particular, I want to start building a picture of how Reece Lumbard went from breaking into the pottery, to winding up dead in the drain."

"Fair enough," the sarge said. "For that, we'll need a brew."

Wendy stood up. "I'll make it. I can talk to Gav while I'm in the kitchen, make sure he knows I'll be over later." She hurried out.

"Keen," the sarge said. "I like that."

Dougie frowned. Was the sarge insinuating that he *wasn't* keen?

He cleared his throat. "So the forensics at the scene include Reece's prints."

"Including one print in blood that isn't his," Tina said.

"Right. Are we any closer to finding out whose blood that is?"

"Nothing on the system." Sergeant Connors leaned back in his chair, so far Dougie thought it might topple.

"What about injuries?" Tina asked. "We're assuming Reece hit Peg Casey with that jug, given his prints are all over it. But did she fight back?"

"It's difficult to tell, from what I saw," Dougie said. "His flesh was bloated from being in the water, and I didn't spot any wounds."

"She might not have drawn blood," Tina said. "D'you think the two of them could have fought, and she pushed him into the river?"

Dougie considered the distance between the pottery and the river. "I don't see how that's possible, given where she was found. He landed a pretty heavy blow on her, and she's over seventy years old."

Tina nodded. "Yeah. It was a long shot."

"Maybe there's an accomplice," the sarge suggested. "Someone else working with Lumbard. The two of them fought over whatever they were trying to steal, and Lumbard ended up in the river."

Dougie looked down at his chilly hands. Sure, Reece Lumbard had broken into the pottery. He'd attacked Peg Casey. But he hadn't deserved to die.

He looked up. "There can't be an accomplice. We didn't find any other prints."

"The accomplice might have had a few more brain cells to rub together," said the sarge. "Worn gloves."

"And there's the blood," Tina said. "That print, in the unidentified blood."

"What have I missed?" Wendy blocked the door open, carrying a tray of mugs.

Dougie turned to her. "We're wondering if Reece Lumbard might have had an accomplice for the burglary."

Wendy put the tray down. "And the accomplice shoved him into the river."

Dougie nodded. Wendy handed out the drinks while each of them pondered what they did and didn't know.

"It all comes down to that blood," Tina said. "If Reece and his killer fought, then maybe he had the other guy's blood on his fingers."

"Might not have been a guy," Wendy said.

"True. Although to push Reece into the water..." Tina turned to Dougie. "How big was Reece?"

"Six-foot-one," Dougie replied. "Well built."

Tina nodded. "I don't see a woman managing to overcome him. But we need to keep an open mind."

"So what next?" Dougie asked.

"Well, Peg Casey certainly didn't push Reece in the river. So either he fell in by accident, or..."

"Or?"

"Or someone else pushed him in. And I know there was a raging storm on, but someone must have seen him."

Dougie's mouth fell open. "The guy who ran into my car."

"That's a solid lead," Tina said. "Follow it up. And we need to find witnesses, anyone who might have seen Reece's accomplice."

"Which includes Annie," Dougie said.

Tina's face fell. "She was there." She sighed. "I'll deal with my mum. Can you guys work on finding other witnesses?"

"Leave it with us," the sarge said. "Let's hope your mother delivers the goods again."

CHAPTER THIRTY-NINE

THE MAN EYED ROSAMUND, his head cocked.

"Digby Durridge-Smythe," he said. "We met at that charity do you attended with David, last Christmas." His eyes narrowed. "Are you two back together, then? Is that why you're here?"

The woman who'd been inside the sitting room stepped out of one of the French doors. "They are not," she said. "David is my partner." She cocked her head. "Surely you're aware of that, Digby, having let this beautiful house to us?"

He gave her a nervous grin. "Shari, of course. You are just as charming in the flesh as in your emails." He stepped past Rosamund and shook Shari's hand.

Rosamund watched, wishing the ground would swallow her up. Why on earth had she decided to come here?

Shari looked at her. "You must be Rosamund. Pleased to meet you." She took a step towards Rosamund, and before Rosamund could do anything to stop her, she had a hand on her shoulder and was planting a light kiss on her cheek.

"Oh." Rosamund blinked back at her. "Yes. I'm Rosamund. David's wife."

"Well..." Shari replied, then smiled. "Yes, of course you are. Legally, at least. And... and did Cameron pass on my message?"

Rosamund sniffed. "He gave me the reindeer, if that's what you're referring to." She hoped Shari wouldn't ask to see it.

Shari shook her head. "Not that. Although I do hope you like it. I bought it in the pottery near your quaint little mill in Lyme Regis. I assume it has some kind of significance, as part of the English Christmas tradition?"

"Errr..." Was that why she'd bought it? And if it was from the pottery, did that mean Annie had sold it to her?

"But that wasn't what I was referring to," Shari said. "I asked your delightful son to pass on my apologies."

"Apologies?"

Shari frowned. "I imagine my relationship with David has caused you pain. And I'm truly, deeply sorry for that." She looked into Rosamund's eyes in a way that made Rosamund imagine she wanted to climb into her very soul.

Rosamund didn't do climbing into people's souls.

"Thank you," she said. "I must say, this is a beautiful house you're staying in."

Property. A safe topic.

"You'll find that the house is mine," Digby said. He looked up at the windows, lined with fairy lights. "Marvellous, isn't she? Wish I lived in her myself, but it's more economical for me to live in the *actual* cottage and rent this place out to tourists." He looked at Shari. "I do hope you like it."

"Like what?" said a male voice.

Rosamund turned to see David coming round the side of the house. He wore the dark green winter coat she'd bought for him five years before: spotted in Harrods, it was real quality, and she was glad he hadn't cast it off.

"The house, old chap." Digby walked towards him and slapped his shoulders. "Wisteria Cottage is a gem, isn't she?"

"She is," David agreed, pushing Digby's hands off his shoulders. "I appreciate you letting us stay here."

The light wasn't great, but David looked well. Better than well. Had the years rolled off him since he'd abandoned his family?

"No problem," Digby said, "for an old golfing acquaintance and member of the local... well, let's say I understand you have a certain standing in this neck of the woods."

David glanced at Rosamund, then turned to Shari with a smile. Rosamund wanted to give an explanation as to why she was here, but Digby had hijacked the conversation.

"Not so sure about that," he said. "Not anymore."

Digby ignored him. "And there's something else, old chap," he said.

David raised an eyebrow. "There is?"

"I wanted to pick your brains, professionally."

"Ah," said David. "Money?"

"Indeed." Digby pushed back his shoulders. "You work in wealth management, yes? Heard you're one of the best."

David smiled. "Well, I wouldn't say that..."

"Learn how to take a compliment, man. Modesty doesn't suit you. Anyway, I need some help with making the most of this place, not to mention my investments and... other assets. I've been so busy with all my activities in the community, I tend to neglect some of the stuff I should be on top of. Tax breaks, efficiencies, consolidation. You know the kind of thing."

"What kind of assets?" David asked, his tone light. Rosamund knew what he'd be thinking; she'd witnessed these conversations before. What he wanted to know was whether the assets had been obtained legally.

Digby counted off on his fingers, gazing upwards. "A couple of local businesses, some holiday lets and longer-term rentals. Part ownership in a boatyard, would you believe? Little bit of farmland. In the middle of sorting out a hotel renovation." His hand dropped. "Those are the biggies. There's some other odds and sods."

David chuckled. Digby had given the right answer.

"Come inside, why don't you?" he said. "There's no time like the present. With a portfolio like that, you'd definitely benefit from some help."

Digby looked towards the house, then at Rosamund. He peered at her for a moment, then at Shari, then back at her.

He turned back to David. "Sorry, old chap, don't have the time right now. But I'll be back tomorrow, if that suits, yes?"

"Er... yes," David replied.

"Cheers. Very grateful." Digby hurried round the side of the house.

"That was odd," David said, looking at Shari.

"*He's* odd," Shari said. "He seemed to think you and Rosamund were an item again, when he saw her here."

David stiffened. "Goodness. What would make him think that?"

Shari gave a nervous laugh. She touched David's cheek in a proprietorial gesture. "Nothing I need to worry about, I hope?"

"Nothing," Rosamund and David said simultaneously.

"I will need to speak to him, though," David continued. "In the morning, maybe. If there's a possibility of a commission..."

Shari frowned. "Tomorrow we have plans to visit Exeter. Christmas shopping."

His shoulders slumped. "You don't need me for that, surely."

Shari looked at him. "Well. No. I suppose I don't *need* you there. But..."

"Good." He kissed her cheek and gave her hand a squeeze.

Rosamund resisted a laugh. So Shari was getting exactly the same treatment she had. Work always came first for David Winters. There would be a commission to be earned on any advice he gave Digby, and the greener the client, the larger that commission would be.

David looked at Rosamund. "What brings you here, Rosamund? Cameron been trash-talking me?"

If he had, he'd have good reason, Rosamund thought.

"No," she said. "I came to see Shari, actually."

"You did?"

"I dropped by to thank her for the kind gift she sent me."

"You did?" Shari said. "But when I saw you, you were—"

"It was very kind of you," Rosamund said. "Not entirely to my taste, I don't imagine David was involved in the purchase. But the gesture is much appreciated."

"Oh." Shari looked confused. "I'm sorry if I misjudged, I meant—"

"You meant well," Rosamund said. "And I wish you the best of luck."

She reached out and gave the younger woman's hand a squeeze.

You're welcome to him, she thought. *I don't envy you.*

"Rosamund," David said. "You can't just leave."

But she was already walking towards the side gate.

She gave a little wave. "Have a good Christmas, David. Be sure to spend more time with your son while you're here, won't you?"

"Rosamund! Stay. We need to talk."

"Oh no, we don't."

"David, darling," she heard Shari say, after she was out of sight. "Let's go into the warmth."

The voices became indistinct. Rosamund smiled to herself as she hurried towards the road. There was David's car again, with the old registration number she remembered. So what had she seen earlier that evening? Had she been hallucinating?

Perhaps she'd been hallucinating for some time. But now...

About one thing, at least, her mind was clear.

Shari was welcome to David Winters.

She, Rosamund, was well shot of him.

CHAPTER FORTY

"Ah." Figgy breathed in the chilly sea air. "You know something, Cameron?"

They were sitting on a bench between Figgy's caravan and the Cobb. They'd gone for a drink in town but had to stop after just one because Christmas meant they were both skint. Figgy had more presents to buy this year and the expense was keeping her awake at night.

"What?" Cameron asked her. His breath clouded in front of him.

"I think I'm the luckiest woman alive." She huddled into him.

He smiled. "You do? And is that because you're currently snuggled up on a bench with me?"

Figgy giggled. "Partly." She swept an arm out, taking in the view. "But also because of this. People pay millions of pounds to live in a location like this, you know. I've seen the property shows."

"Oh, I know." He sighed. "I imagine my parents' house cost twice as much 'cos it has a sea view."

"And I have the best spot in town, all for the price of ground rent on a caravan. And the perfect boyfriend, of course."

"Boyfriend? So we're official?"

Figgy felt her chest tighten. "Oh. Did you not want to...?"

He kissed the top of her head. "I very much *do* want to. And you are the perfect girlfriend, Figgy Edmunds."

She grinned. She really was a lucky woman. There was only one thing spoiling it: her grandparents would never get to meet Cameron and see how much more settled she was now. Or her parents, although she'd made her peace with that long ago.

Cameron gave her a squeeze then stood up, stamping his feet. "Bloody hell, it's cold."

"The Christmas lights do make it feel warmer."

"Ah, the legendary tasteful Lyme Regis lights," he said. "Christmas decorations that even my mother approves of."

"I like them," she replied.

He looked into her eyes and grabbed her gloved hands. Gloves her nan had knitted.

"Something I'm learning about you, Figgy, is that you love Christmas."

"I *adore* Christmas."

"And this year, I think I will, too."

She frowned. "Christmas has been hard for you?"

His gaze dropped. "Last year it was clear my parents didn't want to be within ten miles of each other, let alone sitting across a dinner table and pulling crackers."

That sounded rough. And a long way from Figgy's experience of Christmas.

"You can always spend Christmas with me," she said, her voice not much more than a whisper. Was it too much?

His face lit up. "Oh my God, that would be amazing." He glanced down at the box sitting on the bench. "I think I can even tolerate your tacky decorations."

She gave him a mock punch. "My decorations are not tacky. They're kitsch."

"Is that better?"

She gave a firm nod. "Kitsch is cool."

Cameron laughed. He bent to kiss her, then pulled back. "I need to go to the kiosk," he said. "Sort out Christmas shifts."

"They're open at Christmas?"

"They do a roaring trade this time of year. I'll drop by your caravan after, if that's OK?"

"That would be lovely." She gave his hand a squeeze and turned towards her caravan. As she walked, she became aware of a presence in the air behind her.

She glanced back to see a huge herring gull hovering mere inches from her neck. Kevin, her nemesis. The downside of living on the beach.

She flapped a hand and picked up the pace. "Go away!"

The gull was undeterred. He flew past her, turned and then hurled himself straight at her.

"Arrgh! Kevin, you stupid bird! Stop it!" She turned away from him, bending over and clutching the box. However much Rosamund hated that reindeer, she didn't want to drop it.

Kevin backed off; she'd hit his wing with her hand. She hurried to the caravan, threw herself inside and slammed the door.

"What on earth was that about?" She placed the box on the table and slumped onto the bench seat, panting.

When she'd got her breath back, she stood up and filled

the kettle. Silence. Kevin hadn't followed her, thank goodness.

At this time of year, the seagulls in Lyme weren't as much of a menace as in the summer. With no tourists to steal from, most of them disappeared. Flown south? Figgy wasn't sure.

But Kevin was different. He'd learned that Figgy occasionally left food out – something she knew she shouldn't but couldn't resist. And he'd taken a particular shine to the chocolate digestives she enjoyed.

While the kettle boiled, Figgy pulled the pottery reindeer out of its box. It was surprisingly heavy, and larger than she remembered. There was no way her Christmas tree would hold its weight.

She cast about the caravan, looking for a suitable spot. She smiled.

She walked to the front of the caravan and the broad window facing out to sea. Behind the bench seating that ran along this wall was a deep windowsill.

She placed the reindeer in the centre of the windowsill and stood back to admire it.

Perfect. It complemented the multicoloured tinsel she'd draped by the windows and the twinkling fairy lights festooned around her TV set.

She went back to the kitchen and started making a cup of tea.

Thud!

Figgy gasped, her hand going to her chest.

Thud!

She turned towards the front of the van. Something had hit the window.

Thud!

Figgy ran to the window, waving her hands and shouting.

The seagull ignored her. He drew back, hovered in the air a moment, then dive-bombed the window again.

"Kevin! Stop it! You're going to break the glass."

The seagull gave her a harsh look then took another dive.

This time, the caravan actually reverberated. A bauble fell off her Christmas tree and smashed on the floor.

"No!" She ran to it. Purple glitter, not shatterproof.

"Kevin," she said. "That was my nan's." She thumped on the window. "Go! Go away, you horrible seagull!"

She looked at the bauble, lying in a thousand shards on the carpet. She remembered buying it with her nan, when she was... nine? Ten? Every year, they'd buy one new bauble to add to the tree. This one, bigger and glitzier than most of her collection, had been one of those special ones.

And now the damn seagull had smashed it to bits.

Figgy closed the curtains.

Thud!

She yanked the curtains open and thumped the window. She waved her fist at the gull, then slumped onto the sofa.

"Kevin, what *are* you doing?" she muttered.

He flew away again, twisted in the air and took another dive, and Figgy finally realised what he was aiming at.

The pottery reindeer.

She picked it up. The seagull followed her with a beady stare. Figgy shivered.

"What *has* got into you?"

She threw a blanket over the reindeer and took it into her bedroom, where she hid it in a cupboard. She could hear the seagull's squawks, following her along the length of the caravan.

She returned to the living room. Kevin was outside,

perched on a rock. He stared at her, then at the space where the ornament had been.

"You don't like Christmas decorations, it seems."

The gull let out a high-pitched squawk before flying away. Figgy watched him recede towards the horizon. Her heart was racing.

She shook her head. "Well, Kevin, it seems you share aesthetic sensibilities with my friend Rosamund."

CHAPTER FORTY-ONE

TINA SMOOTHED down her suit as she waited for the front door to be opened. She was beginning to wish she'd delegated this task to someone else.

Don't be a wimp, Tina Abbott.

The door opened, and Annie's momentary confusion turned to delighted surprise. "Tina, love! I wasn't expecting you today." She peered around Tina. "You got the kiddies with you?"

"I'm here for work, Mum."

"Ah." The smile dropped. "That'll explain why you didn't use your key."

"I haven't used my key in almost ten years."

"Well, you should do. Come inside, then. You're letting the cold in."

Tina followed her mother inside and closed the door. She could see why Annie was worried about the cold; the house was boiling.

"You been given a discount by the energy company? It's roasting in here."

Annie turned to her. "Is it? Feels just right to me." She sniffed. "Come on into the kitchen and I'll make us a cuppa."

Tina did as she was told. She lowered herself into a chair and smiled at the sight of Annie's gargantuan pencil case on the table.

"You've been making art with the kids," she said.

"I have," Annie replied. "And I can tell you, those three grandchildren of mine are very talented."

Tina smiled. "Even Daisy?"

"There's a lot to be said for blobbing your open palm onto a sheet of paper, you know. She loves it."

"I know. They all love spending time with their granny."

Annie turned to her. "Do they? I do hope so."

"You know they do. You're a wonderful granny."

Annie beamed. "And I'm very glad to hear it. But that doesn't mean you'll get extra sugar in your tea, girl."

"I don't take sugar."

"You know what I mean." Annie turned back to the kettle. She poured two mugs and placed them on the table.

"Now," she said. "Tell me what work it is that brings you here. Have you found the so-and-so who attacked Peg?"

"We have, but it's not as simple as that. You were at the mill earlier—"

"And I saw what looked very much like a person lying on the ground, under all those sheets. What happened?"

"Mum." Tina leaned back. "I'm supposed to be asking the questions."

"Of course you are. But it was you who asked if I was at the mill earlier."

Tina couldn't remember phrasing it as a question. She sighed.

"OK," she said. "So this isn't public knowledge yet. But we do believe we've found Peg's attacker, yes."

"Good. I knew things would speed up once you got involved, love."

"It wasn't me who found him," Tina corrected. "It was Dougie and Wendy. For a burglary—"

"Aggravated burglary, surely."

Tina's jaw clenched. "It's not a case the MCIT would normally get involved with."

Annie frowned. "But you're here now." She put down her mug. "Oh."

"Oh indeed. The man you saw on the ground. He was most likely the man who attacked Peg. And he's dead. The council pulled him out of the drains, he—"

"He was blocking them," Annie said. "That's why I had to move Peg and Sally's stock."

Tina nodded. "That seems to be the case." Truth was, she didn't know much about the burglary; local police had been working on that.

"Poor man," Annie said. She took a long sip of her tea.

"He attacked your friend."

Annie frowned at her. "Even if he did, he didn't deserve to die." A pause. "So you think he fell in the river? When he was running away from the pottery?"

"That's one possibility."

"And the other is..."

Tina swallowed. "Look, Mum. We're just speculating right now. We don't have nearly enough from Forensics or Pathology to—"

"I know how it works, love. What's your theory?"

"We think that – that Peg's attacker might have had an accomplice. Maybe they—"

"Maybe they shoved him in the river, after he didn't get whatever he was supposed to from the pottery."

"We don't know he didn't find what he was looking for."

Annie shook her head. "Sally said there was nothing missing, when she spoke to Dougie."

"Right." Tina eyed her mum. How was this happening? Sitting across a table discussing theories with Annie, like she was at home with Mike?

She sighed. *She's a witness.* Just a witness. And Tina had questions to ask her.

"Ok, Mum," she said. "You were there, the night it happened. I need to—"

"It wouldn't surprise me, you know."

Tina frowned. "What wouldn't?"

"For people to want to kill each other, over the stock in that shop. I sold the most garish item there for *three hundred pounds* the other day. Three hundred pounds! A hideous pottery reindeer. There must be other things worth a lot more."

Tina nodded. That gave them a motive for the burglary. Maybe for murder, too.

"You were there, Mum," she said. "Did you see anyone, inside the shop? Anyone out the back, after you found Peg? Or while you were walking round there?"

Annie sniffed. "I've already talked to Dougie about this. I heard a bang. That's why I went round the back. But I didn't see anyone."

"Did you see anyone on your way to the pottery? You walked up from the beach, right?"

Annie adopted a wistful look. "Last swim of the year. I'm missing it. The courtyard was deserted. That storm sent everyone inside. But there was the man driving the BMW."

Tina leaned in. "You mentioned that in the statement Dougie took. Can you remember anything more about him? Was it definitely a man?"

"I can't swear to that, but the car... it was flash. Bluey-silver. Tim says he's seen one parked illegally down at the Cobb."

"When?" Tina asked.

"Before I got to the pottery. While I was walk—"

"No. When did Tim see the car? This is Tim at the RNLI station, yes?"

"Yes." Annie smiled. "That's him. I don't know, sorry. You can ask him."

"We will." Tina drummed her fingers on the table. She could hear seagulls shrieking outside. "So, what can you tell me about this man? The one driving the car?"

Annie shook her head. "His face was obscured. He was holding up a towel. At least, I think it was a towel. Maybe a hanky"

"Do you think he could have been nursing an injury?"

Annie shrugged. "Could have, I suppose."

"So, am I right in thinking he was holding the towel, or hanky, to the right side of his face, closest to the driver's window?"

Annie frowned. She gazed out of the back window for a moment, then looked back at Tina.

"Yes," she said. "He was. Which means if your drowned fella was left-handed, he could have whacked him, before the BMW driver pushed him into the river."

CHAPTER FORTY-TWO

ROSAMUND LEANED against her front door, her chest rising and falling.

She'd done it.

She'd faced him.

OK, so maybe she hadn't faced him. Not in the everybody-yelling-showdown way she'd wanted to when he left. But she'd looked him in the eye and...

And she'd been cool.

More importantly, she'd *felt* cool. She'd looked at her husband, her ex-husband, and she had felt... calm.

Not angry. Not as angry as she had been, at least. And not sad. She hadn't suddenly found herself missing him, aching to get him back.

Shari was welcome to him.

She felt a long, slow smile spread across her face.

"You've done it," she told herself, then looked towards the stairs. Was Cameron in?

No, he'd gone out. She hadn't registered where.

She let out a sharp breath and pushed herself off the door. She walked to the kitchen, taking long, slow strides.

She had this. She was going to be OK.

In the kitchen, she went straight to the fridge and brought out a bottle of Sauvignon Blanc. This called for a celebration. She turned to the shelves to grab a glass and...

Wait.

She turned back to the kitchen door.

She'd closed it before going out, hadn't she? She always closed the downstairs doors, to prevent draughts from circulating around the house.

But it had been wide open.

She shook her head. *You're imagining things.*

It would just be Cameron. She could never get him to understand why she liked things a certain way. And closing the doors was one of those things.

Rosamund shook her head, walked through to the sitting room, and sat on the sofa, sipping her wine.

She closed her eyes.

The wine was good. She felt good.

She opened her eyes.

The sitting room door.

That had been open, too.

"Cameron," she grunted. "Why will you never do what I ask you to?"

Rosamund stood up and went back to the kitchen. She scanned it. Had someone been in here? Had she been broken into?

After what had happened to Peg, she had lain awake at night, worrying. When Cameron inevitably left home, she'd be on her own here, in this large house set way back from the road, which quite obviously held items of value.

Her chest was tight.

Stop it, she told herself. *It's just your son.*

She went back to the front door. It had been locked and bolted, just the way she'd left it.

She hurried into each room downstairs and checked the windows. All closed.

She frowned, looking at the stairs.

Are you really this paranoid?

She placed her glass on the hall table and stood on the bottom step.

"Hello?" she called. "Is there anyone up there?"

Was it a good idea to announce yourself to a burglar? Would it scare them away, or would it just make them jump out and attack you?

In Peg's case, it had been the latter.

She swallowed.

Go up. You can do this.

She started up the stairs, her footsteps soft and her progress slow. After a moment she realised that was pointless, after calling out. She ran up the last five steps and hurled herself into her bedroom.

It was empty. The windows were closed.

The same for the other bedrooms, and the bathroom.

You're being ridiculous, she told herself. *Calm down.*

She walked down the stairs, her heart pounding. What if someone jumped out at her from one of the downstairs rooms?

She'd checked the kitchen and sitting room. She knew they were empty. Now she went into the study, also empty. The dining room, which she knew would be clear as it was connected to the sitting room.

Also empty. Windows closed and locked.

You're imagining things.

Rosamund picked up her glass from the hall table and walked back into the sitting room. She sat down again.

Enjoy the wine.

She sipped. It was still good. She was still triumphant.

Focus on that.

She sipped the rest of the wine, glancing just occasionally towards the door.

Wondering.

CHAPTER FORTY-THREE

"THAT'S IT," Figgy said. "I've had enough."

She slammed shut the lid to her laptop and strode to the bedroom.

"Stop it, you idiot seagull!"

She went to the window and hammered on the glass. Kevin, who had been hurling himself at it continuously for the last ten minutes, shrieked and flew away.

How did he know it was there? She was sure he hadn't been near the window when she'd moved the reindeer to the bedroom. And seagulls were stupid birds, weren't they?

Maybe not. Or maybe... could he smell it?

Figgy pulled the ornament from the cupboard. Once again, she was surprised by how heavy it was. She put it to her nose.

Thud!

Figgy almost dropped the reindeer. She placed it on the bed and closed the curtains, her heart pounding.

"Kevin, you gave me a fright."

Thud!

She waved a fist at the seagull, unseen behind the curtains. Sighing, she picked up the reindeer and turned it over in her hands.

Thud!

This was never going to work. She didn't want a Christmas decoration she'd have to keep hidden. But even when she kept it hidden...

Thud!

"Alright, alright," Figgy said. "I'm getting rid of it."

But where?

She couldn't just put it out in the rubbish. Kevin and his seagull mates would tear the bin bag apart to get at it. And besides, it had been a gift...

Yes. She knew just the place.

The first challenge was to get it away from the caravan without being attacked by Kevin. If it was the smell he was following, she'd need to mask that.

And she had the perfect solution.

Ten minutes later, Figgy was outside her van, holding a black sack full of rubbish. It stank badly enough to mask anything, or so Figgy reckoned. The wind had dropped, and the fetid smell of rotting food enveloped her like a fug.

On the top of the next-door caravan, observing her with his head cocked, was Kevin. He watched her for a moment, then flew to the roof of her caravan.

Figgy held her breath, half expecting him to dive for the bin bag and tear it open with his beak.

She waited. He stood on her roof, glaring at her with those bright yellow eyes. Then he took off and did a circuit of her van, no more than a wingspan away from the windows.

He was trying to find the reindeer.

What he didn't know was that it was wrapped inside two

layers of clingfilm, which were inside two plastic carrier bags, which were hidden inside her favourite cake tin.

All of which was wrapped inside a bin bag, buried deep within the bag of rubbish Figgy carried.

It had worked.

She allowed herself a quiet grin and a triumphant punch of the air, then locked up her caravan and headed for the prom.

When she reached the kiosk – shuttered now, it was getting dark – she felt the flutter of wings behind her.

She stopped, clutching the bag, and turned.

Kevin perched on a rubbish bin, staring at her.

Figgy swallowed the lump in her throat. Kevin was beginning to feel almost like a pet. Possibly a more malevolent pet than a guinea pig or a budgie, but still. She felt like she knew him.

But today there was something in those beady eyes she hadn't seen before. And she knew how vicious seagulls could be.

She picked up pace, hurrying along the prom and into town. As she approached her destination, she was relieved to see lights on and people inside.

She ran across the road and shoved open the door to the gallery. She turned and pushed the door shut. Kevin was across the road, perched on a parking sign.

"Figgy?" Helen said.

Figgy leaned against the door, panting. "Thank God," she said. "I'm so glad you're here."

She opened her eyes. Helen was standing behind the counter, looking puzzled. Next to her was Harper, who had a hand on Helen's shoulder. And opposite them both stood Annie.

"Dead," Annie was saying. "They found him in the drain." She turned at the sound of the door closing. "Figgy? Are you OK?"

"Harper." Figgy smiled. "You're back."

Harper exchanged a look with Helen. "I certainly am," she said.

"Figgy, darling," Helen said, "are you quite alright? You look like you've seen a ghost."

Figgy had dropped the bin bag on the floor in her haste to close the door. She waved at it and opened her mouth to speak.

Nothing came out.

Annie took a step towards her. "Sit down, Figgy sweet-heart. I'm worried about you."

Figgy screwed up her face. The ornament she'd hidden inside a bin bag and was now trying to get rid of... it had been a gift from Rosamund. Well, kind of.

She hadn't been expecting an audience for this.

She held up the bin bag. Its contents shifted and the smell intensified.

"Helen," she croaked. "I've got something for you."

"A bin bag?" Annie asked. "What's in it?"

Helen's face was a mask of pure disgust. "I think we know the answer to that from the smell."

Figgy shook her head. "It's a long story. And I can explain. Kind of. But please..." She coughed, wishing she could speak clearly. "Please don't tell Rosamund."

CHAPTER FORTY-FOUR

Tina yawned as she picked up the call. It was only half past five in the evening, but the combination of headlights flashing towards her on the A35 and her permanent sleep deprivation made it feel like midnight.

"Dougie," she said. "What news have you got for me?"

"Your theory that Reece was killed by an accomplice is looking stronger."

She winced as a car came the other way without dipping its beams. "Bloody idiot," she muttered.

"What was that?"

"Sorry, Dougie. A35, you know how it is. What's making it look more solid?"

"I feel for you. Reece has got a definite injury to the back of the head. It's deep, and there's bits of wood embedded in his scalp."

She winced. "And there's nothing that could have inflicted the injury in the pottery? No indication Peg Casey could have done it?"

"The CSIs took a thorough inventory of the place.

Nothing suitable was left there. And this injury... I can't believe a small elderly woman could have inflicted it."

"She's one of my mum's swimmers. Probably stronger than she looks."

"It's not just that. The angle the wound seems to have been inflicted from... Pathology seem to think it can only have been someone taller."

"You got Pathology out there? I'm impressed."

"I think the Exeter office owes the sarge some favours."

Tina smiled. You didn't work as a sergeant for as long as Jim Connors had without making a few friends and earning a few favours. As long as those favours were above board...

"OK," she said. "So there's the wound, and this potential co-conspirator. Do we really think he was the guy in the silver-blue BMW? Reece Lumbard didn't seem the type to hang out with men with that kind of money."

"We don't know how old that BMW is. And Reece might have been working for him. Stealing valuable items to order."

Tina slowed as she approached the first of the round-abouts on the edge of Dorchester. The traffic was moving, at least; she'd be home in thirty minutes.

"More like dealing drugs for him," she said. "The stolen goods would have been funding Reece's habit, if he had one."

"Pathology have taken blood samples, but we don't have the results yet."

"You only found him this morning," Tina said. "You're doing a great job. So we've got the BMW, and this man holding up a towel or handkerchief to what might have been a wound. I suggest you check CCTV, to—"

"To see if we can spot him driving away from the crime scene," Dougie said. "Wendy's already on it. And we've got all local units on the lookout for the car."

"Good." Tina pulled away from the final roundabout, relieved to be free of Dorchester. "Don't forget, there's a good chance we've got this guy's blood. The fingerprint."

"There's no match for the DNA on the system."

She considered. "OK, I'll go into the office first thing. I'll talk to DI Scott about whether we can put a call out for DNA sampling."

"Half the population of Lyme Regis is tourists, this time of year."

"Yes, but how many people come to Lyme to do a bit of shopping then kill someone?"

"Fair point. Let me know how you get on. And I hope Daisy gives you a good night's sleep."

Tina laughed. "As if! I reckon we'll catch Reece's killer long before that happens."

CHAPTER FORTY-FIVE

"Don't worry," said Figgy. "It's just my rubbish bin." She approached Helen with the bin bag held open.

Annie leaned forward. The bag stank. What was Figgy doing, bringing her kitchen waste here?

"Have the council stopped collecting from the caravan park?" she asked. "Because if they have, I'll go and speak to Councillor Durridge-wotsit, give him what for."

"Nobody needs to give anybody what for," Helen said. "But, Figgy, I really would appreciate it if you'd explain."

Figgy began to root through the bag. Annie and Helen both recoiled. Harper laughed.

"You swimmers," she said. "You're all crazy."

"No we blimmin' well are not," Annie insisted. Harper shrugged.

"You're back," Figgy said, again. She looked at Harper, her face alight.

Harper gave Helen what looked very much like a conspiratorial grin, followed by a squeeze of the hand. "I am."

Annie was watching Helen. The last time she'd seen her friend, she'd lost all her colour. Now it appeared to be back, with a technicolour filter applied over the top.

A good sign? She hoped so.

"It really is good to see you back, Harper," she said. "I hope you two have managed to sort out your differences."

"We have," Helen said. "And I'm going to tell you all about it in just a few moments. But first, Figgy, I need you to get that bin bag out of my shop."

Harper leaned into Helen and whispered something into her ear. Helen's eyes widened and she clapped her hands together. She nodded at Harper, who slunk out through the door leading to their first-floor flat.

Annie waited for an explanation. Nothing.

What's going on?

"The rubbish," Helen said. She held out an arm, leaning back so her head was as far from her hand as she could manage. "I'm very sorry you're not having it collected, Figgy dear. But please, next time, can you please just go straight to the bins behind the shop?"

A shiver passed between the women. Earlier this year they'd managed to lose a murder victim in those bins.

Figgy pulled a second bin bag out of the first one. It had a banana skin and a chocolate digestive wrapper stuck to it. She peeled them off and placed them back in the first bag.

"Please," Helen said. "I really don't think—"

"Let me show you," Figgy said. "I've got something for your shop. But I had to hide it."

"Hide it?" echoed Helen and Annie in unison. Helen sounded disgusted. Annie, on the other hand, was intrigued.

"Why did you have to hide it?" she asked.

Figgy opened the second bin bag and brought out a cake tin. Annie recognised it; she'd used it to take Figgy's home-made cakes to Tim in the summer.

A fine way to get a man's attention.

"A cake tin?" Helen said. "Please don't tell me you're going to offer us something out of that. The lack of hygiene..."

Annie sniggered. "All I can say is, thank the heavens Rosamund isn't here to see this."

Figgy gave her a meaningful look but said nothing. She placed the tin on the counter and opened it. Inside was another plastic bag.

Annie tutted. *Will this never end?*

"Don't tell me there's more rubbish in there," Helen said. She kept glancing towards the door where Harper had disappeared. Annie couldn't help but worry that Harper might pull off another genuine disappearance.

Figgy unwrapped the plastic bag, and another one inside it. At last, she placed the contents on the shop counter with a flourish.

"This," she said. "This is what I've brought you. I'll take the rubbish. Of course I will."

"What is it?" Helen gave the object a poke.

"What does it look like?" Annie asked.

Helen looked at her. "A garish pottery reindeer."

"Exactly. And if I'm not mistaken, it came from Peg and Sally's pottery shop." She looked up. "Where did you get it, Figster?"

"Please," Figgy said. "You have to promise not to tell her I'm passing it on."

Annie frowned. "Tell that Shari woman? Did

Rosamund's ex-husband's girlfriend give you this thing? Do you know how much she paid for it?"

Figgy's face fell. "Oh, no. How much?"

"Three hundred pounds."

Figgy's mouth fell open.

"Wait a moment," said Helen. "Why are you bringing it to me? And how does Annie know about all this?"

"I've been working in the shop, remember," Annie said. "I sold it to her."

"For three hundred pounds?" Helen looked aghast.

"There was a price tag on it. I told her the amount, and she paid it."

"But it's hideous," Helen said.

Figgy frowned. "I quite like it."

Helen gave her a puzzled look. "So why don't you keep it?"

"Because I'm not the only one who likes it. It's got Kevin all worked up."

Helen spluttered out a laugh. "Your pet seagull?"

"He's not my pet. Anyway, will you take it, for the shop? Sell it, give the money to charity."

"Or to Rosamund, if she gave it to you," Helen pointed out.

Figgy winced. "I'd rather she didn't know."

Annie slapped a hand on Figgy's shoulder. "You're going to have to get used to having her as a mother-in-law, you know."

Figgy turned the colour of beetroot. "She's not my mother-in-law." The blush deepened. "Not... yet."

"Did somebody say mother-in-law?"

They all turned at the voice. Harper was standing in the

doorway. In one hand she held four mugs, one dangling from each finger. In the other was a bottle of Champagne.

"Oh!" Figgy cried. "Fizz!"

Harper gave her a wink. "Better than fizz, Figgy. Bolly. Nothing but the best for my future wife."

Harper put the mugs and bottle down beside the reindeer. She took a step towards Helen, reached out an arm and pulled her towards her. The couple shared a long, deep kiss.

"Oh." Figgy shifted from foot to foot. Her blush had subsided.

When Helen and Harper had finally drawn apart, Annie put a hand on each of their arms. "Congratulations, you two. This is wonderful news." She gave Helen's shoulder a squeeze.

"I know!" Harper's eyes were bright. Helen was gazing at her, her face one big smile.

Whatever it was that had happened between the two of them, they'd clearly sorted it out.

"So," Harper said as she poured Champagne into the mugs. "Who's going to celebrate with us?"

"I think we all are," Annie said.

"What about Rosamund?" Helen asked. "We should get her down here."

"She can come to the proper celebration, in the Pilot Boat tomorrow night," Harper said. "This is just an impromptu thing."

Figgy looked relieved. "All the best parties are impromptu."

They clattered their mugs together.

"To the happy couple," Annie said. She'd find an opportunity tomorrow to discover how things had turned around so completely.

"To the happy couple!" Figgy echoed. "So does this mean you'll take my reindeer?"

"Of course, darling." Helen laughed. "Right now, I'll take any old tat."

CHAPTER FORTY-SIX

"Hello, sweetheart." Annie held out the two plastic bags she'd brought as her daughter Naomi answered the door.

"Mum." Naomi looked wary. "I don't remember asking you to do my shopping." She glanced over her shoulder into the house. "It's my mum!" she called.

"Christmas crafts, for Poppy," Annie said. "I thought she might like them."

"Poppy already has lots of crafting supplies." Naomi eyed the bags. "I thought you were getting her more for Christmas."

"Oh, that's ages away. Can I come in?" Annie didn't wait for an answer but instead squeezed past her daughter into the hall and through to the kitchen.

Poppy was sitting at the kitchen table, eating a bowl of Rice Crispies. Dougie was at the sink, washing a mug. He turned.

"Annie. I thought I heard voices. Is something wrong?"

"Wrong? Heavens, no. Does something need to be wrong for me to visit my family?"

"But it's half past seven in the morning," he pointed out.

"Granny!" Poppy jumped up and gave her a hug. Annie returned it, grateful that someone at least was pleased to see her.

"Did you walk all the way here?" Naomi was in the doorway behind her. "What time did you leave home?"

Annie placed the bags on the table, and Poppy immediately started rummaging through them. Annie noticed the look that went between Naomi and Dougie.

"By this time," she said, "I've normally had my morning swim, enjoyed a good gossip with the girls, and I'm relaxing over a vanilla latte at the kiosk."

"By this time?" Naomi said. "But it's still dark!"

"When will you be returning to the swimming?" Dougie asked.

Annie glared at him, ignoring Naomi's snigger. "Don't be cheeky. Maybe that's my summer routine I'm talking about, but it makes no difference. I'm a morning lark, and I've spent my entire life walking the hills of Lyme Regis." She lifted a foot and slapped her calf. "An early morning trek up to the edge of town is no challenge."

"I can't sit around and chat," Naomi said. "I've got to get Poppy to her before-school club and then get to work."

"And I've got an early briefing with the sarge and MCIT," Dougie said.

"By which you mean our Tina," Annie told him.

"Not just Tina, potentially."

She raised an eyebrow. "So you've got new evidence? You're closer to finding Peg's other attacker? The man in the BMW?"

Dougie clenched his jaw. "You know that I can't talk about the details of the investigation."

"Not even to a key witness? I was the first on the scene, and without me you wouldn't even know about the man in the BMW."

"He's not the only person we're interested in."

"No?" Annie raised her eyebrows; this was new. "You've got another suspect?"

"Somebody I saw from my car, on the... it doesn't matter." Dougie finished drying his mug and placed it in a cupboard. He walked to Naomi and kissed her cheek. "I'll see you later, love."

As Dougie turned to Poppy to pick her up, Annie looked at Naomi.

"How did you find the science fair? You looked like you were holding your own when I was there."

Annie knew that Naomi had been dreading the science fair, not least because it was the brainchild of the dreadful Fenella.

Naomi shrugged. "It was OK, I suppose. I'm just glad it's over."

"Did you manage to get DNA from any more of our great and good?"

Naomi grimaced. Dougie put Poppy down and looked up.

"DNA?" he said.

Annie nodded. "They were doing an experiment. Taking swabs from inside people's cheeks."

"Mine's still sore." Naomi rubbed her cheek. "The kids got me to do it twenty times at least."

"DNA?" Dougie repeated.

Naomi frowned at him. "Yes, Dougie. DNA. What's got into you?"

"Nothing. It's just... I don't suppose you labelled them, did you? Kept a record of who they were from?"

Naomi shrugged. "No idea. Why?"

Dougie's eyes were narrowed. "Nothing. No. We couldn't..." He looked at his wife. "Can I ask you a favour?"

"Of course."

He nodded, a faraway look in his eyes.

"Those samples," he said. "If you've still got them... don't throw them away."

CHAPTER FORTY-SEVEN

"Sarge," Dougie said. "I've had an idea."

Sergeant Connors turned to him. They were in the team room with Tina, mugs of coffee in front of them all.

"Go on then," said the sarge.

"The DNA," said Dougie. "That bloody fingerprint."

"Please don't say what I think you're about to say," said Tina.

"What?" he asked, adopting his best innocent expression.

"We can't possibly do a community appeal. There's too much movement in and out of the town."

He shook his head. "It's not that. It's the science fair they did at Naomi's school."

She frowned. "What's that got to do with anything?"

"They were demonstrating how to take DNA samples," he said. "There was a whole load of test tubes, apparently." He shrugged. "Maybe they kept some."

The sarge laughed. "Oh, Dougie. I know you want to get this one solved. But we don't have the consent of those people for their DNA to be used in a police investigation. And it wasn't *exactly* taken in controlled conditions."

Dougie sighed. The sarge was right. "OK," he said. "So we still need to find Reece's accomplice. It could be the bloke I almost ran over on Sunday night."

"Bad news there, I'm afraid," said the sarge. "He came forward, phoned in last night. Name's Simon Dalgleish. He's got an alibi for the time running up to when you saw him. He was working in the Pilot Boat."

"We're sure it was him?" Dougie asked.

"He gave me all the details. Talked about how he came out of Sherborne Lane, stopped in front of your car. Blue VW, right?"

"Right."

"That's what he said. Sorry, lad. I don't think he's our man."

"Which leaves the man driving the silver-blue BMW," Tina said.

"Wendy's been asking questions about him," the sarge said. "There have been reports of a similar car illegally parked at the Cobb."

"Who from?" Dougie asked.

"Tim Cromwell at the lifeboat station. He's about as reliable as they get."

"Did he report seeing anyone driving the car, or getting out of it?" Tina asked.

The sarge shook his head. "He submitted his report online. Didn't give any details."

"OK," she replied. "We need to speak to him, see if there's anything else he can tell us." She stood up.

"I still can't believe we haven't picked the car up on ANPR," Dougie grunted.

The sarge gave him a pat on the shoulder. "We'll find it, don't you worry. It's early days yet."

"Dougie," Tina said. "Fancy coming with me to interview Tim?"

He grabbed his coat. "Beats sitting here, watching nothing come in on the number plate recognition."

She gave him a rueful smile. As they made for the door, it burst open.

Wendy rushed inside, her breathing heavy.

"Wendy?" Dougie said. "You OK?"

She grinned. Her cheeks were flushed and her face shone with sweat.

"What is it?" Tina asked.

"The CCTV," Wendy panted.

Dougie frowned. "Which CCTV? At the Cobb? You've found the driver of the BMW?"

She shook her head. "No. The Tuck Shop Café."

"That scruffy café by the mill?" Tina asked.

"Their CCTV isn't working," Dougie said. "The woman working there told you on Monday."

Wendy shook her head. "But it is. She lied."

"She lied?" Dougie and Tina asked in unison.

"She broke the camera herself, on Monday morning."

"That means it *is* broken," Dougie said.

"Maybe," said Tina. "But not on Sunday night. So how d'you know this, Wendy?"

Wendy licked her lips. "I was out on the seafront, just doing my rounds. A lad came up to me. Not really a lad. Will Sampson, he's a delivery driver. He was delivering a parcel to the brewery on the other side of the mill courtyard on Monday—"

"... and he saw her putting the CCTV out of action," Tina finished.

"Yep. He was doing a video of his delivery, no one was in so he needed evidence he'd done the drop. She's in the background, going at the camera with a hammer."

"Wendy, you're a genius," Tina said.

Wendy shrugged. "All I did was let a member of the public provide me with information."

"I don't care," Tina replied. "That CCTV will show us everything."

"It might not," said the sarge. "The place is pretty ropey, their CCTV might be, too."

Tina shook her head. "I looked at that camera. And besides, she deliberately damaged her own property so we wouldn't be able to watch the footage. Which tells us two things."

"The footage will give us valuable evidence," Wendy said. "That's what I thought."

"But what's the other thing?" Dougie asked.

Tina turned to him, eyes gleaming. "Whatever's on that recording," she said, "I'd lay odds it incriminates someone at the Tuck Shop Café."

CHAPTER FORTY-EIGHT

Annie was glad to have a morning meeting with her swimming friends. Figgy was already at the Town Mill Bakery, smiling serenely, when she arrived.

"You look like the cat that got the cream," Annie said after ordering a coffee at the counter and sitting down.

"I've just been for a paddle," Figgy replied. Beside her was a tote bag with a towel inside.

"Ah, a sunrise dip, even if only up to your ankles. That'd be enough to start anyone's day right."

Figgy giggled. "Cameron joined me, he stayed at the caravan last night."

Annie felt her smile widen until it was as broad as her friend's. "Even better than a sunrise paddle." She tapped the side of her nose. "Say no more."

"Is Rosamund joining us?"

"I imagine so. She needs to be brought up to speed with Helen's news, after all."

"Of course." Figgy's smile dropped.

Annie squeezed her hand across the table. "She'll get

used to it, Figgy love. You make her son happy, and what mother is going to argue with that?"

Figgy didn't look convinced. "I've asked Cameron to spend Christmas with me," she said.

"Oh. Now, I'm not sure what Rosamund will make of that. You do realise it's only her second one since David left? And her first since she started getting settled?"

"She won't want to spend it alone."

Annie considered. "She won't. But I could invite her to mine. I've got Naomi coming this year. The girls take it in turns."

Figgy gave her a look. "I can't really picture Rosamund in the middle of a chaotic Abbott Christmas."

"Oi!" Annie gave the younger woman a mock-glare. "I'll have you know my Christmasses are run like a military operation."

"Still. I know my idea of Christmas is nothing like Cameron's used to. I'm not sure he can cope with all the kitsch in my van."

Annie snorted. "He'll get used to it, if he cares about you. And from what I've seen, he very much does."

Figgy adopted a wistful smile. Annie watched her over the rim of her coffee cup, wondering if her relationship with Tim would ever develop like this. She wasn't too old...

"Hello, you two." Rosamund stood behind Annie, looking between the two of them. She seemed out of breath.

"Rosamund." Annie stood and gave her a hug.

Rosamund shrank back. "What's that in aid of?"

"Things aren't easy for you right now. What with David and his girlfriend being in town."

Rosamund looked at Annie for a long moment, then gave a dismissive wave. "You really don't need to worry. I went up to Wisteria Cottage last night – it really *isn't* a cottage, you know – and smoothed the waters with them. And then I..." She shook her head. "No. Don't worry about that."

"Oh." Annie was surprised. "Well, that's good."

"It is. Shari is nice, as it turns out. I don't envy her, having to put up with my ex-husband."

"But you're still married."

"Only legally. He's as ex as ex gets, as far as I'm concerned." Rosamund squared her shoulders. "I'm putting the past behind me. Moving forward with my future."

"I'm glad to hear things are looking up for you," Figgy said.

Rosamund looked across the table at her. "They are. And you and I are in need of a chat. Let me order a pot of tea, and I'll be right back."

Figgy's face fell as Rosamund walked away. She looked like she wanted to bolt.

Annie leaned across the table. "She doesn't bite. Maybe it'll be the good sort of chat."

"No one announces they need a chat, then walks away. Not if it's the good sort of chat." Figgy was breathing rapidly.

"Take deep breaths, Figgy love. You're imagining the worst. Look, here's Rosamund back."

Figgy plunged her hands beneath the table. Rosamund sat down beside her. The emotion Annie could sense pouring off the younger woman was pure fear.

Rosamund wasn't that scary, surely?

"Figgy," Rosamund said, turning to her. "I bumped into Cameron on my way down here. He told me about your early morning paddle."

"Oh, God," Figgy muttered. "I'm sorry. I didn't mean to—"

"What's wrong?" Rosamund put a hand on Figgy's shoulder. She didn't seem to realise that the effect was to make Figgy freeze, like a seagull in headlights.

"I'm happy for you," Rosamund said. "And for Cam. I haven't seen him like this since his dad left. And I can tell you, it isn't his dad coming back that's cheered him up."

"No," Figgy muttered. "He's so angry at him."

"Rightfully so," Rosamund said. Figgy looked at her, brow creasing.

"It's you, Figgy," Annie said. "*You've* made Cameron happy again."

"You have," Rosamund agreed. "It's taken me longer than it should have to accept this. But thanks to you, I feel like I've got my boy back."

Figgy looked at her. "You do?"

"Morning, ladies!"

Annie turned to see Helen enter the bakery. Harper trailed behind, gripping her hand. Both of them were flushed.

All these loved-up couples, she thought. *Maybe I should go and see Tim, see if things are ready to move to the next level.*

Across the table, Rosamund had bent her head closer to Figgy's.

"I'm sorry I was an arse," she said.

Figgy stifled a laugh. "It's OK. You were just protecting him."

Rosamund squeezed her shoulder. "And now we both can."

"Right, ladies?" Helen plonked herself down next to Annie, causing the bench to shake. "Who's for something a bit stronger than coffee?"

Rosamund looked at her across the table, then up at Harper. "You're celebrating Harper's return. Welcome back."

Harper nodded, not pausing in her stroking of Helen's shoulders.

"We're celebrating a bloody sight more than that!" Helen looked between Annie and Figgy. "Have you two not told her?"

"Sorry," Figgy said.

"She's only just got here," Annie added. "We've not got round to it."

"Not got round to it? My goodness, ladies!" Helen stood up and snaked an arm around Harper's waist. "Rosamund, I'm delighted to inform you that Harper and I are getting married."

The people at the neighbouring seats must have been listening in, because a smattering of applause rippled around the bakery. Helen gave a bow, then planted a loud kiss on Harper's cheek. She frowned and wiped off the lipstick.

Rosamund was standing, too, her hands up. "That's wonderful news! Congratulations, both of you."

Helen raised an eyebrow. "You're not freaked out by it, what with you being in the process of getting a D-I-V-O-R-C-E and all that jazz?"

"Goodness, no. I'm better off without David. And you two are clearly better off together."

"We are," Harper agreed, her arm around Helen's waist. Helen turned to look at her, eyes sparkling.

"Very well," Annie said. "Another celebration. The pubs are nowhere near open, so..."

"What do you mean?" Rosamund said. "Another celebration?"

Helen exchanged glances with Annie. "Annie and Figgy here just happened to pop by the shop last night. Figgy had a—"

"Figgy had a question about a suitable Christmas present," Figgy cut in.

"Oh," Helen said. "Yes. For Cameron, right?"

Figgy nodded. "For Cameron."

"OK," Rosamund said. "I suppose I would have appreciated being a part of the festivities, but... well, I was busy. And if we're going to celebrate now—"

"This one's the proper celebration," Annie cut in. "Much more of a thing than last night." She winked at Helen's mouthed *thank you*.

"Very well," Rosamund said. "Where shall we go?"

"The gallery's only around the corner," Helen said.

"I've got plenty of booze in my house," Annie suggested.

"That's kind of you," Helen said. "But do you mind if I ask what kind of booze?"

Annie laughed. "Not your kind, I'm sure. We'll go wherever you want to go."

Helen nodded. "The gallery, then."

"The gallery," they choroused and made for the door.

As they turned right towards the seafront, Annie remembered something.

"Helen," she said, "you told us Harper was missing. She wouldn't return your calls or messages. How did you track her down?"

"I know the answer to that one," Figgy said. "It was that driftwood reindeer, wasn't it?"

Helen stifled a laugh. "It was. Harper took all her stuff except that, and she didn't even leave it in her studio. She put it in my storeroom. So I knew it was significant."

"A clue," Annie said.

Helen rolled her eyes. "Yes, darling. A clue."

"There's a beach at Sidmouth," Harper said. "I collect driftwood there, after storms. I guess my subconscious wanted Helen to find me."

"And I'm damned glad it did," Helen said.

They were outside the gallery now. Helen reached into her voluminous handbag, searching for keys. Harper put a hand into her own jeans pocket and drew a set out.

"Pockets, my love," she said. "So much more practical than that thing."

"Oh, my God."

Annie turned to see Figgy standing a few paces behind them, her eyes and mouth wide.

"Oh my God," she repeated.

"What is it?" said Annie.

"Are you quite alright?" Rosamund asked.

"The reindeer," Figgy said.

Annie nodded. "The driftwood reindeer."

"No. The other one."

"Oh. That." Rosamund grunted.

Figgy screwed her eyes up. "The reindeer. And my bauble. The smashed one. We need to..." She opened her eyes.

"What is it, Figgy love?" Annie asked.

Figgy wiped away a tear.

"Are you OK?"

Figgy nodded. "It's..." She chewed her lip. "It's the key to everything. Or at least, I think it is."

Helen and Harper had gone inside the gallery. Helen put her head out of the door.

"Are you ladies coming?" she asked.

Figgy looked at her. "Have you still got it?"

"Got what?"

"The pottery reindeer. From last night."

"Yes. I've still got it. Actually, Figgy, I've been meaning to—"

"We need to get inside it," Figgy said. "We need to smash it open."

"Smash it open?" Annie asked. "What are you—"

"You gave it to Helen?" Rosamund said. "I don't understand."

Figgy blushed. "I'm sorry, Rosamund. But it was Kevin. That aggressive seagull. He wouldn't leave it alone. He made the caravan shake. It broke things, there was a smashed bauble... I'm not making sense, sorry. But even when I hid it in a cupboard, he was dive-bombing the windows."

"Dex was like that, too," Annie said. "Not so much with the reindeer, but in Peg and Sally's shop. I've had to stop walking him, while I'm looking after the place."

"That's it, then," Figgy said.

"That's what?" Helen asked. "I'm sorry, darlings, but I've no idea what you're on about."

"The reindeer is connected with Peg's attack," Figgy said. "And with the death of the man who attacked her."

"It is?" Annie asked.

Figgy nodded. "We need to smash it open. If I'm right, it'll explain everything."

CHAPTER FORTY-NINE

"Morning, Gail," Tina said as the crime scene manager picked up the phone. Gail Hansford was Dorset's most experienced CSM and someone she'd worked with on plenty of occasions.

"Tina," Gail replied. "How's Christmas prep going in Lyme Regis?"

"Oh, as chaotic as ever. I think my mum's bought half the toys in the town for the kids. Has she seen how small my house is?"

"Don't knock it," Gail replied. "It's only 'cos she loves them. And you."

Tina grunted. She should be grateful, she knew. If Annie could keep out of this investigation until it was concluded, then maybe she'd forgive her for being an overbearing granny.

"In better news," Gail said, "we've done a thorough examination of the car your victim was driving."

Lumbard's red Golf had been taken to the forensics lab in Dorchester as evidence. His mum had not been happy about it: she'd spent at least twenty minutes on the phone to Dougie insisting that it was a violation of her rights as its owner. Even while grieving the loss of her son.

"What did you find?" Tina asked.

"Plenty of prints. Reece's, and his mum's. Dear God, it took Gav ages to convince her to provide us with them. I think she thought he was going to arrest her."

"Her son's dead," Tina said.

"People act weird. She must be in shock."

"Maybe. Any other prints? Please tell me you've got a match for that bloody fingerprint in the pottery."

Gail sighed. "Lots of other prints, like every other car we examine. But no match for that one, unfortunately. We've found some hairs and skin samples, and we can make DNA comparison."

Tina's heart sank. "But you said there was good news."

"Yes. The car had traces of restricted substances. Much more than traces, in fact. Mainly in the glove locker, but some in the boot. And a smaller quantity on the steering wheel, door handles—"

"The surfaces Reece would have touched," Tina said.

"Exactly. I guess there's every possibility that his mum's responsible..."

Tina shook her head. "...but given Reece broke into the pottery and was killed, possibly by his accomplice, it's most likely him. Is it enough for you to be sure he was dealing?"

"It's not so much the quantity, but the pattern. Sure, there's traces on the surfaces. But most of it's in the glove compartment, and not just in one small patch. The inside of it is covered, which is consistent with large quantities of drugs having been transported in there."

"You say restricted substances," Tina said. "Which, exactly?"

"Methamphetamine," Gail said. "Some heroin, but mainly meth."

"OK. So maybe Reece was burgling properties to fund his habit. We know a lot of low-level dealers are recruited via their own addiction."

"Judging by the quantity of drugs I think have passed through that car, I'm not sure how low-level he was."

Tina slumped in her chair. She was alone in the team room at Lyme Regis police station; Dougie had gone out to help Wendy recover the CCTV and interview staff at the Tuck Shop Café, and Sergeant Connors was in a planning meeting for the Lyme Lunge. Although how much policing a bunch of foolhardy swimmers needed, Tina wasn't sure.

"We need to find out who supplied him with those drugs," she said.

"Let me know when you track them down. There'll be forensics, it'll help you make the link."

"Thanks, Gail."

Tina hung up and rubbed her eyes. So Reece Lumbard had been a drug dealer. No real surprise there.

But who had he been working with? And had his supplier decided he was a liability, and pushed him into the river?

CHAPTER FIFTY

ANNIE LOOKED around her group of friends, then back at the object sitting on the shop counter in Helen's gallery.

The four of them stood around it, Helen and Rosamund on one side of the counter and Annie and Figgy on the other. Harper had gone to fetch a tool with which to open it.

"Wait." Helen raised a hand. "I don't want anyone coming in." She walked over to the front door and locked it.

As Helen returned to the counter, Harper entered through the back door, holding a hammer and chisel.

"Where did you find that?" Helen asked.

Harper looked at her. "The shed, next to my workshop."

"I thought you'd taken everything."

Harper shook her head. "Not quite everything. I actually hid quite a bit in the shed, and I took the key."

"For effect," Helen said.

"So I could come back," Harper replied.

Annie exchanged a wary look with Rosamund. Just moments ago, Helen and Harper had been all loved-up. Was trouble brewing?

"Shall we open it, then?" Annie said, keen to break the tension. "I want to know if Figgy's right."

Figgy gave a nervous giggle. "I'm probably wrong, you know. We could be about to destroy an incredibly expensive ornament all because of a daft idea I've got into my head."

"Not daft," Annie told her. "You're never daft."

"I might be this time. And... Look, I know you all think this thing is hideous, but I quite like it."

"I'll do you a deal," Rosamund said. "If you're wrong, and that thing is empty, I'll buy you a replacement."

Figgy frowned. "But that's impossible." She looked at Annie. "It was the only one in the pottery, right?"

"That it was," Annie said.

Rosamund shook her head. "This isn't Sally's work. You've seen her pottery. It came from elsewhere. Maybe it was left in the pottery by the man who attacked Peg. Along with its contents."

"You agree with me?" Figgy said. "You think there's something inside it, too?"

Helen rolled her eyes. "You won't get arrested for saying the word, Figgy. You've described your seagull's reaction to it, and—"

"Not my seagull," Figgy put in.

Helen waved a dismissive hand. "And Annie's described the way her dog's been behaving."

"Again," said Annie, "not my dog."

"Oh for goodness' sake," Helen said. "For the purposes of this conversation, can we just act as if they're your animals?"

"Hey, hun," Harper said. "It's OK." She was next to Helen now, holding her hand. The hammer and chisel were on the table beside the reindeer.

Annie had to admit, she quite liked the reindeer, too.

"You ladies didn't allow me to finish," Rosamund said. "I'm offering to replace it for Figgy because I think I know where it came from."

Annie looked up. "You do?"

Rosamund nodded. "Or at least, I believe I know where you can buy more just like it."

"Where?" Helen asked.

"One of the many fossil shops on Broad Street," Rosamund said. "The one two doors up from the pasty shop. I don't remember its name."

"That's because it doesn't have a name," Helen said. "I keep an eye on all the retail comings and goings along here, and I noticed new owners moving into that unit two weeks ago."

"Just in time for Christmas," Annie said.

"But it isn't open yet," Helen told her. "There's no sign over the door, no name as far as I can tell. I don't even know quite what it's supposed to be selling." She looked at Rosamund. "But you've been in there?"

Rosamund nodded. "I'm not sure I was supposed to. But on Friday I was passing, and they seemed to be open. There wasn't much stock; a half dozen of those reindeer, all slightly different, and some dinner sets. Along with the usual fossil tat and Christmas decorations, of course."

"That all sounds a bit random," Figgy said.

"That's what I thought," Rosamund said. "But you know what Lyme can get like at Christmas."

"So did you recognise it when Cameron brought it home?" Figgy asked.

Rosamund shrugged. "I suppose I did. I assumed Shari had bought it from the new shop. It's hardly the kind of thing you'd expect to find in the Millside Pottery. No disrespect, Annie."

"None taken." Annie had had a thought. "Who was running this new shop? Anyone you recognised?"

"No, sorry," Rosamund said. "I can tell you one thing, though, she was incredibly grumpy."

"She?"

Harper picked up the chisel. "So are we going to break into this thing?"

"Wait," Annie said. "The woman in the shop, Rosamund. Can you describe her?"

Rosamund's brow creased. "Early forties, blonde hair with brown roots. Permanent scowl."

"Did she have a name badge?"

"I didn't see one. Sorry."

"It's OK."

"What are you thinking, Annie?" Helen asked.

"That godawful café by the mill," Annie said. "The place with the broken CCTV." She did air quotes.

"The Tuck Shop Café," Figgy said.

"The reindeer?" Harper asked. She held the hammer in one hand and the chisel in the other.

"Wait, sweetheart," Helen said. "This might be important. Annie, are you saying there's a connection between the shop with the reindeer and the café?"

"I'm not sure," Annie said. "It's the way Dex was behaving, pawing at the side of the building. And when we went in there, there was something off about the place. And the reindeer, with the way Figgy's seagull reacted to it—"

"Not my seagull," said Figgy.

"I know," said Annie. "But we need to tell the police about the shop."

"Really?" Rosamund said. "You want to go to the police, instead of investigating yourself?"

Annie felt her toes curl. "I don't want to annoy Tina any more than I already have. Maybe we should give this reindeer to her, instead of opening it ourselves."

"No," said Harper. "We need to open it."

"She's right," Figgy said. "After all, it's our property."

Helen clapped her hands together. "It *has* passed through each of our hands. And if we gave it to the police and it turned out to be empty, what kind of fools would we look like?"

"That's true," Harper said, jiggling the hammer in her hand.

"Careful, darling," Helen said.

"I work with tools far bigger than this every day. I'm good."

"Let's open it," Figgy said. "Smash it."

Helen smiled, her fingertips together and her hair coming loose. "I second that."

"I agree," Rosamund said.

Annie swallowed. They were right.

Harper looked at her, an eyebrow raised. "Annie?"

Annie nodded. "Do it."

"Stand back," Harper said. "And close your eyes."

The four swimmers each took a step back. Harper pulled a set of goggles from her pocket and put them on.

"Very fetching, darling," Helen said. Harper gave her a wink.

"One... two... three." Harper hit the end of the chisel, her jaw tensed in concentration.

Annie held her breath.

Harper made another hit.

The reindeer shattered into four large pieces, and many smaller ones. The women held their breath.

Harper put down the hammer and chisel and began to peel away the fragments, confirming what everyone already knew.

"Your hunch was right, Figgy," she said.

"Oh, my..." Figgy gasped. She looked at Annie, who was swallowing the lump in her throat.

The reindeer was hollow, but it wasn't empty. Inside was a plastic bag.

The plastic bag had been torn open by one of the shards. Its contents spilled out onto the counter.

"Oh, my God," Figgy said.

"Well, you've certainly set the cat among the pigeons, Figglington," Annie said.

"Have I? Oh no, should we have called the police?"

"This isn't all on you," Annie said. She squeezed Figgy's hand. "And yes, we definitely need to call the police now."

CHAPTER FIFTY-ONE

THE TUCK SHOP Café was closed, as it had been since Monday. It wasn't alone in having closed temporarily, given the flooding, but the other businesses around the mill had since reopened, anxious to make up for lost time.

Dougie had a suspicion that the Tuck Shop Café only opened its doors for the minimum amount of time of needed to be able to claim it was a legitimate business.

He walked around the perimeter of the building while Wendy hammered on the doors. It was an ugly structure, made of flimsy materials and clearly erected in a hurry, in one of Lyme's most picturesque locations.

How on earth had it been granted planning permission?

"Dougie!" Wendy called. Dougie hurried around the building just as the front door opened.

A woman stood in the doorway, blocking the narrow opening she'd made. She was in her early to mid-forties, with lank dyed-blonde hair and a scowl. She wore an apron with an assortment of stains Dougie preferred not to guess at and a name badge that identified her as Millie-Jo.

"Millie-Jo," Wendy said. "I'm glad you're here." She held up her ID. "I'm PC Wendy Sharman, this is PC Douglas Anderson."

"I know who you are," the woman grunted. "Been watching you fannying about with that blocked drain."

Wendy nodded. "We need to speak to you about your CCTV."

Millie-Jo sighed. "Already told you, didn't I? It's bust. Not been working for over a week."

"That's not what we've been told," Dougie said.

The woman looked past Wendy, at Dougie. "No?" she said. "Who by?"

"We have video evidence." Wendy pointed towards the mill. "It shows you tampering with the CCTV camera."

The woman's face hardened. "Don't know what you're talking about."

Dougie sighed. "We can show you the video recording. It very clearly shows—"

"No need to do that," she said. "I remember now." She gave him a grin that exposed yellowing teeth. "I was fixing it. It was broken, so I was getting it working again."

"The video shows you taking a hammer to the camera," Wendy said. She cocked her head.

Millie-Jo gave her a long look. She pursed her lips, clenching and unclenching her fists.

After a long silence, both Dougie and Wendy waiting for the woman to fill it, she finally spoke.

"I told the bastard he wouldn't get away with it. Not long term."

Dougie felt his skin prickle. *Get away with what?*

"Can you explain what you mean?" Wendy asked.

Millie-Jo shook her head. She took a step outside,

pushing Wendy out of the way. Dougie and Wendy exchanged glances as she peered around the courtyard.

There were a few tourists around, but no one Dougie recognised. In the far corner of the courtyard a family was taking photographs of each other against the Christmas lights.

Millie-Jo's nostrils flared. She drew back.

"OK," she said.

"OK?" Wendy asked.

"You can watch your bloody CCTV. See what he's been making me help him with. But I want you to remember."

"Remember what?" Dougie asked.

"Remember that I helped you. When the shit hits the fan and you're arresting people, remember that I helped you."

CHAPTER FIFTY-TWO

FIGGY COULD FEEL her stomach churning.

She couldn't believe things had got this far.

The reindeer had started out as a gift, something that Shari had offered to Rosamund as a peace offering.

Rosamund, of course, had hated it.

And then Kevin...

Well, now at least she knew why Kevin had behaved the way he had.

Stupid seagull.

The four women stared at the contents of the bag that had been inside the reindeer, spilling across the counter.

"So what do we do now?" Helen asked.

"We call the police," Annie said, again.

Helen looked at her. "But won't that get Sally and Peg into trouble?"

Annie shook her head. "There's no way Sally and Peg have anything to do with putting drugs inside that reindeer."

"What kind of drugs are they, anyway?" Figgy asked.

"Crystal meth," Harper said.

Helen turned to her. "How do you know that?"

Harper shrugged. "I watch *Breaking Bad*, remember? I could probably manufacture the stuff, if I put my hand to it."

Helen frowned.

"OK," said Figgy. "So we call the police, and what do we tell them? Why do we tell them we smashed it open ourselves instead of handing it over when we became suspicious?" She felt a sudden wave of panic. "And what about the fact that there are likely to be drugs all over us? Bits of that stuff will have got onto our clothes, onto Harper's hammer and chisel. What if they think we're involved in this?"

Annie put a hand on her shoulder. "Calm down, Figster. Coming forward with information doesn't automatically make you a suspect. You've been watching too many TV dramas."

Figgy swallowed. "I'm still worried about Peg and Sally."

"Peg and Sally's biggest concern right now," Helen said, "is making sure that Peg gets better and they can come home for Christmas."

"Too right," Annie said.

"Look," said Helen. "First things first, we need to tidy that away."

Figgy looked at her. "Shouldn't we leave it exactly as we found it?"

Helen shook her head. "This is my gallery, and in case you hadn't noticed, there are people standing outside the front door, expecting to buy Christmas presents. Now, they can't come walking in here and find a stash of drugs on the counter. Nor can I leave them standing outside for any longer without arousing suspicion. So we need to clean that up, put it somewhere safe, open the shop, and then, as Annie says, call the police."

"Sounds like a plan," Annie said.

Rosamund sniffed. "I'm still not sure."

Figgy could feel her heart pounding. She could understand why Kevin had become so agitated by the drugs, and *she* couldn't even smell them. "Can I sit down?" she said.

Harper came out from behind the counter. "Here you are, Figgy." She pulled a chair towards her.

Figgy gave her a grateful smile. "Thanks, Harper. I'm glad you're back."

Harper shrugged. "Me, too, even with all this."

Figgy allowed herself a smile. "And I'm glad that you and Helen are getting married." She wanted to ask how things had changed so drastically, but she knew it was none of her business.

"Right," said Helen, returning from the door. "The door is open. Are we good to go?"

"We are," said Annie, emerging from the other door that led to Helen and Harper's flat. "I've placed it all in one of Figgy's bin bags. I guessed the police would want to see those as evidence anyway, so it was the safest thing to use."

Figgy swallowed. She didn't like the sound of that. "Do you think they'll suspect me of anything?" she said. "I mean, I live in a caravan. I haven't got a proper job."

"Figgy," Annie replied, "you *have* got a proper job. Just because you work freelance doing something I don't understand, and most of your clients are on the other side of the world, doesn't mean you're not a respectable young woman."

Figgy glanced at Rosamund.

Rosamund gave her a wary smile. "However respectable you may or may not be, Figgy, you have nothing to do with putting these drugs into this reindeer. Do you?"

Figgy shook her head. "No."

"Exactly," Annie said. "I picked the reindeer up when I was working in the shop, and it was heavy. Its weight hasn't changed any since I first came across it."

"So how did it get into the shop?" Helen asked.

"No idea," Annie said. "I found it in the storeroom and assumed it was part of the Christmas stock, and then Shari came along and bought it."

Rosamund rolled her eyes. "Gullible woman. First taken in by my husband and then buying that thing."

Harper had brought Figgy a glass of water. She gulped it down, feeling a little better. She was overreacting. Her friends would look after her, and besides, she'd done nothing wrong.

"OK," said Annie. "I'll message Tina." She pulled her phone out of her pocket. "We tell the police everything we know, and we leave it with them."

"Good morning, ladies," a male voice came from the shop doorway. "What is it you're telling the police?"

Figgy looked up. A man in his sixties was standing just inside the door with an expansive smile on his face. He was wearing red trousers and a white checked shirt underneath a woollen jacket. He had an air of privilege that made her uneasy. She gestured to Harper for another glass of water.

Rosamund stepped forward. "Digby," she said. "What are you doing here? Come to buy Christmas presents?"

"Of course," he replied. "Which one of you is the shop owner?"

"I am," said Helen. She gave Harper a glance. Harper looked at Annie, who moved towards the doorway to the flat.

How much of their conversation had he overheard?

"Anyway, ladies," he said, "you haven't got to the exciting bit yet. Please tell me why it is you want to call the police?"

CHAPTER FIFTY-THREE

MILLIE-JO BROUGHT a laptop out from under the counter of the Tuck Shop Café. It was a surprisingly modern and sleek-looking laptop, and nothing at all like its surroundings.

Dougie sniffed, looking around the café. In another establishment, he and Wendy would take a seat at one of the tables, place the laptop on the Formica tablecloth. But he had a feeling that anything he put on those tablecloths might just stick to them, and that sitting on those chairs might be something he'd come to regret. Once again, he wondered how this place stayed open.

Millie-Jo turned the laptop round to face them. "Here it is," she said. "CCTV footage from Sunday night. I assume that's what you're after."

Dougie nodded.

"We need footage from seven thirty to eight thirty," Wendy said.

Millie-Jo nodded. "I know that."

Dougie looked at her. "Were you here when the pottery was broken into?"

She shook her head. "I've watched it, silly. How d'you think I know? He made me watch it after I'd taken the camera down so I could check whether it was incriminating."

"Who's this 'he'?" Wendy asked.

Millie-Jo gave her an *are you stupid* look. "Digby Durridge-Smythe, of course," she said. "My boss."

"He's the owner of this place?" Dougie asked. "Isn't he one of the local councillors?"

Naomi had said something about him coming to the science fair. In fact, if he remembered correctly, Durridge-Smythe was the father of Fenella, Naomi's nemesis.

"So did Durridge-Smythe ask you to put the camera out of action?" Wendy asked.

"I'm saying nothing," Millie-Jo said, nodding her head.

Dougie rolled his eyes. "It doesn't work like that," he told her. "You can't tell us one thing and then give us something else with your body language. If we take a formal statement from you, it'll all be in writing and official."

She clenched her teeth. "Well, in that case, you won't be taking a formal statement from me."

Wendy cocked her head. "You damaged property and you hindered a police investigation. You failed to tell us that you had CCTV footage from the night the pottery was broken into, and you've been lying to us all along. I reckon we could easily get a warrant for your arrest."

Millie-Jo looked at her, her gaze level. "You think I don't know that?"

Dougie watched the woman's body language. She was calm; too calm.

This was a woman who'd had encounters with the police before and wasn't scared of them. Was there something bigger going on in this café than simply damaging a CCTV camera?

"Show me the footage," he said.

"I thought you'd never ask," Millie-Jo said. She clicked a button on her laptop, and the screen sprang to life.

Dougie and Wendy hunched over it.

The timestamp said seven thirty. The shot was of the courtyard. The angle of the camera meant the pottery was in full view, not only its front windows, but also the side of the building and the route round to the storeroom. They had a perfect view.

"So this is Sunday night, right?" he asked Millie Jo.

She nodded. "Just keep watching."

He exchanged another glance with Wendy and continued to watch. After a few moments, a man appeared. He was young, slim, wearing a hoodie.

"That's Reece," Wendy said. Dougie nodded.

Reece stopped in the middle of the courtyard. He'd emerged from directly under the CCTV camera, as if he was coming from the café.

"Was he in here before this?" Dougie asked Millie-Jo.

Millie-Jo shrugged. "No idea. I wasn't here on Sunday night."

Dougie cast around the inside of the café; no sign of a camera, nothing to record if Reece had been in here, and who he might have been with. And Dougie already knew they'd drawn a blank with CCTV in the lanes leading to this spot.

"Just keep watching," Millie-Jo said. "It'll all become obvious."

Dougie watched as Reece stopped in the middle of the courtyard. He turned his head from side to side, looking back at the CCTV camera; he clearly knew exactly where it was.

He pulled down his hood and walked towards the river. Not towards the pottery, as Dougie had expected.

As he approached the river, there was movement at the bottom of the screen. A car coming into view.

"That's the silver-blue BMW," Wendy said. Dougie nodded.

The car drove into the courtyard and parked at its centre. He could clearly see the registration plate: ON25 DDS. Dougie pumped his fist below the counter.

"Got him," he muttered.

He swallowed, forcing himself to concentrate. *Keep watching.*

A man got out of the driver's door and started walking towards Reece. Reece turned and ran towards the river. The man picked up pace, but he was at least forty years older than Reece. He couldn't keep up.

Then Reece stopped, just as he was about to disappear from view. The man took a few steps towards him.

"Why's he stopped?" Wendy said. "What's the man said to him?"

Reece took a sharp turn to the right and headed past the car on its other side and towards the pottery.

"This is it," Dougie muttered. "He's heading in there."

"Look." Wendy pointed at the screen. Reece's hoodie was bulging, as if he had something underneath it. Something he was hiding.

"What's that?" she asked.

Dougie shrugged. "Damned if I know."

"We always assumed he was going to the pottery to take something," she said. "Maybe he went in there to *dump* something."

Dougie nodded.

Millie-Jo grunted. "Will you just keep watching?"

The man ran towards Reece. He paused for a moment and looked around the courtyard. The CCTV camera caught his face.

"Oh my God," Wendy said. "I know him."

"So do I," Dougie added.

"That's not good," Wendy said.

Dougie shook his head.

Reece had disappeared into the pottery. The man ran after him, and then Reece re-emerged. His hoodie had changed shape. No bulge.

"He's left it in the pottery," Wendy said. "Whatever was under his hoodie."

"But what was it?" Dougie asked. "We didn't look for anything that hadn't been there before the burglary."

"Well, you don't, do you?" she replied.

Dougie eyed Millie-Jo. Should they be having this conversation in front of her?

As Reece reached the front edge of the car, near the riverbank, the older man caught up with him. The man grabbed Reece's hoodie by the neck and tugged at it.

"Why doesn't he fight back?" Wendy asked. "I mean, he's got to be stronger."

"Reece was thin, remember," Dougie said. "And if he was a drug addict, he wouldn't have had much strength."

"Oh, Reece was a drug addict, alright," Millie-Jo said.

Dougie looked up at her. "How do you know that?"

She shook her head. "I'm saying nothing."

Dougie sighed and looked back at the CCTV feed. The fight was continuing. It looked like Reece had laid a punch on the man, who was holding a hanky up to the right-hand side of his face.

"That's what Annie described," Dougie said. "She said she saw the man driving past in the silver-blue BMW holding a hanky up to his face."

"So Reece did that to him," Wendy said. Dougie nodded.

The older man's arm moved. He reached into his pocket and drew something out.

"Can you zoom in?" Dougie said.

Millie-Jo snorted. "Where do you think you are, MI6? We don't have that kind of technology here."

Dougie looked at her, unsure if she was telling the truth. But the Digital Forensics team probably would be able to improve the quality.

"Did he just stab him?" Wendy asked.

Dougie looked back at the screen. "Did who just stab who?"

"You-know-who just stabbed Reece."

They watched as Reece toppled backwards. His arms flailed wildly, reaching for the man's arm. The man took a step back, preventing Reece from getting any kind of purchase.

"Whoa," Wendy said.

Dougie swallowed the lump in his throat as they watched Reece lose his balance and topple backwards into the river.

Wendy looked at him. "Did one of our most respected local councillors just murder somebody?"

CHAPTER FIFTY-FOUR

"Ah, Digby," Rosamund said. "What a fortunate coincidence that you came at this moment."

Durridge-Smythe gave her a puzzled look. "Fortunate coincidence?"

Annie watched as her friend pulled on that posh smile that she hadn't seen her adopt for at least six months.

"Oh yes," Rosamund replied. "I wanted to have a conversation with you about fly-tipping on the beach."

He raised an eyebrow. "What fly-tipping on the beach?"

'You don't know?" Her face was a picture of surprise.

"I'm sorry, Rosamund my dear, but I don't know what you're talking about."

Rosamund gave a light, tinkling laugh. Annie hid her own laugh behind her hand.

"Goodness, Digby, surely you must have heard about it. People have been bringing vans down to the beach at the crack of dawn. Earlier even than my friends and I go swimming."

"You go swimming at this time of year?" he said. "My, my, ladies, you are hardy souls."

Annie gave him an insincere smile. Harper, standing behind the counter, was smacking the hammer against her open palm.

Don't do anything stupid, Annie thought.

"Well, these vans are there before we are," Rosamund said. "Ridiculously early. Three in the morning. I only know about it because I can see it from the window of my house."

At least that made sense. Rosamund's house had one of the best views of the bay in Lyme Regis. You'd be able to see anything that went on at the beach from there. In fact, the only spot with a better view was Figgy's caravan.

"Very well," Digby said. "Tell me more. Obviously, we at the council are very keen to ensure that this kind of thing doesn't happen."

Rosamund gave him a broad smile. "Oh, I'm so glad to hear that. Let me fill you in on the details."

He raised a finger. "One moment, if you don't mind. When I entered the shop, I'm sure I heard somebody talking about calling the police. Is there anything I can help with? Obviously, as a senior member of the local council, it's my responsibility to—"

"Oh no, no, no," said Rosamund. "That was nothing local. Helen was just telling us about something in Dorchester. Over a year ago."

Digby looked at her. "Over a year ago? I'd heard about you ladies solving mysteries, but I thought that only started this summer."

Ugh, thought Annie. How had anyone voted for this pompous idiot?

Helen flicked back her hair, joining in the airy, posh-woman act. "Well, it's nothing you need to worry about."

"Nope," said Harper, clutching the head of the hammer. "Nothing at all."

Durridge-Smythe curled his lip.

"Ah, yes," he said. "Yes, madam." He smiled. "Or is it sir? I wouldn't want to offend."

Harper's nostrils flared. "It's *Harper*," she said. "And I prefer to use she/her pronouns."

Digby's smile thinned. "Very good," he said. "Very modern."

Annie could hear her pulse whooshing in her ears. *How long before Tina gets here? What if he leaves?*

"Anyway," Rosamund cut in. "I was about to provide you with the details of the vans I've seen dumping rubbish down at the seafront."

The door opened. Annie looked past the others to see Tina enter.

Thank God for that.

Tina's gaze darted around the room, quickly taking in what she was seeing: Harper with the hammer in her hand, traces of dust on the shop counter, and Rosamund attempting to engage Digby Durridge-Smythe in conversation. Figgy, meanwhile, sat on the chair Harper had brought her, mute.

Are you alright, Figster?

That would have to wait.

Annie beckoned Tina towards her.

"Come upstairs," she said. "I need to show you something."

Digby gave her a sidelong glance, clearly intrigued. Annie ignored him.

"DC Abbott, isn't it?" he said. "You're Annie's daughter."

"Tina." She gave him a smile. "Annie's daughter and Naomi Anderson's sister, too. I believe you and she met at the Science Fair."

His cheeks reddened. "We did indeed," he said. "I gather she's a superb assistant to my daughter, Fenella."

"A teaching assistant is *not* the same as a personal assistant," Annie said. She knew how Fenella had been treating Naomi.

"Oh, that's not what I meant, of course," Durridge-Smythe replied. "Please, don't misunderstand me."

"What is it you want me to see?" Tina hissed.

Annie gritted her teeth, gave Durridge-Smythe a *butt out* look, and led Tina up the stairs. Harper followed, still pounding that hammer into her palm. Annie wished she'd put it down.

"Which room?" she said.

"Kitchen," Harper replied.

Annie had never been up here. She and Helen always met in one of the local bars or cafés, or at the harbour when they were swimming. The women weren't really in the habit of going to each other's houses. Well, apart from the time they'd gone to Rosamund's to determine whether she might or might not have killed the man they'd found dead in her car.

"Where's that?" she asked.

Harper jerked her head to the right, indicating an open doorway. Annie led Tina inside.

The bag holding the reindeer was on the kitchen counter beside the kettle. Annie pointed at it, not wanting to touch it.

She ran over the last hour in her head. Had she touched the reindeer since Figgy had suggested they should crack it open? No, she didn't think she had. But when Harper had smashed it, fragments of pottery, dust and crystals had gone everywhere. Annie and her friends would have incriminating evidence all over the front of their clothes.

"Open that bag," she told Tina. "But put some gloves on first."

Tina gave her one of her looks. "Are you sure this isn't a wind-up, Mum?" she said. "You've got Durridge-Smythe down there, and now you're bringing me up here and getting me to look into a bag?"

"It's all connected," Annie said. "Durridge-Smythe. He isn't the pillar of the community he likes to paint himself as. We think he..." She lowered her voice to a hissed whisper. "We think he killed the man who attacked Peg."

Tina narrowed her eyes. "What? You're telling me he killed Reece Lumbard?"

"Reece Lumbard?" Annie said. She hadn't been told his name. "Is that his name?"

"It is," Tina replied, her voice firm.

Annie nodded. "Well, in that case, yes. That is what I'm telling you. Have a look in that bag."

Tina pulled a pair of forensic gloves from her pocket. She snapped them on and delved into the bag.

"Jesus Christ, Mum, what have you got in here?"

"If I'm not mistaken," Harper said, "it's a hideous pottery reindeer hiding a bag of crystal meth."

Tina looked at her. "Well, you're not wrong there. How did it get here?"

"Long story," Annie said. "It was in the storeroom of the pottery. And then I sold it to Shari, that's Rosamund's ex's new girlfriend, and then she gave it to Rosamund. Well, she gave it to Cameron to give to Rosamund via Figgy. And then Rosamund didn't like it, so—"

"Stop," Tina said. "How did it get into the pottery? Did this belong to Peg Casey?"

"We don't think so," Annie told her. "My hunch is that – what was his name again?"

"Reece Lumbard," Tina said.

"Reece Lumbard, that's it. My hunch is that he hid this in the pottery. I don't know why, but I'm sure you can work it out. So he wasn't actually trying to steal something, you see. Instead, he was trying to *put* something there. That's why it's so different from everything else in the pottery. That's why it matches the reindeer they've been selling up in that new shop on Broad Street."

"What new shop on Broad Street?" Tina asked.

"Don't you know about that? It's one of those pop-up shops, probably. Run by Millie-Jo, the woman who also runs the Tuck Shop Café. It's been selling these reindeer."

"Slow down," Tina said. "Are you telling me there's a connection between a new shop selling these reindeer and the Tuck Shop Café, and you think that the man who attacked Peg Casey had this reindeer and left it in the pottery on Sunday night?"

Annie nodded vigorously. "That's the theory, yes."

Tina gave her a stern look. Annie stood her ground, resisting the urge to back away.

"I can back her up, if it helps," said Harper. "This reindeer's passed between so many hands I must be one of the few people in Lyme Regis who hasn't had custody of it, but I can tell you none of the swimming club members have got anything to do with those drugs."

"Apart from the fact that there are fragments on your face, Mum," Tina said.

Annie put a hand to her cheek. "Are there?"

Tina raised an eyebrow.

Annie swallowed. "I hope you don't think that means—"

"No, Mum. I don't think that means anything." She sighed. "Who broke the reindeer open?"

"That was me," said Harper.

Tina turned to her. "Why? Why didn't you just call the police, given what you suspected?"

Annie closed her eyes. "We thought there was a chance we were wrong. And if we were wrong, you'd think we were stupid."

"Oh, don't get me started on that," Tina said.

For a moment, there was silence. Tina dragged a hand through her hair. Annie waited for the outburst.

"OK, right," Tina said at last. "What you've told me corroborates other information that the police have."

"What information?" Annie asked.

"I'm hardly about to tell you that. Just leave that bag exactly where it is and ask Helen to get everybody out the shop. Everybody except Durridge-Smythe." She put up a hand. "In fact, no. I'll ask Helen to get everybody out the shop."

She turned her back on Annie and hurried down the stairs. Annie looked at Harper.

"How d'you think that went?"

Harper pursed her lips. "You were trying not to piss your daughter off, right?"

"Right."

"Well, I think you failed there."

CHAPTER FIFTY-FIVE

FIGGY STEPPED out of the gallery, finally confident that her legs would hold her weight.

She couldn't quite believe what had just happened.

Had she really stood there while Harper had smashed open a reindeer full of drugs? And had Rosamund really promised to buy her a replacement?

No. Now that she thought about it, Rosamund had only promised to replace the reindeer if Figgy's hunch about it containing drugs proved to be false.

And Figgy's hunch had turned out to be very much true.

How was it that a stupid seagull with piercing eyes and a taste for chocolate digestives could track down crystal meth? Was this a normal seagull thing, or specific to Kevin?

It didn't matter. The reindeer was gone, and the police would be swooping down on the new shop to take the rest of them in as evidence.

She turned at the sound of sirens, a police car heading down Broad Street.

It pulled up outside the gallery, across the double yellow lines. Annie's son-in-law and his colleague jumped out.

"Is he still in there?" he snapped at Figgy as his colleague hurried into the shop.

"Who?" she asked.

"Digby Durridge-Smythe."

She nodded. "Oh yeah, he's in there alright. And the reindeer with the drugs."

The policeman gave her a look. "How do you know about that?"

"Long story," she said. "My name's Figgy Edmunds. I live in the caravan park on Monmouth Beach." She gestured towards the beach. "I imagine you'll be wanting to take a statement. It might involve seagull behaviour."

He frowned at her. "Are you the one with the seagull they tried to fool with the painted pebbles?"

She grinned. "Yeah, that's me."

"Right," he replied. "I know where you live. I'm PC Anderson, I'll call round later."

He headed into the shop but was stopped by the door opening in his face. His colleague, who was a similar size and build to Figgy but white, came out, with Digby Durridge-Smythe in handcuffs.

Figgy resisted a *Yay!*

PC Anderson gave her a nod and got back into the front of the car. His colleague got in the back with the once-revered, now-disgraced councillor.

The bell sounded over the shop door and a crowd shuffled out: Helen, Harper, Annie, Rosamund, and Annie's daughter, Tina.

"I'll see you at Hill Road," Tina called to the two uniformed officers.

PC Anderson nodded before driving off.

Tina folded her arms across her chest, eyeing the group of swimmers. "I can't quite believe you lot have managed to get yourself involved in yet another murder. We'll be wanting to take statements from all of you." She stared at Annie. "Not least you."

Annie put her hands up. "Don't look at me."

"You were sniffing around the crime scene the whole time."

"To be fair on Annie," Helen said, her movements agitated, "she hasn't had sight of the reindeer since Monday. I was the last one to have custody of it. And you'll find traces of the drugs on my shop counter. I'm just telling you this now so you don't suspect me of being involved with its sale."

She glanced at Harper, who stepped towards her and squeezed her hand.

Was Helen genuinely worried that she might be under suspicion? Figgy had only brought the reindeer to Helen's gallery last night because of her desperation over Kevin's behaviour. Helen really had nothing to do with this.

A van drew up and a ridiculously tall man got out. Figgy reckoned he was almost two feet taller than her. He nodded at Tina.

"Thanks," Tina said to the women. "We'll be in touch." She turned into the gallery with the man.

"He's the forensics chap," Annie said. "Gavin."

"How do you know all this?" Helen asked. Her face was pale and her hand was gripping Harper's. She peered into the shop, watching Tina lead the man through the doorway to the flat.

"I keep my eyes and ears open," Annie said.

Helen nodded. "Should I go in there, keep an eye on them?" she said.

"I don't think they'd let you," Annie replied.

"It'll be alright," Harper muttered. "Stop worrying." She had a messenger bag slung over her shoulder, which she patted. "I grabbed your documents."

Helen's face visibly calmed. "Oh, Harper! Thank you." She wrapped her arms around her fiancée, and they shared a deep kiss. Figgy wondered if Cameron was around. Would an evening out be on the cards?

"So it looks like we'll be in the market for a new local councillor," Rosamund said.

"You should do it," Helen told her. "You'd be perfect."

"Given the nature of our last councillor, I can hardly take that as a compliment."

Helen shrugged. "Take it how you want to, darling. I think you'd be good at the job."

"You would," said Annie. "It would give you purpose."

"You think I don't have purpose?"

Annie raised an eyebrow. "You clean holiday cottages. Is that your life's calling?"

"No."

"Exactly."

Helen let go of Harper's hand and clapped her hands together. "So if we can't go back into the shop until the forensics people have finished, why don't we go to the pub to celebrate?"

Figgy sighed; no date with Cameron. But this was more important.

"Celebrate?" said Rosamund. "I hardly think finding ourselves in the middle of a murder investigation is a cause for celebration."

"They're celebrating getting engaged," Figgy said. "Don't you remember?"

Rosamund straightened. "Of course I remember, my dear. Yes, why don't we all go for a drink at Rock Point to celebrate? My treat."

Figgy looked across the road at the pub. They'd been in the gallery for so long, it was starting to get dark. The lit Christmas tree on the raised pavement across from them twinkled in the early evening light.

She wrapped her arms around herself, allowing her horror at discovering the drugs to give way to excitement at the prospect of Christmas. Christmas with Cameron.

"Rosamund," she said. "Do you mind if I ask you something?"

Rosamund looped her arm through Figgy's as they crossed the road towards the pub. Figgy forced herself to maintain contact. She'd never seen Rosamund hook arms with anyone.

"What would you like to ask me, my dear?" Rosamund said.

"Please," Figgy replied, bristling. "'My dear' makes me feel like I'm sixteen. Carry on calling me Figgy, at least when we're with the others."

Rosamund cocked her head. "You're right. I need to get past your relationship with my son and remember that you were my friend first."

"I'd like that," Figgy said.

Annie was standing at the door of the pub, holding the door open for them. Figgy and Rosamund squeezed through side by side. Figgy smiled at Annie's raised eyebrow.

"So," said Rosamund as they approached the bar. "What is it you wanted to ask?"

"Well," said Figgy, "it's something I've already mentioned to Cameron. It's about Christmas."

"Oh?" Rosamund's voice had hardened.

Figgy forced herself to continue. "I asked him if he would spend Christmas with me. I wasn't exactly looking forward to spending it on my own in my caravan, and I love Christmas. I really do. It reminds me of my nan."

"I'd love for you to spend Christmas with Cameron," Rosamund said.

"Really?"

A nod. "But on one condition."

Uh-oh.

"Which is?" Figgy asked.

"Instead of Cameron spending Christmas at your van and you having to cook a turkey – I assume you cook a turkey?"

Figgy nodded. "A tiny one. Well, a chicken, really."

"Indeed. In what I can only assume must be a tiny oven."

Figgy nodded.

"So I thought. So why don't you come to mine for Christmas Day? I have plenty of space."

"That's very kind of you," Figgy said. "But I suspect my Christmases are a bit different from yours."

"Hmm."

"And that's why we're going to bring Christmas to you," Annie said.

Rosamund turned to her. "I'm sorry?"

Annie clapped her hand on Rosamund's shoulder. "I'm not taking no for an answer, Rosamund. We're all having Christmas together this year. I know I'm supposed to have Naomi, but you know what? I fancy spending it with my mates instead. You know what kids are like, they like being in their own place. So you cook the turkey, I'll bring all the trimmings. Figgy can bring some decorations. And Helen..."

Helen glanced at Harper. "What were we planning, sweetheart?"

Harper shrugged. "Looks like we're planning Christmas at Rosamund's, doesn't it?"

Helen planted a kiss on Harper's cheek. "That sounds perfect."

CHAPTER FIFTY-SIX

Dougie walked into the team room and threw himself into a chair.

"Oi," said Wendy. "You don't have to be so bad-tempered."

"Don't I?" he said. "You haven't seen the lawyer Durridge-Smythe has hired. I reckon his left sock is worth more than the contents of my entire wardrobe."

She shrugged. "Doesn't matter how expensive his socks are. He's up against CCTV showing his client pushing Reece into the river."

Dougie shook his head. "I watched it again. The two of them fought. A good lawyer will make out that it was self-defence. Durridge-Smythe had a wound on his face, after all."

"And Reece had a stab wound."

"We didn't see one."

"It wasn't apparent, what with him having been in the water. And the dark hoodie disguising the blood. But don't worry. Pathology have been on the phone. He was stabbed in the stomach, and they're saying that's the cause of death."

"Not drowning?"

"Not drowning."

Dougie stood up and punched a wall.

"That's no way to react to good news," Wendy said.

"Sorry, Wendy. I think I've got too much pent-up frustration with this case."

"Remind me to never let the sarge recommend you for a transfer to CID, if this is how you react."

He slumped back into his chair. "Sorry, Wendy. I didn't mean to... I'll be fine."

"Good. 'Cos it's Christmas. Season of good cheer, and all that."

Dougie shook his head. "I don't think I'll be cheerful till the CPS have agreed to prosecute."

"Which they will, given Millie-Jo's evidence."

"She didn't seem like a woman who wanted to make things official."

Wendy shrugged. "She's changed her mind. Talking to the sarge now."

Dougie stood up. "Really? Shouldn't one of us interview her with him? We were the ones who went through the CCTV with her, after all..."

Wendy gestured for him to sit down. "The sarge isn't interviewing her. It's just a preliminary chat, explaining the process to her. He's going to put her in a nice office somewhere with a cup of tea, and then you and Tina will go in and talk to her. Before the main event, after Durridge-Smythe has finished with his lawyer."

"Me and Tina? Not you?"

Wendy shook her head. "You and Tina."

"Are you…?" he began, feeling awkward. "Are you pissed off that it's me, and not you? Who made that decision, anyway?"

"Tina did. She seems to think Millie-Jo will respond better if there's a man in the room. And sadly, I'm inclined to agree with her."

"Sorry, mate."

"Well, yeah. I'm the one who gets to take statements off all those swimming club lot. So I guess I get the scraps."

"Again, sorry." Dougie knew how challenging it would be to get a coherent narrative out of his mother-in-law. And some of the others were quite frankly bonkers, especially that art gallery one.

His phone rang.

"It's Tina," he said.

"Probably conferring with you about the interview."

He shrugged and picked up the call. "Hey, Tina. How's it looking at the gallery?"

"Very good," she said. "There's a significant quantity of crystal meth here, even with half of it having been spattered all over the shop. And the pottery reindeer has prints all over it, including some that are a match for Reece."

"What about Durridge-Smythe?" Dougie asked.

"His prints aren't on the system yet," she said.

"We've got his DNA. Or at least, Naomi has. That fingerprint, the blood…"

Tina laughed. "Yes, I heard all about the science fair. But let's take a sample the official way, yes?"

Dougie nodded. "So we definitely think Reece dumped the reindeer at the pottery before he died? Trying to hide it from Durridge-Smythe, maybe?"

"My theory is that he was in some sort of trouble with

Durridge-Smythe and wanted to keep him from getting his hands on the drugs for some reason. So he hid them in the pottery, but then was confronted by the man."

"Who stabbed him."

"We don't know that for sure," Tina said.

"Pathology have spoken to Wendy. Stab wound to the stomach."

"Ouch. Poor Reece. He might have hit Peg Casey over the head with a jug, but..."

"...but he didn't deserve to die. I know." Dougie realised he hadn't called Dorchester Hospital to check on Peg's progress for a couple of days.

"OK," Tina said. "Right now, Durridge-Smythe is being briefed by his lawyer. Our theory is he stabbed Reece, then followed him into the shop where he saw Peg on the floor, and fled, leaving his print on the shelf."

"After which Reece staggered out and fell into the river," Dougie added.

"Poor bugger."

Dougie sighed. Reece Lumbard had dealt drugs. He'd attacked an innocent old lady. But he hadn't deserved to die in a freezing river.

"I gather you want me in the room when you get a statement from Millie-Jo?" he said.

"Please," Tina replied. "Wendy says she responded more favourably to you."

"Not so sure about that, but happy to help. How are we going to get her to talk?"

"From what we know, she's been working at two businesses, both fronts for drug dealing. There are all number of crimes we can charge her with. But we can be lenient, if she helps us. This is a murder investigation, after all."

"Won't she just go out there and sell more drugs, if we don't stop her?"

"We do have to bear that in mind," Tina said. "But my hunch is that Durridge-Smythe was the one pulling the strings. Maybe, like Reece, she was an addict who he was able to manipulate."

"She doesn't look in the best of health."

"Exactly. Look, I've got a few more things to do here, then I'll be over for the interview. Can you get her into a suitable room, make sure she doesn't go anywhere?"

"No problem. Thanks, Tina."

"What for?"

He hesitated. "You brought me and Wendy in on this like we were members of MCIT, or at least CID. You could have got your own lot in and left us to do the grunt work."

"You know the geography, and you know the people. MCIT would be mad to ride roughshod over you. I think DCI Clarke'll take this over now, while she waits for a new DI to start. God only knows what this would have been like if DI Patterson was still in charge."

Dougie had heard plenty about DI Hannah Patterson. Especially now she was back in Devon, just over the border.

"Well, thanks anyway," he said.

"My pleasure, Dougie. You and Wendy did a great job."

CHAPTER FIFTY-SEVEN

ANNIE SMILED as her daughter entered the pub.

"Tina love," she said. "We're celebrating Helen and Harper getting engaged. And Rosamund's paying."

"Only for one round," Rosamund said.

Annie gave her a stare. "We're still on the first round. What will you have, Tina?"

"I can't join you for a drink," Tina said. "Still working. But congratulations." She gave Helen a kiss on the cheek, then awkwardly shook Harper's hand for a moment before the two of them grinned and gave each other a hug.

"So," Helen said. "What did you find in the gallery?"

"You're right. There was a significant quantity of crystal meth in that pottery reindeer," Tina said. "And we've been able to get prints from it. Including all of yours, I'm afraid."

"Anything else?" Helen asked, bobbing from foot to foot. Annie wondered what was getting to her; was it simply the police being in her shop, or something more?

"Just the prints and the drugs," Tina said. "Why, is there something else you haven't mentioned?"

"Oh, no," Helen said with a high-pitched laugh. "Just ignore me."

Tina frowned. "Good. So I've asked Wendy Sharman to visit each of you to take statements. Please try and make some sense of how each of you ended up with the reindeer in your possession. We will be checking that your stories are coherent and don't contradict each other too much."

"Do we need to stay away from each other until Wendy takes the statements?" Figgy asked. "Contamination of evidence?"

Tina smiled. "You're witnesses, not suspects. It's not as severe as that. Besides, you've been in here drinking for the last hour, so if I wanted to separate you, I've missed the boat. But Wendy will be expecting you all home for a visit within the next hour."

Annie grunted. "But we're celebrating."

"A man died, Mum."

"True."

"It's fine," Helen said. "You'll all be at the wedding, anyway."

"You've set a date?" Figgy asked.

Helen and Harper exchanged a look. "We thought Christmas Day."

"Christmas Day?" Rosamund said, aghast. "But you're all supposed to be at my house on Christmas Day. How am I supposed to host a wedding?"

Helen put a hand on her arm. "Don't worry, darling. The wedding will be on the beach. Later in the day."

"Is that legally binding?" Tina asked. "Sorry, none of my business."

Helen held her head high. "Do I look like the legally binding sort? You know me and Harper. Free spirits. Making our commitments to each other in public is enough." She looked at Harper. "Isn't it, sweetheart?"

"It is." Harper smiled and put an arm around Helen's shoulders. "And she's adding me to the title deed for the gallery, so there's that, too." She grinned.

Annie laughed. Should she laugh? She wasn't sure.

"Right," said Tina. "So you're all going to be home in the next hour. Wendy will want to know what you saw, and how you came to have the drugs in your possession."

"But we didn't know about the drugs," Rosamund said. "At least not until Figgy..."

"It was Kevin," Figgy said. "He was acting weird, dive-bombing the caravan. And Annie's Dex was, too."

Tina frowned. "You worked out that there were drugs inside the reindeer, because of a seagull and a labrador?"

"A very clever labrador, I'll have you know," Annie said. "Maybe I'll suggest to his owner that he becomes a sniffer dog."

"Please, no," Tina said. "I'm assuming you're not going to claim that your seagull is a very clever bird?" she asked Figgy.

Figgy chuckled. "Not my seagull. And to be honest, I can't decide if he's a stupid bird, or actually a genius."

Helen spluttered. "Stupid. Remember those painted pebbles."

Figgy shrugged. "True."

"I spoke to Digby last night," Rosamund said. "He was asking David for investment advice. And... Oh, my." She put a hand to her face.

"What is it, Rosamund pet?" Annie asked. "You've gone pale."

Rosamund shook her head. "The car. I thought it was David's, but it had the wrong registration plate." She turned to Tina. "I remember it. ON25 DDS. Is that Digby's?"

Tina scrolled through her phone. "It is."

"So that's the car Annie saw on Sunday night."

"It is. And I imagine we'll be taking a statement from David as well. Is this David Winters, your husband?"

"Ex-husband, Tina dear. Very much ex."

"Sorry."

"It's alright," Rosamund said. "You weren't to know. And there's something else."

"Yes?" Tina nodded.

"After I visited Wisteria Cottage, I think I was broken into."

Annie gasped. "You didn't say anything about that. My goodness, were you hurt? Was anything taken?"

Rosamund shook her head. "Nothing was taken. To be honest, I thought I was imagining things. But the doors into all the rooms were open. And I always close them. You see, I told Digby about the reindeer. Not directly, of course, but Shari mentioned it, while he was there. So he'll have thought I had it."

"You didn't have it?" Tina asked.

"Figgy had it by then. I'd given it to her."

"Which was when the seagull went after it," Figgy said.

"You're sure you were broken into?" Tina said.

Rosamund nodded. "Cameron wasn't in while I was out, and... I have a camera doorbell, Tina. I didn't think to check it, but I'm sure..."

"Thank you," Tina said. "I'll let Wendy know, she can check it when she comes for your statement. You'll be first on the list."

"Of course."

Tina gave her a tight smile. "All of you get home soon, yes? No more celebrating until Wendy has your statements. I'm hoping to have enough to prosecute, before his lawyer gets his claws in."

Annie gave a mock salute. "No more celebrating until we've been good girls."

The swimmers laughed. Tina sighed.

CHAPTER FIFTY-EIGHT

FIGGY AND CAMERON HELD HANDS, swinging their arms as they walked down the hill towards the beach. She felt pleasantly full and slightly tipsy, as well as deliriously happy.

"That went OK, don't you think?" he asked.

She looked up at him. "I thought it went wonderfully."

"Are you sure? She wasn't too... regimented?"

Figgy squeezed his hand. "Your mother is always going to be regimented. But today she was a lot more laid-back than she normally is."

"Not as laid-back as Helen and Harper, though. With this hippie beach wedding that isn't a wedding."

"As far as they're concerned, it *is* a wedding. Don't forget, only a few years ago, they wouldn't have been able to have a wedding at all."

"True. But wouldn't you think that would make them want to have a proper wedding even more?"

Figgy laughed. "Have you met Helen? She's a bohemian. No tradition for her."

"True."

Figgy stopped walking, and waited for Cameron to do the same. She stood on her tiptoes and tugged on the lapel of his coat, bringing him down to her for a kiss.

"Now, now, you two," came a voice. "We don't want to end up with a double wedding."

Figgy turned to see Annie coming down the hill behind them.

"You caught up," she said.

"Only because you two keep stopping for a snog. And because your mum's dishwasher meant that my offer to do the washing up only took five minutes."

"She let you load the dishwasher?" Cameron said.

Annie laughed. "Of course not, silly. I started clattering plates around and she told me she'd take over. Apparently, she knows her system, and she doesn't need me interfering with it."

"Oh, she knows 'her system' alright," he said, doing air quotes. "No one messes with my mum's systems."

Annie smiled at him. "She did well today. It can't have been easy having us all in your house, knowing that your dad and his girlfriend are just a few miles away in that mansion."

Cameron frowned and looked down at the ground.

"Are you OK with that?" Figgy asked.

He shrugged. "They've invited me for lunch tomorrow. Apparently, they've bought me a present."

"I just hope it isn't a pottery reindeer," Annie said.

"Or a stash of drugs," Figgy added.

A car pulled up beside them and the window slid down.

"Get in, all of you," Rosamund said. "You'll catch your death."

"I've spent all my life living by the sea," Annie replied. "I can cope with a bit of a breeze."

"This is more than a bit of a breeze," Rosamund told her. "This is a full-on gale."

"Do you think Helen and Harper did the right thing, going ahead in this weather?" Figgy asked.

"Don't worry," Rosamund said. "Helen told me they'd spoken to the owner of the Kiosk. Hot drinks and sausage butties all round, once the ceremony's over. And big orange umbrellas in case of rain."

"This weather will wreak havoc on umbrellas," Annie said.

"Sausage butties?" Cameron said. "I don't think I could eat another thing."

Figgy gave his hand a squeeze. "We can feed them to the seagulls if it's too much."

"And encourage Kevin? No thank you."

"Come on then," Rosamund said. "Get in."

They all piled into the car, Annie in the front and Figgy and Cameron snuggled up together in the back. Rosamund drove into the Cobb Gate car park at the bottom of the hill, which was otherwise empty.

"I still can't believe you continue to park here," Annie said.

Rosamund looked at her. "It's like riding a bike. You just have to get straight back on again."

"You're comparing falling off a bike to having a man crawl into your car and die in the passenger seat?"

Rosamund shrugged. "It's the most convenient car park."

Annie shook her head. "Rosamund Winters, ice queen. You certainly suit your name."

"Is that really what you think of me?" Rosamund pulled into the space nearest the beach and stopped the car.

"It's not, Rosamund love. Not really. Not anymore."

Rosamund narrowed her eyes. "Good."

Annie turned to the front of the car, her face lighting up. "Tim!" She threw open her door and hurled herself into the arms of Tim Cromwell, who was waiting outside the car.

"Hello, ladies," Tim said as the rest of them piled out of the car. "Hi, Cameron."

"Hello, Tim," Figgy said. Cameron gave him a nod.

Figgy liked Tim. She'd sat with him outside the lifeboat station after her nan died. His son had died in a tragic accident years earlier, and while that was a much harsher memory than the death of a woman in her eighties, it meant he understood that sitting and staring at the sea was sometimes exactly what she needed.

"Figgy," he said. "Did you enjoy your Christmas?"

"I did," she said. "It was marvellous."

"And so was mine," he replied. "Rosamund, I'm very grateful you let me be a part of your gathering."

"Annie didn't exactly give me a choice," Rosamund said, then caught herself. "I mean, it was a pleasure having you there. Good to have another man in the house."

"Oi." Annie pulled Tim close to her. "Don't you go getting any ideas, Rosamund Winters."

Rosamund smiled. "I can see how much Tim cares for you, Annie. I wouldn't dream..."

"And a good job, too." Annie grabbed Tim's hand and gave it a loud kiss. He chuckled.

"Right," he said. "We've commandeered the lifeboat station where there's a bit more shelter, but the staff from the Kiosk have brought refreshments. Come and see how magical the place looks."

They all made their way along the prom, battling the

wind. The Kiosk was shuttered, which caused Figgy a moment's panic, but Tim reassured them.

"They've brought some parasols and deckchairs along to the boathouse," he said. "It looks as orange as the beach on a summer's day."

At last, they reached the lifeboat station at the mouth of the Cobb. The doors were open, festooned with fairy lights.

"It looks lovely," Figgy said.

"Kitsch enough for you?" Cameron asked.

"Weddings aren't supposed to be kitsch," she replied.

He raised his eyebrows. "No? Well, that's good, I guess."

They stepped inside the shop and walked through to the area where the boat was housed. Fairy lights had been hung from the ceiling and draped over the boat. In the far corner, behind the boat, deckchairs and parasols had been set out. The whole space glowed.

"Oh," said Figgy. "This is beautiful. Who did it?"

"Mainly me," Tim said. "I snuck out after Rosamund's delicious turkey dinner and got it set up when I saw the weather forecast. Let's just hope we don't get called out."

"Oh," said Figgy. "Do you think that's a possibility?"

"In this weather, callouts are more frequent. But Christmas Day is normally quiet. And besides, there's a plan in place for if we have to stop things."

"Tim Cromwell, you are an extremely talented man," Annie said. "And a very thoughtful one."

He flushed.

"Here they are," Figgy said. She gestured towards the boat. Helen emerged from one side of it – starboard? Figgy wasn't sure – and Harper from the other.

She hugged herself. *How romantic.*

As they reached the front of the boat, Helen and

Harper caught sight of each other and smiled. Helen was wearing a flowing cream dress with embroidered seashells and waves. Harper wore a pale grey suit with a white waistcoat beneath. They both looked perfect. And they were both grinning like their faces might split.

Figgy wiped back a tear. *Don't cry.*

"It's OK," Annie whispered in her ear. "They're happy tears. Let them flow. I know I will."

Figgy turned. Annie was behind her, clutching Tim's hand, tears pouring down her face. She turned to the side to see Cameron beside her and Rosamund beyond. They shared a smile, then Cameron gave Figgy a wink.

Figgy caught movement at the door to the lifeboat station; someone was outside.

"Are we expecting anyone else?" she asked.

Annie grinned and turned towards the door. "I was hoping they'd make it." She walked to the door and opened it for two more arrivals; Peg and Sally. Peg had a walking stick and was leaning on her sister, but was smiling.

Rosamund stepped forward. "Peg," she said. "How are you? You're home?"

Peg waved her stick dismissively. "We can do all that afterwards. Ignore me. Focus on them." She nodded towards the boat, where Helen and Harper stood.

Helen and Harper walked to the front of the boat. A woman in a flowing green dress was waiting for them: the celebrant, Figgy assumed.

Behind her, she heard a sob. Annie. She tightened her grip on Cameron's hand.

Figgy let out a long, slow breath. She felt like she might turn to jelly, she was so happy.

The perfect Christmas, the perfect boyfriend, and the perfect group of friends.

We hope you enjoyed reading *The Shattered Bauble*. We have another mystery for you, *The Missing Corpse*, which you can get for free as ebook or audio from our book club or you can buy in paperback from book retailers. Read it for free at: rachelmclean.com/the-missing-corpse.

Happy Reading,
Rachel and Millie

READ A NOVELLA, THE MISSING CORPSE

When one of the members of the swimming club takes on a new job cleaning holiday lets, she expects her biggest challenge to be working her way through six cottages before the next guests arrive.

She doesn't expect a mystery.

Why is a picture in one of six identical cottages very slightly different to the others? Who is the mysterious woman who let herself in and cleaned before Rosamund got there? And what's that awful smell in cottage number one?

As Dorset Police investigate two murders they suspect of being connected with organised crime, Rosamund's mysteries may be more serious than she thinks. Will she and her swimming buddies be about to solve a double homicide?

Download the ebook or audiobook of *The Missing Corpse* for FREE at rachelmclean.com/the-missing-corpse or buy in paperback from book retailers.

ALSO BY RACHEL MCLEAN

The DI Zoe Finch Series – buy from book retailers.

Deadly Wishes

Deadly Choices

Deadly Desires

Deadly Terror

Deadly Reprisal

Deadly Fallout

Deadly Christmas

Deadly Origins, the FREE Zoe Finch prequel

The Dorset Crime Series – buy from book retailers.

The Corfe Castle Murders

The Clifftop Murders

The Island Murders

The Monument Murders

The Millionaire Murders

The Fossil Beach Murders

The Blue Pool Murders

The Lighthouse Murders

The Ghost Village Murders

The Poole Harbour Murders

The Chesil Beach Murders

The Beach Hut Murders

...and more to come

The McBride & Tanner Series – buy from book retailers.

Blood and Money

Death and Poetry

Power and Treachery

Secrets and History

The Cumbria Crime Series by Rachel McLean and Joel Hames – buy from book retailers.

The Harbor

The Mine

The Cairn

The Barn

The Lake

The Wood

The Port

The Marsh

ALSO BY MILLIE RAVENSWORTH

The Cozy Craft Mysteries – Buy now in ebook and paperback

The Wonderland Murders

The Painted Lobster Murders

The Sequinned Cape Murders

The Swan Dress Murders

The Tie-Dyed Kaftan Murders

The Scarecrow Murders